CHLOE'S PEOPLE

CHLOE'S PEOPLE

Mary Street

CHIVERS

THORNDIKE

This Large Print book is published by BBC Audiobooks Ltd, Bath, England and by Thorndike Press®, Waterville, Maine, USA.

Published in 2005 in the U.K. by arrangement with Robert Hale Limited

Published in 2005 in the U.S. by arrangement with Robert Hale Limited

U.K. Hardcover ISBN 1–4056–3105–8 (Chivers Large Print)
U.K. Softcover ISBN 1–4056–3106–6 (Camden Large Print)
U.S. Softcover ISBN 0–7862–6979–0 (General)

The text of this Large Print edition is unabridged.
Other aspects of the book may vary from the original edition.

Set in 16 pt. New Times Roman.

Printed in Great Britain on acid-free paper.

British Library Cataloguing in Publication Data available

Library of Congress Control Number: 2004110552

ONE

It was an honour, Miss Johnson told me, to be befriended by a great lady such as Miss Helen Waring, but after six months of enduring that lady's determination to find a husband for me, I felt it was a friendship I could do without.

'Thus far,' I told Miss Johnson wryly, 'she has attempted to match me with Mr Fairbrother, Mr Cross and Mr Bateman. Now, she thinks Mr Kilroy would do very well.'

It was Christmas Eve and I was enjoying a few blessed days of freedom from the Warings. Miss Johnson and I were alone in her parlour, comfortable and warm, with a bowl of walnuts, glasses of Madeira, coals burning rosily in the grate and a branch of candles to light up the game board.

We were engaged in backgammon. As I shook the dice, Miss Johnson tossed nutshells into the fire, plucked nervously at her muslin cap and said, 'My dear Chloe, with Mr Kilroy you would be very well established.'

'I shall not marry without liking, and I do not like him.'

'He is not the most agreeable gentleman,' Miss Johnson admitted. 'It is regrettable there are so very few gentlemen of marriageable age, these days.' She sighed. 'So many promising young men have been lost in these dreadful wars.'

We were drawing to the close of the year 1813, a year that had marked the Battle of Vitoria and the Battle of the Nations. Many were predicting the fall of Napoleon in the coming year but, to me, the notion of peace was strange. Our nation had been at war with the French all my life and many young men had been killed in the fighting.

In church, we sent up prayers for those engaged in the perilous task of warfare; those from our parish who fell had their names read out and we prayed for mercy on their souls, but it could not be said that here, in Gloucestershire, the high affairs of state touched us to any significant degree. The only vexation to young women was a scarcity of young men to fall in love with.

'Miss Waring,' I said, 'is not a lady to be put off by such circumstances. She thinks it not beyond her powers to bring about my marriage. *My* marriage,' I added with emphasis. 'She would not consider any of these gentlemen for herself.'

Miss Johnson said, 'Miss Waring is a lady, Chloe. Moreover, she has wealth at her disposal: her marriage is not a matter of urgency. I confess, I know not why you have taken her in such dislike when her dearest wish is to see you comfortably established.'

'Her dearest wish is to meddle in matters which do not concern her.'

Miss Johnson fluttered a protesting handkerchief and repeated that Miss Waring wished to see me well married and comfortably established.

'But which of her choices would consider me a suitable match? I am a nobody; I have no money and no relations that I know of! What will recommend me to the kind of suitor Miss Waring has in mind?'

During my early years, I was raised by my nurse, Emma Gooding, the only mother I have ever known. She, however, was too old to have been my natural mother. She died, aged sixty-two, when I was seven years old. After that, the rector's wife escorted me three miles to Stellham, a village in Gloucestershire, and placed me in a boarding-school for girls, run by Miss Johnson. There, I was educated in a useful way until I was sixteen and there I remained as a parlour boarder.

An unknown person had determined this, had paid for it all, and also provided me with clothes and a modest allowance. I called that person my Somebody. When I reached an age to understand such matters, I thought my Somebody was my father, who paid to keep me out of the way. I suspected my birth was illegitimate and that I was an embarrassment to him.

Miss Waring was an embarrassment to me, but when I said so, Miss Johnson became quite alarmed. 'My dear, I beg you will have a care!

3

It would not do to offend her.'

'Aye, that is the trouble, there is none who dare to speak their minds to her. She is too used to having her own way.'

Miss Johnson was flattered to be noticed by the Warings. Whenever they were short of company, she was called upon to dine, or to take tea and make up a four at cards and listen and defer to the opinions of Mr Waring and his daughters.

She had asked permission to take me there one evening last June, shortly after the marriage of the older Miss Waring. The wedding celebrations were over, Miss Jane Waring was now Mrs Helcott and gone away, and the remaining Warings were feeling flat and in need of company.

'I venture to hope,' Miss Johnson confided, 'that Miss Helen will like you, for her friendship could be most advantageous to your situation. I do not despair of it, for now her sister is married, she will be in want of a companion.'

I had not objected to the friendship, at first. I admired the superior elegance of their house, with its large rooms and fine furnishings and beautiful ornaments. I enjoyed the delicate fare they pressed upon me and I envied their many conservatories and their gardens with fine lawns and fountains and the stand of mature oaks and chestnut at the end.

Miss Waring, three years my senior, was a

pretty girl, two inches shorter than myself, her figure nicely rounded and sturdy. She had fair hair, soft blue eyes, regular features and a fine complexion, all assisted by the most becoming fashions. Her deportment was elegant and she had easy, polished manners. In these matters I admired her and learnt much by observation. But, as we became better acquainted, I found certain aspects of her character were irksome to me.

She was over-inquisitive and there were times when she attributed the worst possible motives to the conduct of others. Her wealth and position brought constant deference, which led her to suppose that she was wiser than other people.

When she enquired about my family she was dissatisfied with the brevity of my story and asked, 'Have you never tried to discover your parents?'

I had, and met with checks in every direction. The financial arrangements were dealt with by an attorney who spoke of 'his client'. This client demanded from Miss Johnson written reports on my conduct and progress but these, too, were passed through the attorney and we could not find out his identity.

I said, 'I am given the name of Smith which, whether it be truth or convenience, leaves me sadly placed to investigate.'

She acknowledged this and admitted my

conjectures about my Somebody were probably correct. 'We may, however, be thankful that he does not neglect his duty to provide for you.'

Her family was of consequence in our neighbourhood. Since she had determined to befriend me, it was necessary for her to think me worthy of her friendship. Now, purely because of her own vanity, she determined that my father was a high-born gentleman, most likely an aristocrat.

'For there is something of the patrician in your features, dear Chloe, which speaks of distinguished breeding, however unfortunate your poor papa's morals. Well, I must do the best I can to see you become well connected.'

With this in mind, she attempted to promote my marriage. She chose gentlemen of minor consequence, all of whom would, in my opinion, exercise prudence in money matters when choosing a wife. Moreover, they would look upon my origins as a possible source of trouble and scandal should my parentage become known.

When I said so, Miss Waring steered me towards a looking-glass and bade me to take note of my own beauty. 'Your figure is most pleasing, your features are distinguished, your dark hair and eyes are everywhere admired and your complexion is flawless. I declare, any gentleman might fall in love with you, and love, my dear Chloe, makes a mockery of self interest.'

She was persuaded one of them would fall in love with me and frequently made me blush by parading me before the gentlemen, pointing out my best features, as though she was selling them a horse.

Hoping to dissuade her, I began to find fault with my suitors. Mr Fairbrother, I declared, was too fond of eating. 'Already, he grows stout. Consider what his form will be in ten years' time.' I shuddered. 'I think I could not bear it.'

I disliked the flighty Mr Cross and detested the pompous Mr Bateman and I hid a smile when she told me, crossly, that it would be my wifely duty to correct the failings of my husband.

'A lady in your situation cannot afford to be too nice in her notions,' she told me severely. 'It is of the utmost importance for you to become comfortably established. Only marriage can save you from penury.'

I thought penury preferable to marriage with Mr Bateman but I did not say so for I had learnt how she would lecture me on all the evils of remaining single.

Miss Johnson said she meant well and I suppose she did, but my patience was sorely tried when she advised me to detach myself from my friends.

I thought of Mary Hughes and Rachel Todd and Sally Carter and I shook with anger at

Miss Waring's careless presumption. These friends had been fellow boarders at Miss Johnson's school and had often been so obliging as to invite me to stay in their homes during the holidays.

Everywhere I was welcomed and made to feel at home. Their mothers had taught me domestic skills: from them I had learnt of baking bread and pies, of churning butter and straining cheese, how to manage pigs and poultry and dress a joint, how to cultivate vegetables and fruit, and how to make preserves.

If their kindness had made me a little tearful for having no family of my own I had, at least, had glimpses of family life and formed certain aspirations for my future.

I had less faith in securing the kind of gentleman Miss Waring had in mind than I had in the notion that my abilities would bring prosperity. Miss Johnson had seen to it that all her charges were competent needlewomen. This, and the knowledge I had acquired away from school might, I felt, render me very acceptable to a man who would value my homely talents.

So I was indignant when Miss Waring expressed the opinion that such acquaintances would do me no good in polite society.

At first, I could not answer her with civility. I bit back my temper, however, knowing Miss Johnson would be grieved by any falling out with the Warings.

In the end, I said that upon marriage I would defer to my husband. But in the meantime it would be most unbecoming in me to repel those who had shown me nothing but kindness.

I remained in correspondence with my friends, despite Miss Waring's displeasure. To own the truth, I had begun to find my situation intolerable, unwilling to continue my association with that lady but unable to end it on account of Miss Johnson.

Two days ago the Warings received their Christmas visitors, a party consisting of relations and high-born friends. Miss Johnson was not required and neither was I. We made our own merry party, and contrived to spend Christmas agreeably.

Lady Pascall was one of the Warings' guests. One day she suffered a fall and hurt her ankle. This caused consternation, for the Warings's party were to attend a ball. Clearly, Lady Pascall could not go and, clearly, she could not be left alone.

Miss Johnson was summoned to keep her company. Miss Johnson was suffering with dyspepsia, a result of Christmas indulgence in her fondness for pastry.

Which is why, on that bleak December afternoon, I was obliged to forsake my book and the warmth and comfort of the parlour to trudge a mile and a half over frost-hardened mud, with my breath hanging misty in the air, to mind my manners and act as unpaid companion to an old lady, whilst the rest of them sallied forth from Stellham House in pursuit of gaiety.

On the way, I had a most peculiar encounter.

The sound of hoofbeats taught me that someone on horseback was approaching from behind. I paused and stood aside to let him pass. He cantered towards me, touched his hat as he went by, then, with a loud oath, wheeled his mount around and came to halt in front of me, blocking the path.

'What are *you* doing here?' he demanded.

'Sir?' I stared at him, perplexed. By his clothes and the quality of the beast he was riding, I guessed he was one of the gentlemen visiting the Warings, a tall, broad-shouldered man, dark-haired and handsome, but flushed and angry.

'Why are you here? Come, Isabella, what trickery is this?'

'No trickery, sir, and my name is not Isabella. I fear you have mistaken me for another.'

'Upon my soul!'

He dismounted and hitched the reins over a convenient branch. Then he strode towards me and since he appeared so angry I was alarmed and took a step backwards. He caught me, ignoring my protests, and with his hand beneath my chin he forced my head upwards, pulled at the strings of my woollen bonnet and uncovered my head.

His annoyance was increased. 'I know you too well, my girl, so do not think you are disguised by wearing such shabby garments! Where are your parents? Have you no thought for their distress when your mischief becomes known?'

I struggled unsuccessfully; he held me fast, myself panting in astonished outrage and he increasing in temper.

'Unhand me, sir! I know not who you think I am but I assure you, never have I, until this moment, set eyes upon you. Upon my soul, this is too much!'

He sucked in his breath. 'Isabella, I warn you—'

How this altercation might have ended I know not, but at that moment I was relieved to espy someone I knew.

'Mr Draper,' I called. 'Mr Draper, would you be so good as to assist me?'

'Why, Miss Smith, are you in trouble?'

'Miss Smith?' ejaculated my captor. *'Miss Smith?'*

Mr Draper joined us. He looked the gentleman up and down and evidently thought better of fighting him. Instead, he said peaceably, 'Come, young master, there is no call to be treating a poor young woman in that rough unmannerly fashion just because she has

11

no family to protect her.'

'Ha! That is what she has told you, is it?'

'Mr Draper, this gentleman has mistaken me for some acquaintance of his. Would you be so good as to tell him who I am and—and'—my voice rose in pain as he tightened his grip on my arm—'and—and how long you have known me?'

'Eh, Miss Chloe, I am puzzled to remember how long that is. Ten years, or thereabouts, I reckon. You were just a little maid of seven or eight . . .'

It was enough to convince the gentleman of his mistake. I was released and he took a step backwards, regarding me in astonishment.

'Thank you, Mr Draper, I am obliged to you.' I rubbed my arm and turned to the other. 'I trust you are satisfied, sir?'

'I can scarce believe it,' he muttered. 'There cannot possibly be two of you!'

Outraged as I was by his rough handling, curiosity got the better of me. Instead of delivering reproofs, as I should have done, I said, 'Am I so much like your Isabella?'

'She is not my Isabella,' he said coldly.

'Well, then, who is she?'

'More to the point, who are you?'

Mr Draper was a courteous man and took it upon himself to introduce me to my assailant. 'This is Miss Smith, sir, who is boarder at Miss Johnson's school.' Then to me, he added in some concern, 'Are you going home, Miss

12

Chloe? Would you wish me to walk with you?'

'I thank you, but no. I am on my way to Stellham House.'

'Are you indeed? And what is your business there?'

That was the other, who had yet to speak a civil word to me and I was more outraged by his continuing rudeness than I was by his initial mistake. Now, I said haughtily, 'I have yet to learn how my business can possibly be of any concern to you?'

'Upon my soul, you are very pert for a schoolroom miss.'

I felt my colour rise. 'I am not a schoolroom miss,' I said indignantly. 'I am a parlour boarder.'

'A subtle distinction.' He bowed and there was something insolent in his expression. 'I must try to remember.'

'And you consider yourself a gentleman, do you?'

These pleasantries were interrupted by Mr Draper. 'I can walk with you to Stellham House, if you wish, Miss Chloe.'

'No need for that,' pronounced my opponent. 'I am going there myself, I will escort Miss—er—Smith.'

I lifted my chin. 'I believe I would prefer to be escorted by Mr Draper.'

He stared at me in blank astonishment. Then his features were transformed by a grin, reluctant at first, but slowly widening into rueful acknowledgement.

'Aye, no doubt. Upon my soul, I believe my wits have gone a-begging! Marcus Redgrave at your service, madam, and I beg you will excuse my incivility. Come, I mean you no harm, you need have no fear of me. Besides, I want to talk to you.'

'Ah, but do I want to talk to you?'

He regarded me in some amusement. 'Yes, I think you do.'

Odious man! He was right, of course, I did want to talk to him for I was consumed with curiosity about the lady to whom I bore such a remarkable resemblance.

I turned to Mr Draper, thanked him for his assistance and told him I would accept the gentleman's escort. Mr Draper remained undecided and I spent several entertaining minutes hearing Mr Redgrave assure him he did not mean to murder me.

'Though I cannot wholly blame him for his suspicions,' he said, when Mr Draper finally went away. 'He must have thought me a dangerous lunatic.'

There was something so engaging in his smile that, in spite of his rough handling, I found myself smiling in return.

'Mr Draper is not alone in that apprehension,' I informed him. 'Have you conceived a particular attachment for my bonnet, sir, or may I have it back?'

'What? Oh, I beg your pardon!' My bonnet

was restored to me and I put it on. He watched me in some curiosity and said abruptly, 'Who are you, Miss Smith?'

'That,' I said, 'is something I would like to know myself.'

His eyes widened. 'Do you not know?' he demanded. 'How can this be? No, wait! I recall now, that fellow Draper said you had no family to protect you. I confess I dismissed it as falsehood, at the time. You are an orphan, I collect?'

There was little point in refusing him my story, for he could have it in an instant from Miss Waring. Besides, I thought I would learn more by being frank with him. As we set off, with him leading his horse, I told what I knew.

'Curious,' he remarked, when I had done.

'I certainly am,' I said. 'It occurs to me that I might have some common ancestor with the lady you call Isabella, and if you would be so good as to tell me something of her—'

'I would not advise you to seek out Isabella,' he said.

I understood his meaning and I was nettled. I said, coldly, 'I assure you, sir, I have no wish to encroach upon her, or her family. Ever since I came to understand such matters, I have supposed my birth is illegitimate and I can easily comprehend how my existence must mean trouble and scandal for someone! All I wish is a little intelligence.'

'This intelligence I will give you,' he said.

'Isabella Harcourt is trifling and silly and has a capacity for childish mischief which too often goes beyond what is pleasing. She has a liking for complicated jests,' he added, 'which is why I so far forgot myself as to accost you in such an unseemly way! The resemblance is quite remarkable. You could be her—'

He broke off and gasped and looked at me again.

'Her twin?' I prompted. 'Is that what you are thinking?'

He was pale and his lips were tightly compressed together. He shook his head, and his voice sounded hollow. 'You are like enough to be her twin, but I think you are not.'

'I cannot be her twin,' I said, 'for I comprehend she was legitimately born, and to gentry?' He nodded and I went on, 'As her twin, there would be no objection to my birth so why should we be separated? No, it cannot be so, though I may be her half-sister, born out of wedlock. Are you acquainted with the lady's father, sir? Would you say that was possible?'

He shook his head, frowning, so lost in thought that he did not hear me. When he spoke, it was not to answer my question. Instead, he demanded to know how old I was.

'My eighteenth birthday occurred on the tenth of November.'

'Not her twin, then. Isabella is younger by six months.'

'What of her father, sir? Could he be—?'

16

'It is not possible. She takes her looks from her mother.'

'Oh!' The implications struck me immediately. 'That makes nonsense of my supposition. There may be some connection, nevertheless. Can you advise me, sir?'

'They are considered a respectable family,' he said, but there was a faint hint of disapprobation in his voice. 'Her father, Sir William Harcourt, is a distant cousin of mine. Her mother, I fear, is something of an invalid, and Isabella . . .'

He paused and I said, 'What of Isabella?'

He regarded me in a sombre fashion. 'You are not like her,' he said abruptly.

'Well!' I said indignantly. 'Am I expected to believe you, after all that has passed?'

'In appearance, you resemble her exactly. But you are not like her. Do not ask me how I know! Ten minutes ago, I was certain you were her. Now I am aware of a difference in your demeanour, but I can say no more.' He frowned over it. 'It may be the expression in your eyes, I cannot tell.'

'I do not know the lady, so I cannot assist you. I may never meet her, but sir, I would know what you can tell me.'

He regarded me sombrely and seemed reluctant to speak. My voice rose a little. 'You must see how I wish to know more!'

'But would it profit you to know more?'

'I do not seek to profit, only to learn a little.'

17

'Well, I give you fair warning,' he said, 'should Isabella discover your existence, she will make use of your resemblance and involve you in many schemes designed to confuse and deceive and none of them to your advantage. It will do you no service to be mistaken for Isabella!'

'That,' I spoke feelingly, 'is something I have recently discovered!'

He grinned as my shaft found its mark.

'As for your own antecedents,' he went on, 'there may be a connection with her mother's family but I think—indeed, I am certain—you would be unwise to pursue it.'

'You mean they would dislike it.' I sighed. 'I cannot blame them, I suppose. But how I wish I knew more! You cannot know how uncomfortable it is, sir, to have no family.'

'A family can be more of a curse than a blessing,' he informed me, smiling. 'Do not repine, Miss Smith. My advice to you is find a good man, marry him and make your own family.'

'Perhaps, one day, I will,' I said. Then, concerned in case I had given him a mistaken impression, I went on, 'I hope I have not led you to suppose I am unhappy, sir. I am provided for and I do have good friends. Well, I am grateful for your information.'

We turned into the gravel drive to Stellham House. My companion said, 'Your errand is to Miss Waring, I take it?'

'I expect to see Miss Waring, but my errand is to keep Lady Pascall company this evening.'

At that, my companion stopped and stared. 'Is it, indeed? Well, well!' He seemed about to say something more, but he checked himself and spoke brusquely, 'Well—go on, do not wait for me, I must see this fellow settled in his stable.'

He turned to lead his horse away, but I was alarmed about what might arise should Miss Waring learn of my resemblance to another and I halted him and begged him not to mention it.

He slanted a quizzical look at me and I blushed, unwilling to venture a frank opinion of the lady who was, after all, his hostess. I went on in some embarrassment. 'Miss Waring has been very kind to me but sometimes she has—er—fanciful notions! It is the kind of story that would appeal to her and she can be very persistent and—er—'

'Tiresome?' he suggested. He laughed at my expression. 'Very well, Miss Smith. Your secret is safe with me!'

TWO

I stood by the window in Miss Waring's dressing-room, looking out at the frost-whitened lawns. It was barely four o'clock, but it was growing dark. Behind me, the room blazed with light from a multitude of candles.

Miss Waring was taking more than usual care with her appearance in preparation for the ball. Her golden hair was taken up at the back and arranged in artful curls at the front, with little blue flowers pinned here and there.

'Now, Chloe, tell me what you think of me in my ball-gown!'

She wore a blue silk gauze hung over an underdress of pink satin. The effect was pleasing but elusive, the colour seeming to change with every movement.

I felt a twinge of envy and a sudden plunging of my spirits, but I admired her and told her what she wanted to hear, that it was very fine, it became her admirably and she would be the most sought after lady at the ball.

She deliberated over an array of scent bottles, choosing at last frangipani. She slipped on her gloves, smoothing them to the elbow and pronounced herself ready. Her maid came forward to slip a pelerine of dark blue velvet over her shoulders.

All this was to assist her in her new ambition of captivating the gentleman who, unbeknown to her, I had met with on the way. I had learnt he was not, as I had previously supposed, a plain Mr Redgrave, but a Sir Marcus Redgrave, baronet, with estates in the county of Derbyshire.

I had said nothing of my encounter with the

gentleman, knowing she would be offended to learn he had spoken to me and knowing also that she would subject me to ruthless questioning. I had no wish to tell her what I had learnt, but no wish, either, to involve myself in falsehood.

Upon my arrival, she had invited me to her dressing-room and spoken of her designs upon Sir Marcus quite openly, seeming unaware that her maid had ears. I was not at all pleased to be her confidant in this matter.

'I shall be Lady Redgrave!' she announced. 'I confess, the notion of a title pleases me. I cannot imagine why dear Papa never made a push to get one.'

Never have I regretted my lowly estate more than I did at that moment. Chafing at the curb I must put on my tongue, I said, 'Once you told me you had determined never to marry.'

'That,' she informed me, 'was before I saw him. Now, I am quite determined upon it.'

'Before you saw him?' I blinked in some surprise. 'Do you tell me you had never met him before? How is it you have a stranger with you, at Christmas?'

'Well, he is not a stranger, not exactly, because he is acquainted with my brother, Mr Helcott.'

He was there because Lady Pascall, an old acquaintance of Mr Waring, had announced her intention to pay them a visit. This left the Warings in want of a gentleman to make up

21

the party and somehow, Sir Marcus had been prevailed on to join them. He came with the Helcotts, Miss Waring's sister and brother-in-law. Miss Waring had met him for the first time only two days ago and had, she said, fallen instantly in love with him.

'I declare, never have I set eyes on a gentleman who pleased me better. How fortunate is my colouring, for it is well known that dark gentlemen have a preference for fair ladies. And I have the advantage of being pretty. It will be quite astonishing if he does not fall in love with me.'

I had previous experience of Miss Waring's sublime confidence in her own powers: now, without knowing exactly why, I felt a most reprehensible desire to give her a jolt. 'I take it the gentleman has formed no previous attachment?'

'I think not, for why, then, would he spend Christmas here?'

'In matters of the heart many things can go awry.' I spoke with all the wisdom a circulating library could impart. 'He may have quarrelled with his true love, but it does not follow that he no longer cares for her.'

I beamed at her, but she was shaking her head, so I went on, warming to my theme, 'He may have determined, in a heated moment, to remove himself from her presence and to accept your brother's invitation as being altogether fortuitous! He wishes nothing more, at this present, than to avoid all painful reminders of her.'

I kept my countenance, despite the look she gave me and continued soulfully, 'Try as he might, he cannot forget her, and when circumstances bring them together again, as they must, they will be reconciled and live happily ever after.'

Pleased with my powers of invention, I almost believed it myself, but Miss Waring was not impressed. 'My dear Chloe, there are times when you allow your imagination to run away with you. I advise you to check such wild flights of fancy.'

Coming from one who had, not so very long ago, blithely determined my father was a duke, I felt this was rather strong. I controlled my features with an effort.

'Sir Marcus is not engaged and for very good reason! His fortune is reduced, for his father gambled away a large part of it. Fortunately, he died before he could completely ruin himself. Sir Marcus has a competence, no more. He can afford to marry only where there is fortune.'

'He should have little difficulty there.' Still hopeful of jolting her out of her complacency, I went on, 'After all, he has a title to assist his cause. And he is as handsome—er—according to the way you describe him! There must be at least one rich lady eager to place her fortune at his disposal.'

'Not so,' she told me. She was quite firm about it and quite insensible of her own mendacity. 'It is a depressing fact, my dear, that in such a case, a gentleman's attentions may be suspected. I am persuaded Sir Marcus would not wish to be thought a fortune hunter!'

'Indeed, he is in a sad case! He cannot afford to marry a poor lady and his pride will not allow him to pursue a rich lady!' I shook my head. 'He had better remain single.'

'I am determined he shall not. I have fortune enough and he will marry me.'

I raised my brows. 'You would not wish to be married for your fortune, surely?'

She gave a little trill of laughter. 'Nonsensical girl, of course I would not! But should he come to like me, there will be no difficulty. Already, I have begun to show him little attentions, just to enourage him, you know! I depend upon you to assist me, Chloe, if you will.'

'I? Assist you? I cannot feel it is in my power to lend assistance in such a matter.'

'Of course it is!' She looked surprised. 'Speak of me when you converse with him, increase his good opinion of me.'

I had difficulty in silencing the gurgle of laughter that rose in my throat, for in that instant I recalled how Sir Marcus had, with one word, expressed an opinion much in accordance with my own.

Tiresome!

I said only that I was unlikely to find myself conversing with Sir Marcus but, if I did, I would do my best.

She appeared satisfied and went on to talk of her hopes and expectations of dancing with Sir Marcus at the forthcoming ball. When she was ready, she picked up her fan and said she would take me to Lady Pascall.

As we descended the stairs, she said, 'I fear you will spend a dull evening listening to Lady Pascall's gossip, but you may be certain of a good dinner.'

Lady Pascall and I were to dine together, just the two of us, because the rest of the party were engaged to dine with the family giving the ball. Since they would be late returning, a bedchamber had been prepared and I was to remain overnight.

'I have told the servants to be certain there is a good fire in your room and hot bricks to warm your bed,' she said. 'Such a dreadful frost! At least there is no snow.'

'I fear you will have a cold journey.'

She said with fur-lined cloaks and hot bricks in the carriage, they would do very well. She led me to the room where Lady Pascall was sitting. 'Oh! Oh, Sir Marcus! I had not expected to find you here.'

He had been sitting with Lady Pascall, but he rose as we entered the room and offered a slight bow. 'Miss Waring,' he said, 'and

Miss—er—?'

'This is Miss Smith, come to keep Lady Pascall company.'

'Ah, quite. Delighted to make your acquaintance, Miss Smith.'

'Sir.' I curtsied, at once conscious of his elegance. A very fine gentleman indeed, with a figure that showed to advantage in ballroom finery. He had none of the extravagances of fashion, no jewels, no tassels, just a froth of snowy white cravat surmounting a cream and gold waistcoat: coat and breeches were black, his calves encased in white stockings and on his feet he wore black shoes with silver buckles.

I became miserably conscious of my own gown of blue serge, homemade and looking dowdy at the side of Miss Waring's fairy-tale appearance, even though I had trimmed the sleeves with ribbon. But when I looked directly at him, I was startled to see him flicker an eyelid.

Fortunately, Miss Waring had not noticed. She was now enquiring of Lady Pascall's comfort and ushering me towards her. I was introduced, made another curtsy, and was graciously received.

She was a slim lady, who looked much younger than her seventy years: she sat in a winged armchair with a footstool supporting her bandaged ankle and, despite her enforced repose, she had an air of vigour about her.

I liked her immediately. Her smile reached her eyes, and her eyes danced, conveying a message that she and I were about to enjoy a far more entertaining evening than the poor fools who were venturing out in search of amusements.

'I had expected a Miss Johnson,' she said smiling, 'but a Miss Smith will do very well. What is your name, child?'

'Chloe, madam. Miss Johnson is unwell, which is why she has not come herself. She asked me to pass on her compliments.'

I was obliged to step aside, because Miss Waring began fussing around her, rather needlessly, I felt. It might have been embarrassment in the presence of Sir Marcus, but I had the uncharitable notion that her design was to impress him with her thoughtfulness for others.

I glanced at him, but I could not tell how far he admired Miss Waring. He was still, perfectly at ease and looking amused. He had been blessedly silent on the subject of our previous encounter, with only a brief secret acknowlegement that he remembered it.

Now, for the first time, I was struck by how little information he had imparted. Apart from hearing his opinion of Isabella Harcourt, I had learnt only that I might be related to her mother's family. He had put no name to them and he had not told where they came from.

I wondered if Lady Pascall might enlighten

me further. But she had been quite unsurprised by my appearance so I had to assume she knew nothing of Isabella.

A servant came in to say the carriages were waiting. We heard sounds of voices and laughter as the rest of the party congregated in the hall. Lady Pascall assured Miss Waring that the screens were placed exactly where she wished, that she had no need of another shawl, that she had all her cordials to hand and she was sure Miss Smith would look after her very well.

Sir Marcus ushered Miss Waring away, favoured Lady Pascall and myself with a smile and a quirk of the eyebrow and bowed himself out of the room.

Lady Pascall motioned me to a chair placed opposite. 'Now we may be easy and comfortable together,' she said. 'You and I are going to become great friends, Miss Smith. You shall begin by telling me all about your life in Miss Johnson's boarding-school for girls.'

I could not feel it was a subject to interest her greatly, but she was smiling and attentive so I told her about the school, spoke affectionately of Miss Johnson and recollected a few diverting moments for her entertainment.

Since she knew where I came from, I wondered how much more she knew. 'Has Miss Waring spoken of me, madam?'

I thought it unlikely and I was not surprised

28

when she shook her head. I had been mentioned only as 'Helen's little friend, Miss Chloe Smith' and it was Mr Waring who spoke of me, when someone remarked that Helen must be lonely now her sister was married.

'I have known George Waring for many years,' said Lady Pascall, 'and I know he assisted Miss Johnson with a loan when she first set up her little school. Not unnaturally, she feels a sense of obligation. She will make herself useful to all the Warings and I can easily comprehend how she would introduce one of her favourite girls as a suitable friend for Miss Waring.'

'It was very kind of Miss Johnson to think of me,' I said.

'I have no doubt she meant it kindly,' said Lady Pascall. She sighed and eased her position. 'For my part, I find Miss Waring a tiresome creature and her father does nothing to check her. I wonder why I said I would spend Christmas with them?'

'Perhaps it seemed a good idea, at the time?' I suggested.

She chuckled. 'Perhaps it was a good idea, since it brought me to meet Miss Chloe Smith. You do not like Miss Waring either, do you?'

'I should not say so, madam. She has been kind to me.'

'She makes use of you and she patronizes you,' she retorted, 'and you bear it for Miss Johnson's sake!'

I was startled at her swift and accurate reading of my situation. But I made no answer. I could not prevent Lady Pascall expressing her opinions, but she would not draw me into open disloyalty.

Perhaps she understood this, for she added thoughtfully, 'To be fair, I doubt Miss Waring understands herself. In that lady we see overweening conceit and only moderate intelligence. It is not a happy combination.'

'I believe she means well.'

'That makes her dangerous,' she said. 'Now she is setting her cap at Sir Marcus. Will she get him, do you think?'

'Perhaps you should ask Sir Marcus,' I said demurely.

'I cannot; he is not here. Come, tell me what you think?'

'Well, she is very pretty,' I said carefully, 'and she has the advantage of birth and fortune. Do you know how far Sir Marcus can be influenced by such matters? I do not.'

'Nor I. But I do know his standing with Miss Waring is enhanced by his title. I am afraid she can be very persistent. Upon my soul, I can find it in my heart to pity Marcus!' Lady Pascall laughed. 'We must rescue him, Miss Smith.'

For the first time, I was stung into a retort. 'From the little I have seen of that gentleman,' I said, 'I very much doubt he stands in need of rescue. I am persuaded Sir Marcus is perfectly capable of taking care of himself.'

THREE

Upon retiring for the night I lay awake on purpose, stretching between fresh lavender-scented sheets, watching the shadows, and savouring all the luxury of having a fire in my room, linen-wrapped hot bricks in my bed and a goose-feather mattress to sleep on.

In the morning, hot water for washing would be brought to my room and clean towels and, when I went downstairs to breakfast, there would be a choice of nice things to eat, eggs and ham, or chops, or salted herrings. There would be hot rolls and butter, preserves, plumcake and even toast.

Earlier, when I saw the dinner which had been ordered for Lady Pascall and myself, I had felt some compunction for not defending Miss Waring more vigorously. As I helped myself from a dish of mutton steaks and cucumber, I attempted to rectify the matter, praising her thoughtfulness in ordering dishes to which I am extremely partial.

'A lemon soufflé, too! Such a treat!'

Somehow, Lady Pascall had directed this into an enquiry of the fare served at Miss Johnson's school. I assured the lady that we were well provided with wholesome and nourishing food and we always had eggs for breakfast on Sunday.

She had looked amused. 'And the rest of the week?'

'Porridge, madam, as a rule. But now we have eggs twice a week, since my bantams began laying.'

Her eyes widened. 'Your bantams?'

I told how I had learnt the care of poultry from Rachel Todd's mother and, when I became parlour boarder, I persuaded Miss Johnson to allot a corner of her garden to my enterprise.

'I thought it would be a useful thing to do,' I explained. 'And the children like to help.'

A joiner had built the chicken coop. I watched as he did it and I told Lady Pascall that, with instruction and practice, I might become adept at joinery myself.

A fork clattered against Lady Pascall's plate. 'Joinery?' she exclaimed. 'Upon my soul what have I—?' She checked herself and stared at me. Then she shook her head and repeated, '*Joinery?* I trust Miss Johnson did not encourage you in that?'

I shook my head. 'She says it is not a suitable occupation for a female and everyone else says so, too. But I think that is a great piece of nonsense, one of those absurd dictates of society which people accept without considering the matter at all! I do not see why a lady should not turn her hand to anything her strength is equal to.'

She stared at me in fascination. 'That point

of view had not previously occurred to me,' she admitted. 'But joinery? Oh dear!' She began to laugh. 'Can you picture Miss Waring busy with hammer and nails?'

I giggled. 'I confess, it takes a stretch of imagination.'

'Joinery,' marvelled Lady Pascall. 'How old are you Chloe? Eighteen? How did you come to have such an independent mind? It cannot be Miss Johnson's influence, I am sure.'

'N-no,' I said slowly. 'Unless it is because she . . .' I hesitated, not quite certain of myself, expressing thoughts that were only half-formed. 'I have great regard for her, but her concerns are the children, always, and she has become rather juvenile herself. I do not blame her, for how could she help it? But in recent years, I have begun to feel that I am older than she is! Can you understand that?'

She nodded. 'You have outgrown her,' she said. 'Tell me, what other talents do you have?'

I answered briefly, feeling that I was talking about myself too much and Lady Pascall could not possibly be as interested as she seemed. But she had a delicate way of encouraging confidences and by the time we had finished dinner, she had learnt more than I wished to tell.

Her questions ended when we settled again at the fireside. The backgammon board was placed between us, though we paid less attention to the game than to conversation.

She kept up a lively flow of talk, speaking of the theatre, of music, of art, of poetry and literature, taking me into realms where, I was obliged to confess, I had little knowledge.

She did not mind. She talked and I could have listened for ever, but her ankle began to pain her. I persuaded her to take laudanum, which eased her but made her drowsy, and shortly thereafter she determined to retire for the night.

Servants carried her upstairs on a chair. I followed to be certain of her comfort, but her maid knew better than I how to attend to that, so I wished her goodnight and retired, not unwillingly, to my bedchamber.

I had noticed that Lady Pascall, for all her questions, made no enquiry about my family. She said nothing, asked nothing, but I was very sensible that she knew my situation.

And why should that perturb me? Never had I concealed the facts, for there was no sense in it. In a small place like Stellham, everybody knew everything and strangers could learn it all in minutes. Yet in Lady Pascall there was something alert in her manner towards me, something that went beyond the common interest and I was puzzled.

Was it because I resembled the unknown Isabella? Sir Marcus had been with Lady Pascall, and he must have mentioned our encounter. Indeed, it would be astonishing had he not.

Sir Marcus would give full value to the story and tell how I accounted for myself. If Lady Pascall was acquainted with the other lady, she would be amused and intrigued by the likeness.

As I lay awake watching the firelight cast shadows on the walls, I toyed with the idea of an encounter between myself and my likeness and I giggled, picturing her astonishment. What would she say?

When I fell asleep I had confused dreams about another like me, who was not me, dressed in a ballgown of blue gauze over an underdress of pink satin. She was dancing with Sir Marcus whilst I, envious in blue serge, watched from a distance.

I was roused, briefly, by babble and laughter from the party returning from the ball. Somewhere, a clock struck three. And when I woke again, at seven o'clock, I thought none would emerge from their bedchambers before noon. I would be spared from hearing Miss Waring's account of the ball.

I shivered when I rose from my bed. Frost had painted the windowpanes with crystal ferns and feathers. Outside, icicles hung from the sills, every tree and bush wore frills of ice along its branches, and the lawns were salt-crusted white.

When I went downstairs, I was surprised to discover Sir Marcus already at breakfast. After the usual civilities, I enquired after last night's ball and remarked how delightful Miss Waring had appeared in her ballgown.

He agreed to it, without any sign of particular animation, and added that all the ladies had been very fine. 'Balls, you know,' he added, smiling at me, 'are held expressly for that purpose. An excuse for ladies to flaunt their finest.'

'I beg your pardon, I thought they were held for the purpose of dancing.'

'No.' He shook his head, a faint hint of mockery in his tone. 'Dancing is merely to parade the finery.'

'Well, sir, I hope you did your duty and gave every lady her opportunity to do so.'

'Indeed I did. I admired all of them.'

'All of them?'

'Every one. You would not believe how many compliments I paid last night.'

I giggled, wondering what Miss Waring thought of that. I thought Sir Marcus was teasing her, well aware of her design.

I could think of nothing to say in response, so I became intent on ham and pickled damsons and bread rolls and butter. And it was he who spoke first, asking how I liked Lady Pascall.

'I liked her very much indeed,' I said.

'So you passed the evening agreeably?'

'We did, until her ankle began to pain her. I persuaded her to take laudanum and retire.'

'Do you think she liked you?' he asked abruptly.

I was surprised. 'I saw no evidence of dislike. Whether she was taken with me in any particular way, I know not. Since I am unlikely to have ado with her in any particular way, I cannot think it matters.'

'You might have more ado with her than you think,' he said, frowning. At my look of enquiry, he added: 'She is—she is obliged to remain here until her ankle is mended, longer than she meant. Your company may be required on future occasions.'

'If she does not object, I do not. I liked her.'

'She is a very likeable lady,' he agreed, smiling.

'Well, then.'

'She is also a lady of somewhat frightening subtlety. Do not mistake, I know no ill of her. She has understanding above the ordinary and she has her own way of arranging matters.'

I had been about to bite into a bread roll. I returned it to my plate and gave him my full attention. He was frowning and it seemed to me he looked a little puzzled.

'Speak plainly, sir. Do you mistrust the lady?'

'No, I would not put it as strongly as that: let me say, rather, that I fall short of understanding her.'

'Have you known the lady for long, sir? Were you acquainted with her before you came to Stellham?'

'I have known her all my life,' he said. 'My dealings with her were occasional, as one would expect with an old lady and a young man. In recent months, I have come to know her better; I suspect she determined that I should.'

I was diverted. 'You think she is setting her cap at you?'

He laughed. 'No, I do not accuse her of that.'

'She might have designs on you,' I said. Clearly he suspected some design, if not the one I had attributed to her. I was disposed to tease him so I went on, 'I have often seen old ladies become girlish in the presence of a personable young man. The years just fall away from them! The lady may have determined upon you to give her a new lease of life.'

He answered with similar nonsense and I revised my opinion of him, setting aside the annoyance of our first encounter because the circumstances had been peculiar.

Here he was, a baronet, and a handsome young man, but he did not patronize nor did he look with high-born disdain upon a nobody such as I. Indeed, he gave every appearance of enjoying my society and had borne my pert remarks with good humour.

In our conversation I attempted to further Miss Waring's cause, though without enthusiasm. I was pleased he showed no sign of admiring the lady. I felt he would be wasted on her.

Upon discovering I was about to walk back to the school, Sir Marcus insisted on accompanying me. 'No,' he said, when I protested against the need, 'I cannot allow you to walk alone. Who knows what might befall you?'

'Indeed!' I said mischievously. 'I might be mistaken for some other lady and set upon. In such a case, your protection will be invaluable.'

'Vixen!' He grinned, not at all put out. 'No, but the ground is treacherous in this frost. A slip, a fall, and you could lie hurt and unable to move for some time before you were discovered. You will accept my escort, Miss Smith.'

I was moved by his concern, though it might have been his way of making amends for yesterday's attack. And, I confess, I was not averse to spending a little more time in his society. 'Very well, sir, if you insist.'

When we parted to put on outdoor clothes I saw the maid who said Lady Pascall was awake. I went to her room.

She was propped against her pillows drinking cocoa. She said she had passed a comfortable night and her ankle was easy. 'You are leaving? But not alone, a servant must escort you.'

'Sir Marcus has been so obliging as to offer

39

his escort.'

'Has he indeed?' I could see this intelligence pleased her. Perhaps she thought it would annoy Miss Waring.

She charged me with her compliments to Miss Johnson and said I must visit her again whilst she remained in Stellham. 'And will you inform Sir Marcus there is a matter I wish to discuss with him? Ask him to join me, upon his return.'

Sir Marcus looked amused when I gave him the message. 'Now what could that be about, I wonder?' But he spoke as though he knew very well what it was about.

When we stepped outside, the cold was blade sharp, stinging the throat, freezing our cheeks. Eyes smarting, we set off, breathing shallow to lessen the shock of taking freezing air into our lungs. Above, the sky was blue and sunlight glittered against the ice, but there was no warmth in it.

The ground was icy, but we could pick a way across the frozen surface of a mud path and, when we reached the village, householders had made the way easier by scattering ashes.

We discussed the likelihood of snow, and exchanged stories of previous winters. Our discourse was easy and I had no feeling of awe at being escorted by a gentleman of rank. We exchanged some banter and laughed with each other and I wished other gentlemen were as pleasing. So many people looked blank and uncomprehending when I ventured humour; it was refreshing to find someone quick of understanding.

He came indoors, by no means loath to warm himself at Miss Johnson's fire. I was diverted to see Miss Johnson behaving in the girlish way I had described at breakfast.

Miss Johnson offered wine and biscuits and asked me to arrange a screen against the door so that Sir Marcus (the poor fragile creature!) should not be troubled by a draught.

I did that and excused myself. Before taking off my outdoor clothes I went to check on my bantams, threw them some corn and broke the ice on their water dish.

Miss Johnson's nerves were overset to the point of illness by the sound of doors banging, a consequence, I suppose, of some distressing events in her youth. This might be considered a handicap for one who was mentor to twenty girls, but all had the matter explained and were shown how to open and close doors quietly, and strictly forbidden to slam. This was one of the few rules (apart from those laid down in the Ten Commandments) which she insisted upon and, since her kindness inspired real affection, there were very few transgressions. Indeed, when I was a younger pupil, we competed to be the quietest.

After one year in her establishment, I had it down to a fine art. After eleven years it was a habit and though I have since been accused of being stealthy, I make no apology for it.

Now, my silent entry into her parlour, and the screen I had placed earlier, left the others unaware of my presence. And I was halted, because Sir Marcus was talking about me.

I picked him up in mid-sentence. '. . . and I mislike what I hear of Miss Smith's unknown benefactor, hiding behind an attorney and keeping the child ignorant of her beginnings!'

'It is not difficult to guess the reason for that, sir.'

'Hmm. Well, I will not say you are mistaken. She would need his consent should she wish to be married, I presume?'

'I have always presumed so,' said Miss Johnson, 'and Chloe has a strong sense of what is due: she would ask his approval.'

There was a sound of his fingers drumming on the table. 'What would she do if consent or approval was withheld?'

'She would wish to know the reason. But if she chooses a respectable young man, why should it be withheld?'

Sir Marcus gave a sardonic laugh. 'Why, indeed?'

At this point I became aware I was eavesdropping, but I waited, curious, remembering my likeness to Isabella and wondering if he knew something I did not. After a pause, he spoke again. 'What more do you know, ma'am?'

Miss Johnson used a great deal of

circumlocution to tell him she knew nothing at all. Whilst she talked, I turned and rattled the door handle, letting them think I had just entered.

My indignation with Sir Marcus had surfaced again, because I was certain he had thought about my resemblance to Isabella Harcourt, and had some suspicion of my origins. Yet he told me nothing and I could only suppose he mistrusted my assertion that I had no wish to encroach on the family.

Later, when Miss Johnson told me what he said, I softened again. 'He thought it a shame no one would own you, that you were alone with none to care what became of you. He wanted to know everything I could tell, which is very little, as you know.'

I was moved that he should express such sentiments, but I only said, 'Why should he be concerned with my affairs?'

'Most people are inquisitive, my dear. I told how Somebody, who we presume is your father, provides for you and takes an interest in you, which is true, because he always wishes to know of your progress, even though he uses an attorney as go-between. As for having none to care what became of you, I told him I cared and I was certain your Somebody did, too!'

He had not told how he had mistaken me for another, and when I spoke of that encounter, she looked perplexed.

'Isabella Harcourt? I have no knowledge of

her. Did he say who her father was?'

'Sir William Harcourt, but he did not say whether knight or baronet. Not that it signifies, because he is not my father. Sir Marcus said Isabella took her looks from her mother.'

We talked it over. Miss Johnson, with unusual decision for her, declared she would inform the attorney what had occurred and urge him to persuade my unknown Somebody to make all plain. But I knew, without knowing how I knew, that he would not.

FOUR

Often, during the following week, I went to keep Lady Pascall company. Sometimes we played cards or backgammon, sometimes I read aloud to her, but for the most part, we talked.

Miss Waring was much occupied with others, and I noticed she had an air of excitement and triumph: Sir Marcus had been persuaded to remain after other guests had departed.

Lady Pascall had her own view of the matter. She had quickly discerned that I had no great opinion of Miss Waring and she had advised me that I did myself no service with her by my scruples. With her, I should speak as

I thought. 'For you may depend upon it, she has very few scruples about anyone.'

'Madam, I do not model my conduct on that of Miss Waring.'

'Oh, hoity-toity!' She looked amused and continued to speak ill of Miss Waring, doing so with some wit, diverting me until, at last, my own opinion of the lady escaped me.

Now, she spoke in some disapprobation. 'Really, it is quite embarrassing, the way that girl is setting her cap at Marcus! But you need not concern yourself, my dear. His attentions are no more than the civility required of a guest.'

'Should I concern myself?' I asked. 'Let him marry her and take her away to Derbyshire; I would not wish her back.'

'When he marries that girl, I shall wash my hands of him,' said Lady Pascall. 'He will not do it! He has too much sense.'

I sighed. 'Then I shall have to look about me to find some other husband for her,' I said, and we laughed rather more than was seemly. By this time, Lady Pascall knew all Miss Waring's intention to dispose of me in marriage.

'Her attempts to captivate Sir Marcus have given me respite from her exertions,' I said. 'Though I fear I shall hear much when he takes his leave. How long does he remain here, madam?'

'He came with the Helcotts and it is only

45

proper that he remains with them,' she said. 'Mrs Helcott would further her sister's cause, but Mr Helcott means to leave very soon.'

'And I shall be left to nurse Miss Waring's broken heart.'

'As to that, Chloe, it can be avoided. I have a scheme I wish to put to you and I hope you will not dislike it.'

To my astonishment, she offered to take me with her, to her house in Bath. I would be employed as her paid companion.

'We could deal together tolerably well, think not you?'

'Certainly, madam, but I do not—I h-had no thought—'

'I know,' she said, 'that a staid old lady is not an ideal companion for a young person, but neither is Miss Waring a congenial friend. In Bath, you will make friends better suited to your disposition and there are amusements too, which cannot be found in Stellham. You will not find me demanding, you will have opportunity to enjoy yourself.'

'B-but Miss Johnson,' I said weakly. Then, foolishly, I added, 'My b-bantams!'

'Someone will take on the bantams,' she said with a smile. 'And Miss Johnson's concerns are with the children, rightly so. She is fond of you, but you cannot remain with her always.'

I shook my head in bemusement. 'I fear I am being very foolish,' I said. 'I can scarce take it in.' But already I felt a fluttering of excitement. Bath! Second only to London in fashionable circles, a place I had never thought to see.

When I returned home, I told Miss Johnson. 'I own, I would like to go! Must I ask permission of my Somebody?'

Miss Johnson plucked at her muslin cap, a habit when she was anxious. 'I am not perfectly certain as to whether you need permission, Chloe dear, but it would be civil to inform him and ask his approval. But are you certain, absolutely certain, that you wish to take up the offer? A paid companion is a lowly creature, my dear; you will not be considered anyone of consequence in Lady Pascall's circle of friends.'

'Never will I be of consequence anywhere in the world,' I said. 'For all that I have been educated and have a benefactor, I am little more than a village girl. Here, I act as unpaid companion to Miss Waring and I own I prefer Lady Pascall's society! To be paid, simply for being a companion and running errands, is not an offer I can afford to despise.'

'Lady Pascall is old,' she said. 'She may live for many years but—I am sorry to be brutal, Chloe—but what will become of you when she is taken?'

'I had not thought of that,' I said. But I thought of it now, and I felt a cold wind of loneliness pass across me. Always, I felt the

47

want of family to turn to. But I rallied myself, as I always did, and said, 'In such a case, I shall be obliged to seek another situation, I suppose.'

I watched in fascination as Miss Johnson was roused to unaccustomed anger. 'Sir Marcus was right!' she said. 'Your father should do more than provide for you. Well, I wish you to remember, Chloe, that you are not without friends and, should you find yourself in need, you may find refuge with me.'

'Dear Miss Johnson!' I felt tears prickle under my eyelids. 'How kind you are!'

'I had hoped a respectable marriage for you,' she said. 'I hoped Miss Waring's friendship would secure you a place in society and I confess I do not comprehend why you have taken her in dislike, or why you feel obliged to earn your bread.'

'At this present, I do not,' I said. 'I know I could remain here as parlour boarder, but I confess I feel—' I broke off. It would be ungracious, after Miss Johnson's kindly concern, to admit I felt stifled. 'I would like to see a little of the world,' I said, 'and it will do no harm to accept Lady Pascall's offer. Whilst she lives, I am assured of a situation. Moreover, I shall be well paid and I might easily save myself a little nest egg, and that, you know, is a very real consideration for someone in my circumstances. Only consider, madam, she has offered me a hundred and fifty pounds a year! How should I spend so much, when I am to live in her house at her expense?'

Lady Pascall called to see Miss Johnson. I was not present as they talked but, mindful that her ankle was tender, I went outside to assist her into her carriage when she left.

Her eyes widened as I half lifted her and set her gently into her seat. 'How strong you are! And you look such a fragile creature.'

'I am fortunate indeed that I have always enjoyed good health, madam.'

Miss Johnson looked more cheerful. 'Chloe will always carry my younger girls when they tire of walking,' she said.

'A pleasing lady,' she said later, of Lady Pascall. 'She feels you will have more opportunity to make friends, in Bath. And, Chloe dear, do look at the gentlemen whilst you are there. Lady Pascall says she will not stand in your way should you find someone to whom you could become attached.'

I smiled absently. Miss Johnson, like everybody else, thought marriage essential for a woman of slender means. I knew she would have married herself, but that her young man was killed in a naval battle against the French.

Since yesterday, when I realized I would have money to save, I had been toying with other ideas to secure my future, should marriage elude me. With my savings I would purchase a parcel of land and begin a modest

49

enterprise of my own.

My imagination leapt forward. I had pleasing visions of keeping poultry and growing vegetables and fruit. My vision soon expanded to include an orchard and greenhouses, an employed labourer and a shop where I sold my own produce.

I kept the idea to myself. The time for such a venture was not yet, but it was comforting to have a scheme for the future, a thought of something I could do for myself should I, in later years, find myself alone and unemployed.

Miss Johnson wrote to my Somebody, telling him that I meant to accept Lady Pascall's offer. This appeared to win approval, for he sent a bankers' draft of £50 so that I could purchase whatever I needed in the way of items and apparel.

'You need a new portmanteau,' said Miss Johnson, ticking off items on her fingers, 'and an umbrella, new boots and a good warm cloak. Gloves, scarves, a bonnet, a shawl and a couple of servicable gowns, for we have not time to make them, though we must sew you some night attire. The girls can do the hemming.'

Herself being needed in the school, she procured a lift on a farmer's cart and sent one of the teachers, Miss Terrance, with me into the nearest town. Together we spent a delightful hour choosing among the items in the linen draper's shop.

Miss Terrance did not approve of the gowns available and advised me to leave the purchase of new gowns until I reached Bath. 'For although the clothes there will be more expensive, you will have more choice and, if you are uncertain, you can ask the advice of Lady Pascall's maid.'

The following day, I went to Stellham House to speak with Lady Pascall and there I discovered Mr Helcott and Sir Marcus preparing their departure. Miss Waring was in bed with a cold and Mrs Helcott meant to remain with her.

'Of all the odious ill fortune,' complained Miss Waring when I was shown into her bedchamber. She was propped against pillows, with shawls around her shoulders, rubbing a reddened nose with her handkerchief. There was a strong smell of camphor in the room.

'What fates determined I must catch cold at this present?' she sniffled. 'Sir Marcus was on the point of declaring himself and now my brother-in-law means to whisk him back to London without so much as a by-your-leave!'

'You should not repine too much,' I soothed her. 'If he has formed a strong attachment, he will contrive to meet you again, you may depend upon it. It is fortunate,' I went on, 'that he is a friend of your brother-in-law, for that situation must provide opportunity.'

'Aye, and Jane has invited me to visit with her in London in the spring,' agreed Miss

Waring. 'But who knows how many shameless hussies will be throwing out lures in the meantime?'

I could easily imagine what Lady Pascall might say to that. But Miss Waring was unwell and I had no wish to distress her, so I said only, 'If he can be lured by shameless hussies, then perhaps he is not quite the gentlman you first thought him?'

Miss Waring sneezed and said, 'I have observed there is something flirtatious in his manner towards other ladies. Has he attempted to flirt with you, Chloe?'

'Me? Goodness, no, he would not take the trouble. I have scarce seen anything of him.'

'And now you go to Bath with Lady Pascall,' she remembered. 'Well, I quite understand, dear Chloe, for there you will meet more gentlemen than live in this neighbourhood and I do not doubt that at least one of them will fall in love with you! But I shall miss you. I shall be left quite alone!'

A tear trickled down her cheek and, I confess, I was moved. Perhaps she held me in more affection than I thought. I said, 'I will write to you and tell you of my doings.'

'Indeed, you must. I quite depend upon it.'

'In the spring you go to London,' I continued bracingly, 'where you yourself might captivate other gentlemen besides Sir Marcus, perhaps a lord or an earl or even a duke! You know, your cold may be a blessing in disguise. I think you would be throwing yourself away on a mere baronet.'

I had spoken jestingly, with the intention of diverting her, and I was shocked when she accepted my words as though they were meant. Struck by the notion of future greatness, she said, 'It is possible. Yes, I believe it is possible.'

So much for Sir Marcus! When I left her, she sent her maid for fashion journals so she might study what gowns she would need for captivating her duke.

A servant told me Lady Pascall was in the morning-room and that Sir Marcus was with her. I assumed he was taking his leave of her, and I hesitated, unwilling to intrude.

I decided to wait in the hall. I sat down, reflecting how easily I became disgusted by Miss Waring and how fortunate it was that Lady Pascall had offered me the means of escape.

I would have the means of escaping matrimony, too!

I do not wish to give the impression that I disapprove of marriage. I believe it can be agreeable between two people who have a strong attachment for each other.

In our society marriage is often a businesslike arrangement, undertaken for social advancement, or for financial gain. Worst off are those poor creatures who are obliged to marry to preserve themselves from want, and I had been very sensible that a lady in my situation was considered just such a one.

I am, I confess, exceedingly puzzled by those ladies who can view the prospect of their own nuptials with equanimity, even with pleasure, when they are chosen by some man for whom they can have no good opinion.

Yet the alternatives are few. If we are accomplished we may be employed as governesses or schoolteachers: if we are old enough, we may be employed as chaperon to some well-to-do young lady: if we are young, without great accomplishment, we may be paid companions to old ladies, and think ourselves fortunate to find a situation at all.

I was more fortunate than most, for I liked Lady Pascall and, more importantly, she liked me. I did not despise the opportunity she had offered, but I had no wish to remain a paid companion for ever, moving from one employer to another.

My mind was occupied with my own enterprising scheme, when Mr Helcott walked past me and entered the morning-room. I heard him tell Sir Marcus he had ordered the baggage placed in the carriage.

After exchanging a few words with Lady Pascall, he came back into the hall, speaking to me only to ask where his manservant had got to. Before I could answer, this man appeared at the top of the stairs with a set of valises.

Other servants came, carrying more baggage, Mr Helcott went away and in the bustle, no one shut the morning-room door.

Left alone again, I could hear the talk within, but Lady Pascall was speaking of a child's claim to an inheritance, a matter which did not concern me, so I pursued my own thoughts and paid no heed to their talk until my name was mentioned.

Lady Pascall said, 'I am persuaded my little Chloe has wit enough to be invaluable, but I would have your assistance, also. Do you understand me, Marcus?'

'Oh, I understand you!' Sir Marcus made an explosive sound. 'But my advice is to let well alone for I doubt you understand as well as you think. Bellamy is wholly without scruple!'

Lady Pascall's voice was tight. 'Who should understand that better than I?'

A gasp, then a pause. 'Yes, of course. I beg your pardon.'

There was a moment of silence, then a sob, wrenched with anguish, escaped her, then another, then a shuddering intake of breath. I listened, aghast at the workings of her grief and wondered what had brought about this dreadful pain.

She regained command of herself but her voice was subdued. 'I have need of a gentleman I can trust and you have your own cause. Why should not the two of us unite against him? It is better to set right one injustice than none at all.'

'Would we set anything right? We could do

more harm. Had I none but myself to consider I would not hesitate, but I fear for the child should Bellamy get wind of what you are about.'

'How should he get wind of what I am about?'

'You cannot be certain he will not. You play a dangerous game, madam.'

'Dear Marcus, life itself is a dangerous game.' Lady Pascall sounded impatient. 'So far, I have used my wits and contrived without mishap and I shall continue taking every precaution. What would you have me do? Let him triumph, and deprive the child of all that is due? He shall not, I will not endure it! It is time for a reckoning!'

'I do not gainsay you,' said Sir Marcus. 'Indeed, I would say a reckoning is long overdue. But others have moved against Bellamy without success. And do you have the right to risk an innocent life in your contest with that man?'

'I have it on good authority there has been one attempt on that innocent life,' she said. 'There is danger, I grant you, and it pains me that I must put the child at risk, but I have no right to sit on my hands and do nothing. Once, he suspected me, but I took pains to conceal my intentions—'

'Ha! That is not all you have concealed, as I well know!'

'I know you disapprove, but if I have erred,

it was for the sake of safety. I saw no alternative. I have been patient; I have informants; I have laid my scheme well. Also, I have the advantage of age, Marcus. Bellamy does not see me as a threat.'

'Would it not be better to wait until the child comes of age? As matters stand at this present . . .'

'That will not happen for many years. Dear Marcus, have you not observed that I am an old woman? How much longer will I be spared? Besides, there have been occurrences in recent months, others have schemes, too. Should I delay, the matter could be taken out of my hands. No, I must act now. Make up your mind, Marcus, and do it quickly, before Helcott drags you away. I own, I would prefer to have your assistance, but I go ahead, with or without it.'

'I cannot disguise I have reason to wish that man at Jerico,' said Sir Marcus thoughtfully. 'But the child . . .'

'The child needs more protection than an old woman can offer. I have loyal servants, they will do much, but you can do things they cannot do. If you would be there, Marcus, it would be a kindness.'

'Madam, you leave me no alternative.' A thread of humour ran through his voice. 'What a managing woman you are! Very well! You may count on such assistance as lies within my power.'

'Excellent man! I knew I could depend on you. Well, then, go now and attend to all your own business, for you must join me in Bath, very soon.'

'I am persuaded,' said Sir Marcus sardonically, 'that my health will benefit from taking the waters!'

FIVE

After Sir Marcus had taken his leave I joined Lady Pascall. I told her my belongings were in order and it was arranged that we should leave for Bath on the following day.

I was awkward and distressed, partly by what I had overheard and also because I had caught myself eavesdropping again. Something must have shown in my expression for she said, 'Chloe, dear, why do you look so despondent? Do you regret your decision to come with me?'

'No, indeed,' I said, though I was in some pertubation of mind. Since Lady Pascall had misread my expression, I took advantage of her mistake. 'No, but I confess I feel saddened to leave Miss Johnson—and—and—all my other friends at the school. It has been my home for so many years, you see.'

She laughed gently. 'So you are homesick even before you leave home?' she quizzed me. But she understood and said I should go now, to make the most of my last day with them.

I was thankful to get away for I needed solitude to consider all I had heard. It seemed that, without my knowledge or consent, I was being drawn into dangerous intrigue. Whatever she was about, I had not been informed of it. Yet I was part of her scheme, expected to assist without guidance.

Or was I? Perhaps I was presuming too much and my employment was no part of her design. I was her paid companion, a lowly creature, as Miss Johnson had pointed out. What were such dealings to do with me?

'My little Chloe has wit enough to be invaluable . . .'

It had been the only mention of me, a kindly mention, but it suggested that, though I might be useful on occasion, I was not an essential part of the affair.

No concern of mine then, and it was not as though she was about anything underhand. On the contrary, it seemed she had intention to move against a dangerous and unscrupulous man and she meant to restore a child to his rightful inheritance.

A child who might be endangered by the scheme, if Sir Marcus was not mistaken. He had been drawn in, not because he approved, but because he would exert himself on the child's behalf. That was much in accordance with my observation of him and, I confess, I felt a secret thrill of pleasure to learn that he would join us in Bath.

I was indignant, all the same, to learn that Lady Pascall would place a child in peril. I had not thought her so heartless. Then I remembered her grieving sobs and chided myself for judging her: I knew none of the circumstances.

No longer ashamed of eavesdropping, I determined I would not hesitate to learn more by the same means. After all, what were scruples when a child's life was in the balance? I would discover this child and lend my own vigilance to the protection Lady Pascall had arranged.

With a mind so occupied, I had covered the distance to the school without even being aware of it. Indoors, some half-dozen girls were occupied in sewing for me, which made me feel guilty for having done so little of the work myself.

'I do not object,' said Alice Barnes, snipping off a thread. 'I recall how often you have helped me. Oh, but we will miss you! Will you write to us, Chloe?'

I promised I would and shed a tear at the affection shown by the girls. Later, I wept again, when, led by Miss Johnson, they sent up prayers for my continuing health and safe-keeping and presented me with a writing case (with my name embroidered on the cover) and a pen and inkwell.

'For you to remember us by,' they said, and

through my tears I said I would treasure their gifts, always. Grieving for what I was to leave behind, I lay awake a long time, that night.

Next morning, a village boy took my baggage to Stellham House. Later, Miss Johnson walked there with me and repeated her offer of a refuge, should I find myself in need.

'I know what it is to be at my wits' end,' she said. 'I would not wish that feeling on you, Chloe. Remember, you are not without friends.'

'Dear madam, how could I forget? You are so kind to me.'

At Stellham House, I had to take leave of Miss Waring, who was still laid up with her cold, and then of her father, and lastly of Miss Johnson herself. It was half an hour before I cimbed into the chaise and when we set off, Miss Johnson stood waving her handkerchief until we were out of sight.

'An exhausting business, leave-taking,' observed Lady Pascall. 'No one quite knows how to go about it.'

'I fear that is true,' I agreed.

Lady Pascall fell into abstraction and did not rouse herself until we reached the posting inn. There, she declared she needed respite from being jolted, so we took coffee and then she asked me to accompany her on a stroll.

I enquired of her ankle but she said she would do very well with the support of my arm.

'I have been forced to be idle for many days,' she observed, 'I am stiff for want of exercise.'

We took a turn around the market square. As we did so, she said, 'There is something I wish you to understand, Chloe.'

'Yes, madam?'

I thought she might now be meaning to speak openly of her design against the man named Bellamy, but it was nothing like that. Instead, she said, 'I do not wish it known in Bath that you are my paid companion: you are never to speak of yourself as such. Society will be told that you are my young friend from Gloucestershire who is visiting with me.'

This was so unexpected I could not answer. I recalled Miss Johnson's words: '. . . *A paid companion is a lowly creature . . .*' Was Lady Pascall so far considerate of those beneath her that she would take pains to spare them the disdain of others?

'Do you understand me, Chloe?'

'Certainly I understand your wishes, madam, but I am bound to say I cannot comprehend your motive?'

'Indeed, there is no accounting for it,' she said, with a chuckle. 'You may put me down as an odd, eccentric creature who must be humoured at all times. But you will oblige me.'

'Certainly, madam.' But I foresaw complications. 'What am I to say should anyone enquire of my family?'

'Say your people live quiet lives in

Gloucestershire.'

With a pang, I thought of Miss Johnson and all the others. 'That is true enough, I suppose.'

'You are one of the Gloucestershire Smiths.'

Her tone made this pronouncement seem humorous and I dissolved in a fit of giggles. Her age did not make her immune to impulsiveness, for she said suddenly, 'Chloe, you are like a breath of fresh air! How I shall enjoy having you with me at la—at Laura Place.'

I revised my conjectures. She would take no pains for such as Miss Waring, only for those she liked. I was pleased that she liked me enough to preserve me from high-born disdain.

It was dark before we reached the house in Laura Place, and in the light of flambeaux I caught only a glimpse of my surroundings, tall, elegant houses set around a fountain. Then there was all the bustle of servants bringing in the baggage, and I was shown to a bedchamber, unexpectedly luxurious, lit by many candles and already warm with a fire in the grate.

A maid brought hot water, took my cloak and bonnet, then began to unpack my belongings. Her eyebrows rose as she took in my garments. 'I beg your pardon, miss, but I fear your raiment is not what a young lady should be wearing in Bath.'

'Indeed, I know it!' I said quickly. 'I mean to

purchase new apparel as soon as I may. I understand there are some excellent dressmakers here in Bath?'

'Indeed there are, miss. No doubt Lady Pascall will advise you.' She lifted a gown of blue calico, shook it, smoothed out the creases and laid it out with a shawl of a darker blue. 'Might I suggest you wear these this evening?'

I was amused. 'Certainly, if you think them suitable.'

'No, miss.' She pursed her lips and shook her head. 'They are not what I would consider suitable. However, we must do our best with what is to hand.'

Uppish creature! Did all Lady Pascall's servants give themselves such airs?

As I washed, she waited by my side to place a towel in my hands. She helped me into my gown, tweaked it here and there, and arranged the shawl around my shoulders. Then she picked up my comb and brush, asking how I wished my hair dressed.

'I am quite accustomed to doing it myself,' I said. 'Have you no other duties to attend to?'

'Certainly not, miss!' She appeared offended. 'I am engaged by Lady Pascall to be your personal maid.'

'What?' I confess I was astounded. Was it usual for a lady to engage a personal maid for her paid companion?

'I had no notion she meant to do such a thing! But how did she do it? It was only a week ago I—only a week ago she invited me to visit with her.'

'As I understand, miss,' the maid said, 'Her Ladyship wrote her instructions to her man of business, who engaged me on her behalf. I assure you, miss, I am well acquainted in matters of fashion and I do know how to look after a young lady.'

'I am sure you do,' I said. I looked at her: I judged her to be around thirty years old, a thin woman, very much on her dignity, perhaps because she was in a new situation. 'So you have been in this house for only a few days?'

'I arrived yesterday, miss. My previous situation was with Lady Rufford. She will give me a good character, should you wish to enquire of her.'

When I asked why she wished a new situation, she told me Lord Rufford was in reduced circumstances through losing heavily at play. 'It was a wrench to leave Lady Rufford, miss.'

'I am sure it was. Well, I hope you will find your present employment congenial. What am I to call you?'

Her name was Jane Farley and Lady Rufford always called her Farley. I said I would call her Jane. 'The name pleases me and it suits you.'

She ran a wet comb through a few wisps of my hair, teasing them into little curls across my forehead. The rest she drew back and coiled into a bun—she called it a chignon—which she embellished with a length of blue ribbon. She stood back, appraising her handiwork, not satisfied but obliged, by the absences of fripperies, to leave me as I was.

When I asked my way to the drawing-room she said a footman would conduct me. 'Will that be all, miss?'

I let her go and though I should have been mindful of my duty to Lady Pascall, I confess I did not hasten to join her. I was wholly bewildered by the way matters were going and I needed a few minutes of solitude to compose my mind.

I had, during the conversation with the maid, been hard put to disguise my astonishment at the splendour of my bedchamber. It was larger than Miss Waring's and furnished in a style of elegance which surpassed it.

The bed, a fourposter, was hung with silk damask; it had a matching coverlet and the pillows were edged with lace. Underfoot was a thick carpet and the furniture, which included a cheval looking-glass, was expensively elegant in highly polished mahogany. The candles were the expensive kind, made of paraffin wax.

I took a deep breath and seated myself by the fire. Why had Lady Pascall determined I should be so cosseted?

No one was to know I was a paid companion and, presumably, that included her servants.

After a few moments of reflection, I reached a conclusion. Lady Pascall would know how servants gossiped and how that gossip was repeated in other ears.

Bath society was to see me as 'her young friend', a guest in her house, but eyebrows would be raised should anyone learn I had no maid or that my quarters were plain and spartan.

Clearly, Lady Pascall had no qualms as to my conduct in society. I thought I could acquit myself in a manner befitting a lady, but I was uneasily considering the cost of being fine.

I was reluctant to abandon my scheme of saving my salary: even if I did, I had not sufficient money to purchase modish attire. I could purchase material and copy the fashions, I supposed, but Jane Farley, already scandalized by my apparel, would be even more scandalized by this. It would give rise to the kind of gossip Lady Pascall wished to avoid.

'You may put me down as an odd, eccentric creature who must be humoured at all times . . .'

I could not help liking Lady Pascall, but with all these surprises, I became convinced she had some design.

I recalled what Sir Marcus had said of her. *'She is a lady of somewhat frightening subtlety . . . I fall short of understanding her.'*

He understood her now, I thought. He knew she had a scheme to undo a dangerous man and she had made him part of her scheme. Was my employment also part of that scheme?

Once before I had that idea and dismissed it. Now I revised my opinion. The lady wished me accepted in polite society and I saw no reason other than she wished my assistance to protect the child she had spoken of.

I abandoned my conjectures when I heard a clock chiming the hour. It was time to go downstairs. I stood, catching sight of myself in the glass and, in that moment, I was reminded of another lady, one who resembled me, the wayward Isabella.

My confusion increased. Did that resemblance bear any part in Lady Pascall's reckoning? Or was it an entirely different matter?

SIX

'Ah, there you are, Chloe, my dear.' Lady Pascall was seated by the fireside in a small sitting-room at the back of the house. There was a decided twinkle in her eyes as she looked at me. 'I trust you found your room to your liking?'

'Indeed I did, madam, but I—' I stopped because the entrance of a footman silenced my protests. I accepted a glass of wine and spoke of trifling matters until we were called in to dinner. Here, Lady Pascall talked of less trifling matters, such as the invitations which had been sent, and which we should accept, and what I was to wear for Lady Wilton's rout.

She thought a gown of burgundy-red silk would become me very well. 'And perhaps . . . perhaps something just a little less fine for the public assemblies,' she added. 'With your dark hair and fair complexion, I believe most colours become you.'

She talked of muslins and cambrics and silks and velvet cloaks and more besides. I had not the means to pay for half of it but, mindful of the servants, I said nothing. Instead, I regarded her calmly and steadily and she looked mischievous because she knew I meant to take her to task.

It was a long time before I had opportunity to speak what was on my mind: only when we returned to the sitting-room could I approach the matter.

'Madam,' I said, 'I would do much to please you, but it is not within my power to be so fine. I can sew myself some new clothes and I shall pass myself off with credit, I hope, but I cannot undertake to set myself up in high fashion.'

'My dear child,' she said in some amusement, 'who said you had to purchase your own finery? If it pleases me to indulge in such whims, why should I expect you to pay for them? Tomorrow, we go to Madam Devant's establishment on Milsom Street. I am persuaded she will have everything we need.'

'I have some money, madam. My Somebody was so generous as to make me a handsome present.'

'But I think,' she said gently, 'that your Somebody did not understand how I wish you to appear to advantage. Keep your money for such trifles and fripperies as take your fancy. I assure you, there are many such things to be had in Bath.'

I wrangled with her, saying that her expenditure must be paid back from my salary. She would have none of it and this led to a discussion of the other luxuries she had arranged for me, my bedchamber and the provision of a maid.

'This is not usual treatment for a paid companion.'

'Well, if it comes to that,' she retorted, 'yours is not the usual behaviour of a paid companion! Most of them are perfectly willing to take everything they are given, usually with an excess of gratitude!'

I stiffened. 'Madam, I hope I am not ungrateful. I protest only because you indulge me too much.'

'A little indulgence will do you no harm,' she said. 'And why should I not make you comfortable?'

I regarded her searchingly and here a wish to speak my mind overcame me to the point of recklessness. I said, 'Madam, I cannot help

70

liking you, but I am by no means certain I approve of you!'

This brought a peal of laughter and she was so overcome that it was several minutes before she recovered. 'And what have I done to earn your disapproval, Miss Paid Companion?'

'You have some scheme which involves me but of which I know nothing,' I said, again risking dismissal almost before my employment was begun. But she did not deny it; she said nothing, and her expression was one of attentive amusement so I went on, 'I am to be disguised as a lady of fashion and to accompany you in society, with none to know my true situation. I am uneasy about practising such a deception . . .'

She raised her eyebrows. 'Where is the deception?' she asked coolly. 'We shall not broadcast your story, but neither will we speak falsehood.' Mischief returned to her smile. 'Besides, my dear, for all you know, you may be high-born yourself!'

'I do not depend upon it, madam.'

She chuckled, diverted by my tone of voice. 'Well, you have beauty and such an air of distinction that I am persuaded you will be admired! Do not look at me like that, Chloe. I am not Miss Waring, I do not presume to choose your husband.'

'No, but . . . What is your purpose, madam?'

'One that is, I own, completely selfish! Never had I the pleasure of sharing feminine

71

matters with a daughter and I confess I envied those who did. Now, I can make up for all I have missed. I shall go shopping with you and choose all manner of fripperies, and it will delight me to see you attired in a becoming way and take you about the town.'

Certainly she wore an expression of pleasurable anticipation and it might seem strange that, at eighteen years old, I could understand how she felt. Perhaps it was because I too felt the want of family.

'You have no daughters, madam? What of your sons?'

I was shocked by the change in her expression: all the humour and liveliness drained from her countenance. Now, she looked her age and her skin, in the light of the candles, looked like crumpled paper. She said, curtly, 'I had but one son. He died only two months after his father.'

'I am very sorry to hear it,' I said soberly.

She nodded absently and fell into a brooding, remembering silence. I saw she was distressed and I waited uncomfortably, feeling I had blundered. To lose both husband and son within such a short space of time must have been a terrible grief. Now, I wished I had had the sense to provide myself with some intelligence about her family. I could have learnt of this from Mr Waring, had I thought to ask.

After an interval of silence, she stirred

72

herself and said, 'Joseph, my husband, had been ailing many months before he died and I grieved for him, of course I did, but I was prepared for his end. But for Thomas, I was happy. He was married to a fine girl and now in possession of the title, with many schemes for modernizing the estate. He was killed, he and his wife and their unborn child when . . . when . . .'

So strong were her emotions that her breathing became laboured and her hand went to her chest. She could not speak and I feared in case she took a seizure. I poured a cordial for her: her hand was shaking too much to hold the glass, so I held it for her and urged her to calm herself and drink.

It took a long time: I asked if I should send a servant to fetch her physician, but she shook her head and her hand grasped mine and I held it, kneeling beside her chair, utterly at a loss to know what to do.

She became easier, but she would not speak again until she was fully in command of herself. Then she said, 'Chloe, my dear, I beg your pardon! I had not thought I could become so overwrought, after all these years. They say time is a great healer, but sometimes,' she added, bleakly, 'it is not true.'

'Was it a long time ago, madam?'

'Sixteen years, no, closer to seventeen years now,' she told me. She saw my eyes widen and smiled, though without humour. 'Aye, I know

73

how you, at eighteen, must think that a long time, but at my age, years pass quickly. I am accustomed to my loss, though the manner of it still has power to haunt me.'

Her breathing became laboured again, though it was not as bad as before. I urged her not to speak of it, but she said I should hear it from her and not from the gossips and sensation-mongers. 'For it caused a great sensation, at the time,' she added bitterly. 'Everyone was talking of it! You are too young to remember, of course.'

She talked with difficulty, pausing when her feelings threatened to overwhelm her and I listened in appalled silence as she disclosed a monstrous, nightmare story.

Sir Thomas Pascall and his young wife, Laura, had been in their chaise returning from a neighbourly dinner party when the carriage had suddenly and inexplicably been engulfed in flames. The terrified horses bolted and the coachman was flung from his box into the hedgerow before he had grasped what was happening.

This man, a reliable and devoted servant, was the only witness to the event and his distress was so overpowering that he had scarce been coherent. Shocked, entangled in a thorn bush, terrified and helpless, he had seen crazed, screaming horses galloping to get away from the fire which they drew along behind them, the wind of their speed fanning the flames, the carriage, a grotesque moving bonfire, bouncing and lurching as it was dragged at breakneck speed into the distance.

'When they found them,' said Lady Pascall, in a voice which was tight with the effort of control, 'when they found them, the carriage was toppled on its side, burnt to charcoal. One of the horses was dead, the others had to be destroyed. Thomas and Laura were . . . they would not let me see the remains.'

The remains! The word conjured up a picture of something incomplete, all that was left being unrecognizable, inhuman, blackened, distorted and hideous. I felt a sob rise in my throat, tears came to my eyes, and I sat on the arm of her chair and gathered her into my arms.

To lose the people one loved best in the world was hard to bear. To lose them in such a way was to be haunted for ever by imaginings of the terror they experienced.

My imagination was tormenting me, as it took me to share their last minutes. I was within the burning coach, I saw how the searing heat scorched their skin and their lungs, and how their eyes were blinded by the brightness of flame. With hair and clothes on fire, making feverish efforts to save themselves, with nothing to grasp hold of, everything aflame, they were flung backwards and forwards within the inferno as the runaway carriage swayed and bucked like a ship in a storm.

My tears were spilling over but I was recalled to the present when I felt the rigidity leave Lady Pascall: she relaxed and a slight movement indicated she wished to be released. I let her go and returned to my chair, but I watched her carefully as she settled. She looked tired, but composed.

At length, she spoke, and there was a strange note in her voice as she asked, 'How could such a thing happen, do you think?'

I was startled by the question, for it had not crossed my mind to wonder how the fire was begun. 'Was not the cause determined afterwards?'

'It was accounted for,' she said. 'It was said that an upflung stone broke the glass in a carriage lamp and the lamp-oil made the fire. That explanation satisfied the magistrates: never did it satisfy me.'

'How could they believe that?' I asked indignantly. 'Such a fire would not instantly engulf the carriage; they would have had time to smother the flames, or at least time to escape!'

'I told them so,' agreed Lady Pascall. 'I was not heeded.'

'How, then, do you think it happened?'

'That is a matter which has occupied my mind for many years,' she said. 'But still I have only my conjectures.'

Her tone suggested she thought it was the

76

work of unscrupulous hands and when I said so, she admitted it.

'No one could be so depraved as to do such a thing!' I exclaimed, but she shook her head.

'We live in a wicked world, Chloe. Only consider! How could a carriage take such a blaze of its own accord?'

'A lightning strike might have done it.'

'It was not thunderstorm weather; there was no lightning.'

Lady Pascall seemed determined to convince me that someone had cold-bloodedly set the carriage on fire. I thought of what I had overheard and the man named Bellamy and a hollow opened up in the pit of my stomach, for I guessed she blamed him.

I was unwilling to follow her. I said, 'I cannot imagine how anyone could contrive such a fire. Even a man lying in wait with a firebrand could not make an engulfing blaze, such as you describe. Surely, it was an accident?'

'What accident could make a sudden engulfing blaze?'

I thought about it. 'Could they have passed through a pocket of marsh gas?' I asked. 'Strong enough to be ignited by the carriage lamps? Is that possible?'

Lady Pascall congratulated me on having an intelligent thought, but told me there was no source of marsh gas at the place where the blaze was begun.

I attempted to think of other ways such a accident might occur, but I knew my ideas were verging on the preposterous and, in the end, I conceded defeat.

'You are right, the carriage could not have ignited unless someone was at work.' I felt the colour drain from my cheeks as I understood my own implication. 'Somehow, someone murdered them. Who wished them ill, madam?'

'Someone who had much to gain by their deaths. The Oakwood Pascall estates are considerable and the fortune is not to be despised. Not that he got his hands on the fortune,' she added. 'I took care of that! But he wants it, still.'

The man named Bellamy, I guessed again, and I was right. The title had died with her son, but Conrad Bellamy, cousin to her husband, took control of the Pascall estates.

'There was no entail, nothing to prevent the property passing to a female,' she explained, 'or, as in Conrad's case, through the female line.'

'So you suspect villainy on his part, madam?'

She gave a bleak smile. 'I know enough of his character to be certain of villainy on his part.'

She spoke of iniquities. Tenants, who had their lives made unbearable, were forced off the land to find work in the new

78

manufactories. 'My poor husband would have thought shame to treat his people so,' she said sorrowfully, 'and the land has suffered, too. Yet I was powerless to stop him.'

She told me of another occasion, when simple peasants had turned up a hoard of ancient silver coin with a plough, and he had taken it by convincing them it was worthless.

'He boasted of it,' said Lady Pascall in disgust, 'and said they would spend their gains in the alehouse, had he not had it from them. There is more;' she went on, 'it would take an age to tell you the whole. He enjoys inflicting suffering on others and always, he profits. He is utterly ruthless.'

'So it would seem,' I agreed. 'A man who would do such things must lack conscience, but would he go as far as murder?'

'Someone murdered them, my son and his wife!' Her voice rose. 'Murdered them in the most horrible way imaginable.'

I could think of nothing to say. My reservations about accepting the unknown Bellamy as murderer were undermined by my secret knowledge that Sir Marcus knew him for an unscrupulous man. And he had profited by these deaths.

Lady Pascall must know more about it than I. Now, trembling with suppressed anger and grief, she said, 'I would have justice, but I fear his crime will never be proved. Very few share my opinion of the matter. Most believe my grief brought me to make hysterical accusations and even those who dislike Bellamy will say they saw him elsewhere at the time.'

'If he was responsible,' I suggested thoughtfully, 'he must have taken care to be seen elsewhere at the time. In which case, the fire must have been started with some hidden device. Is that your conjecture, madam?'

She nodded. 'It is, but I cannot find out how it was done.'

I had thoughts of gunpowder, or oil or paraffin, concealed about the coach and somehow set alight, but I knew too little to venture any useful opinion, and I said so. 'A gentleman might have better ideas as to how it could be contrived.'

She had asked two gentlemen of her acquaintance to apply their minds to the matter. They had been diverted, forgetting the horror which prompted her question, treating it as a puzzle to be solved.

'Between them, they invented a number of ingenious devices. They drew diagrams: one suggested a burning candle attached to the hand of a clock. The other suggested magnesium. They talked of potassium, of paraffin, of glycerine, and of gelatin. My head was spinning long before they had done.'

'It sounds very complicated,' I agreed. 'Did they, in the end, make any determination?'

'Only that any such device must have been

situated beneath the coachman's box,' she said. 'With every one of their own inventions, they found difficulties. But,' she added with some deliberation, 'they were discussing the matter for no more than half an hour. A man with murderous intent might spend weeks perfecting a scheme, and Bellamy is not without ingenuity. Certain I am he devised the means.'

'Even allowing that,' I said, 'how could he place his device on their carriage without anyone remarking him?'

Lady Pascall said he would find a way. I did not contradict her though, to me, the question produced a difficulty just as awkward as the other. But she was tired, worn out by journeying and by the pain of recollection. She said she was ready to retire for the night.

I escorted her to her bedchamber and was startled when, upon wishing me goodnight, Lady Pascall clasped me to her in a warm, affectionate embrace, and kissed my cheek.

'Dear Chloe,' she said. 'I cannot tell you how happy I am to have you with me.'

I confess I was moved, but I was too surprised to show any grateful response. I could only stammer that I was very happy to be here and I covered my confusion by asking if there was anything I could do for her before retiring.

She said not, but on the way to my own bedchamber I saw her maid and stopped her, explaining how her mistress had, that evening, been distressed by her memories. 'Can you persuade her to take a sleeping draught?'

She nodded. 'Leave it to me, miss.'

Settled into my own bed, I began to ponder the perplexities of that day. But the room was warm and the bed was luxurious with a deep goosefeather mattress and if I had any sensible thoughts, I cannot remember them. In no time at all, I drifted into sleep.

SEVEN

At breakfast Lady Pascall showed me the latest edition of the *Bath Chronicle*. In the arrivals column the world was informed that Lady Pascall had returned to her house in Laura Place, accompanied by her young friend, Miss Smith of Gloucestershire.

'Is this your doing, madam?' I frowned. 'It rather makes me out to be a lady of consequence.'

'I wish you accepted as a lady of consequence, and why not?' She regarded me quizzically. 'As such, you will receive more admiration, more invitations, more proposals of marriage.'

I spluttered over my cocoa. 'P-proposals of marriage? How am I, in my situation, to entertain proposals of marriage?'

'You will accept them, of course, each and every one of them.' I gasped, but Lady Pascall's chuckle held a certain relish. 'I cannot quite determine whether you are a shocking flirt or a heartless beauty. What say you?'

'I believe you have me confused with someone else.'

'Hmm. Yes, a heartless beauty with an acid tongue.'

I stared at her smiling countenance. After hearing her dreadful story, I was shocked by her present insouciance. Last night I had seen all her grief and distress, yet this morning she appeared to be in high spirits.

I became impatient with my own judgements. Who was I to tell her how to bear the unbearable? It was fresh to me but it had happened to her a long time ago and if she had found a way of composing herself to meet everyday life, so much the better.

Now, she reminded me that today we were to visit a dressmaker who would transform me into a lady of fashion.

I must have looked a little startled for she chuckled and said, 'Surely you had not forgotten? What an odd creature you are, Chloe.'

'I had not forgotten, madam, but my mind has been occupied with other matters.'

'Matters of greater importance, perhaps?' She was in her mischievous mood and she shook her head and tut-tutted. 'I fear you are confused as to the priorities in our society, my dear. You must learn that fashion, and only fashion, is of any consequence. No other consideration signifies a button.'

She was half joking, half serious, but she meant a warning by this observation about the shallowness of polite society.

Perhaps there was shallowness in my own nature, for I cannot disguise how I felt a pleasurable surge of excitement at the prospect of wearing fashionable attire and another surge of excitement because I was to be introduced to a way of life that I had thought impossible to attain. I was to attend balls and parties and routs and concerts. In the summer, there would be picnics and excursions and, Lady Pascall told me, we would visit the Sydney Gardens, where there would be public breakfasts, country dances on the green and firework displays.

These delights were not, as a rule, permitted to the Chloe Smiths of this world. They would come to an end one day but, whilst I could, I would enjoy the pleasures and entertainments.

I no longer protested at Lady Pascall's intention to bear the cost because, though I did not perfectly understand how, I was of the opinion it was all part of her scheme to bring the man, Bellamy, to justice. If she was right about his guilt, then I had no quarrel with her intention.

After breakfast she ordered her carriage and sent me to put on outdoor clothing. As I went, I wondered about the inheritance she meant to restore to its rightful owner and whether that inheritance was, in fact, Oakwood Pascall. Since the younger Lady Pascall had taken her unborn child to the grave with her, who was the boy who now had a claim to it?

I could not ask, for that would betray I knew what I should not and I had no wish to admit how I had overheard.

I ran downstairs when I heard the carriage stop outside the front door. We set off, with Lady Pascall pointing out the residences of her friends, the house where Admiral Nelson had once stayed, the Pulteney Bridge and the general direction of the Pump Room and the Cross Bath.

I was fascinated by my first glimpses of the city in daylight. There seemed to be miles of splendid mansions and people in magnificent clothes, liveried servants, army and naval officers in uniform, gentlemen with snowy white neckcloths and polished topboots and ladies wearing pelisses and bonnets and scarves in a bewildering variety of colours.

We passed sedan chairs and windowed shops and everywhere there was tumultuous noise: noise from gaily coloured carriages and their fine, glossy horses, noise from wagons and drays, iron-clad wheels rumbling over the cobbles, noise from milkmen, newsmen and muffin-men shouting their wares.

Lady Pascall appeared to find entertainment in watching my reaction to all this novelty. I saw her amusement and felt myself blush. 'You must think I am a regular country bumpkin.'

'Not a bumpkin, no,' she assured me. 'It is natural to be excited on your first visit to a city.'

'Natural, but perhaps not fashionable,' I said, smiling. 'I shall confine my displays of excitement and enthusiasm to moments when we are alone. In company I shall declare the city has nothing to redeem it and pretend languid boredom.'

'You learn quickly,' she approved, and we laughed together.

I could not pretend boredom when we arrived at Madam Devant's establishment. Lady Pascall had sent word to expect us and the proprietor came forward to greet us and we were ushered to an upstairs room, so bright with chandeliers and mirrors and gilt chairs that I supposed myself in a ballroom.

Lady Pascall dismissed a white gown trimmed with pink roses. 'It is too commonplace, and too girlish,' she pronounced. 'Not for you, my dear. You are going to be elegant and stylish.'

'I—er—am I?'

'Certainly. Everyone will talk of the

beautiful and enigmatic Miss Smith. Duels will be fought over the colour of your eyes.'

'How nonsensical you are!'

I spoke peaceably, but mischief was in her smile. I tried gown after gown, some figured, some braided, some adorned with knots of ribbon or spangles or pearls. Lady Pascall expressed her opinion. Gowns she deemed insipid or gaudy or commonplace quickly disappeared. Others were set aside as she approved.

The pile of approved gowns increased: I wondered how to choose and discovered, to my consternation, there was to be no choosing. Lady Pascall meant to purchase all of them.

'No, no!' I exclaimed. 'Madam, it is far too much!'

'Certainly, I think we have enough in muslin and cambric,' she said, as though agreeing with me,' but you will need two or three special gowns for important occasions.'

Madame Devant sent her girls scurrying and entered into a discussion with Lady Pascall as to the rival merits of silk, satin and gauze and how cherry-red would become Miss Smith admirably.

A turquoise silk embroidered with silver thread met with approval, but another gown, the cherry-red Madame had recommended, did not. 'Too fussy,' declared Lady Pascall. 'I prefer Miss Smith to be elegant. Frills and flounces do not become her so well as plain simple lines.'

'All gowns are becoming to Miss Smith,' wheedled Madame Devant and Lady Pascall agreed, but still rejected the cherry-red. In the end, I was provided with a flame-coloured silk and a dark-green gauze over an underdress of gold satin.

I thought we had finished at last, only to discover we had scarce begun. I needed an evening cloak, pelisses, pelerines and spencers and shawls. I needed bonnets, gloves, muffs and scarves. I needed boots, half-boots, shoes and dancing slippers. I needed hair ribbons and combs, fans and feathers, and silk stockings. During the next three hours we patronized most of the shops on Milsom Street and Lady Pascall hired a hackney carriage to convey all our purchases to Laura Place.

No one mentioned anything as ungenteel as prices, but my reckoning put her expenditure at several hundred pounds and I confess I was uneasy. She, however, was satisfied and rubbed her hands together and said, 'An excellent morning's work! I declare, I have not enjoyed myself so much these many months.'

'I doubt I have ever enjoyed myself so much,' I said. 'I was taught one should not wish for worldly goods, but I have discovered there is a great pleasure in having them! Oh, but, madam! Such extravagance! I am persuaded you should not have spent so much. You could have purchased material for me to copy the fashions.'

She chuckled. 'I was not educated in Miss Johnson's school of strict economy.'

She turned to instruct her coachman to drive through the streets to show me the landmarks of the city. As we set off I enquired where she had been taught and discovered she enjoyed reminiscing about her early days. She talked of all the changes she had witnessed in the course of seventy years, breaking off only to show me places of interest in Bath.

We drove uphill and along Bennet Street, where she pointed out the Assembly Rooms. 'Tonight, we visit the Upper Rooms,' she told me. 'Private balls are usually much nicer than public assemblies, and when you begin to make your mark as a lady of fashion I have no doubt there will be a good many invitations, but the assembly rooms will suffice for now. In January, the rooms are not so crowded as they become later in the year, and all the better for that. You are certain to stand out.'

It occurred to me that Lady Pascall was treating me less and less like a paid companion: one might almost believe I was a young lady of consequence and she was my chaperon.

'Which reminds me,' she added suddenly, 'I forgot to ask how well you dance. Were you taught? Or do I need to engage a dancing master for you?'

'There may be new dances I am unfamiliar

with,' I admitted, 'but I know most of the country dances, and the quadrille.' I stole a sidelong look. 'I know how to waltz, too,' I said.

'Of course you do,' she agreed. 'Any self-respecting young lady must take pains to learn a dance that is frowned upon by her elders.'

'Will I be permitted to waltz?'

'Not immediately,' she said. 'It would be most improper of me to allow it. You may waltz with Marcus, however, if you can wait until he comes to Bath.'

I gasped, astonished by the way my insides lurched at the idea of waltzing with Sir Marcus. Recollecting I knew of his coming only by eavesdropping, I said, 'Does he come to Bath?'

'I believe he has some design of coming,' she told me. 'We may expect him sometime next week. And Chloe, my dear, may I beg you will not mention it when you write to Miss Waring.'

I turned to look through the carriage window as we proceeded around the King's Circus and the spectacular Royal Crescent, and though I exclaimed at the magnificent architecture, the greater part of my mind was taken up with the wholly vain notion of myself, resplendent in a fashionable gown, dancing with and being admired by Sir Marcus Redgrave.

Not until we had descended to the Grand

Parade, did I shake off these ideas, daunted by the recollection that Sir Marcus, by his own admission, was used to admiring and complimenting the ladies. My emergence into the world of fashion would make no lasting impression.

I turned my attention to the present as Lady Pascall pointed out the great medieval abbey. 'Queen Elizabeth called it "The Lantern of the West",' she told me. 'You see how the windows are arranged, so you can see right through? When lit inside, it has the appearance of a lantern.'

Back in Laura Place, Lady Pascall informed me she meant to rest during the afternoon in order to be fresh for the evening. I escorted her upstairs and left her outside her bedchamber.

In my own room, Jane teased my hair into curl papers. And when I was dressed in a yellow figured muslin, a painted fan in my hand and my dark hair arranged in a cascade of tumbling ringlets, I saw in the looking glass an elegant stranger, someone I felt I did not quite understand.

Lady Pascall was pleased with my appearance. By her design, we were late arriving at the assembly rooms and a considerable press of people were before us.

'Good heavens, madam,' I said in astonishment, 'you told me the rooms would not be crowded.'

'When they are crowded,' she said, 'they are much worse. Upon my soul, is that Marcus? I had not expected him so soon.'

It was Sir Marcus, elegantly attired in ballroom finery, as I had seem him once before. He was dancing with a lady dressed in pale pink, smiling and attentive until the dance obliged him to turn. Then he caught sight of us, missed a step, inclined his head gravely and turned back to his partner.

An unexpected feeling flitted through me, a quicksilver feeling, but urgent and bruising. I swallowed and sat down.

'Emily Pearson,' said Lady Pascall, identifying the lady. 'An improvement on Miss Waring, but not by any significant degree. Insipid creature! She has nothing to say for herself.'

Subdued, I said, 'Sir Marcus might welcome that.'

'I take leave to doubt it. He should choose his partners with more care.'

'I have it on very good authority that he takes pains to oblige all the ladies with dances and compliments, just as a gentleman should.'

Lady Pascall gave me a suspicious look. 'Who told you that?'

'He did.'

'Indeed? Then it must be true.'

We were approached by some acquaintances of Lady Pascall. I danced with a gentleman who asked me, Sir Marcus danced with another lady and then I was introduced to someone else and danced again, so it was some time before he approached us.

He bowed over Lady Pascall's hand: he told me he was very happy to see me again and enquired after my health. Upon being quizzed by my companion, he said he had made an excuse to leave Mr Helcott at the earliest oportunity. Lady Pascall appeared to be diverted by this intelligence.

'He is not the most congenial companion, I take it?'

'He is the greatest numbskull I have ever been obliged to endure! With the exception of myself, that is, for taking up your suggestion that I should cultivate his acquaintance.'

'Poor Marcus! I fear I am a great trial to you.'

I followed this exchange with interest. Having only a passing acquaintance with Mr Helcott, I had formed no opinion of him, so I had not wondered at the friendship between the two men. It appeared Sir Marcus had taken pains to know the gentleman, presumably at Lady Pascall's suggestion.

Sir Marcus followed another suggestion from Lady Pascall and asked me to dance. I would have preferred to have him ask of his own accord, but I did not mention it. 'Why,' I asked, as we took our places, 'would Lady Pascall wish you to cultivate Mr Helcott?'

'She has her own way of arranging matters.'

'Yes, I recall you said that once before. I have since discovered she has a most insistent way of arranging matters! You, I collect, are not at all surprised to find me disguised as a lady of fashion. I confess it surprises me.'

He laughed. 'You make a very convincing lady of fashion.'

'How could it be otherwise?' I said drily. 'Lady Pascall arranged the matter.'

'But why should it displease you?' He slanted a quizzical look at me. 'Never before have I known a lady complain of being fine.'

The dance took him several paces away. When we reached a point where we could converse, I said, 'I do not complain of being fine, as you very well know. But I can easily comprehend that I am being managed!'

He said, 'We are all managed to some extent: by circumstances, by other people, even by the weather.'

'That is not what I meant.'

'I know what you meant. Do not make yourself uneasy. Lady Pascall has a sincere affection for you.' He smiled. 'In some respects, you and she are very much alike, you know.'

'Indeed? Do you know me so well? Or have you mistaken me for another?'

He shook his head and would not answer. As the dance obliged me to turn, I dismissed all the questions that were crowding my mind, knowing very well that a ballroom was not a place to satisfy my curiosity. Instead, I asked him where he was staying in Bath.

'I am staying,' he said importantly, 'in the most elegant, fashionable and expensive hotel in town.'

I raised my brows. 'The Christopher?'

'I see you have a grasp of these matters.'

'My maid has an inexhaustible flow of such information. The Christopher is but a step away from Laura Place, after all.'

'Another fortunate circumstance,' he agreed gravely. 'I am persuaded we shall meet very often.'

'Then I have nothing left to wish for.'

He grinned, not displeased by my gentle mockery, and I smiled back, liking his humour and his easy manner. It occurred to me then, that Sir Marcus and I had dispositions to suit each other: it was a great pity, I felt, that we were so far removed in birth and consequence.

I knew I would see Sir Marcus very often, for he was in Lady Pascall's confidence. Something stiffened within me, putting me on my guard, reminding me that I was only little Chloe Smith, a lowly creature, a nobody, here on false pretences.

Since Lady Pascall desired it, he would condescend to notice me and he would do so with grace and good humour. I felt his charm, I enjoyed it, and I knew my own folly! He might like me, but he knew the truth about me: I thought him not above enjoying a lighthearted dalliance, but a titled gentleman would never have serious design on such as I.

Later, Sir Marcus escorted Lady Pascall and myself to the tea-room. There, my two companions pointed out different people, warning me to beware of one, expressing approbation of another, and dismissing others as dull, or trifling, or silly.

On returning to the ballroom, two gentlemen by the name of Crabtree approached us, father and son. After some civilities, the younger Mr Crabtree engaged me to dance.

He seemed a well-disposed young man, though lacking conversation. I attempted to help matters along: I asked him how long he had been in Bath, and heard a great deal about his mother's rheumatic pains, which brought them here, six months ago, so she could get relief at the Cross Bath.

I expressed proper concern and after a silence I told him I was but newly arrived and gave him my impressions of the city.

'So Bath pleases you?' he said. 'I am very happy to hear it. Lady Pascall expressed doubts as to whether you would come. My mother assured her all would be well. "You may depend upon it", she said, "a young lady who has spent all her life quietly in the country, will be only too pleased to sample the gaiety of the fashionable world". And, of course, my mother was right.'

'Indeed, in such a case, she could not be mistaken,' I said smiling.

In all this, I felt a vague sense of puzzlement, though I could not identify the cause of it. It was not until the music ended and I was returned to Lady Pascall that I gradually came to see the implications in what Mr Crabtree had said.

Unless he spoke falsehood, and there was no reason why he should, then Lady Pascall had been discussing with Mrs Crabtree, her own wish, or intention, of bringing me to Bath.

This conversation, it appeared, had taken place when Lady Pascall was previously in Bath. Which meant she had formed her scheme *before* she went to spend Christmas with the Warings, before I met her, even before I knew of her existence.

A long tremor of apprehension shuddered through my insides. My meeting with the lady was not happenstance. Lady Pascall had known of me before we met and had the design of knowing me better, of bringing me hither. All was her contrivance!

'I wonder why I said I would spend Christmas with them?' . . .

'Perhaps it was a good idea, since it brought me into contact with Miss Chloe Smith!'

Had she chosen to spend Christmas with the Warings because she had the express intention of drawing me in?

'She has her own way of arranging matters.'

She had persuaded Sir Marcus to cultivate Mr Helcott and I now suspected her design was to procure for him an invitation to spend Christmas with the Warings.

Was that also something to do with me?

Once again, I recollected how Sir Marcus had spoken of her. *'She is . . . a lady of somewhat frightening subtlety. She has understanding above the ordinary and she has her own way of arranging matters.'*

How did she know of me, and why had she made such a determination to seek me out? What was she about?

EIGHT

It was late when I finished writing. The embers in the grate had crumbled to ash and the room was chilly, but I had thrown a shawl across my shoulders, unwilling to leave the task half-finished.

With the intelligence gained at the assembly, confusion had crowded upon confusion, and only one clear thought had emerged. I determined to begin a journal, to write down everything that occurred in the hope of making better sense of it. After retiring to my bedchamber, I sat down to record the events of the past few weeks and all that I had learnt during that time.

Shivering, I wiped my pen, covered the inkwell and tidied the writing desk, moving the branch of candles to the table by my bed. Then I slid into bed, grateful for the warmth of hot bricks as I read through my own composition.

At the assembly, with people around us, I was unable to confront Lady Pascall. I made polite conversation and danced with the gentlemen who asked me, but my attempts to dismiss the matter from my mind were wholly unsuccessful. That strange intelligence would intrude and I knew my curiosity would give me no peace until I had heard what Lady Pascall had to say.

Sir Marcus had intended to walk to his hotel but Lady Pascall insisted on taking him up in our carriage. He enquired if we meant to visit the Pump Room, she said we did and, as we parted, we agreed it was likely we would meet again very soon.

At Laura Place we two sat down to discuss the evening. No better opportunity would offer to mention what was on my mind, for I had a clear sight of her countenance.

She was well pleased, gratified by the presence of Sir Marcus, and the way I had been admired and the compliments she had received on her young protégée. Archly, she asked me which gentleman I liked best.

I think she would have been pleased had I expressed a preference for Sir Marcus, but I only said, 'My acquaintance with all of them is of such short duration that I have not determined to like one above the others.' Then I added pointedly, 'I did find Mr Crabtree's discourse interesting.'

She began to laugh. 'I shall begin to think you a very odd creature indeed, if Mr Crabtree interests you. He is attentive to his mother and eloquent on the subject of her indisposition, but most young ladies find him very dull. Do tell me, what exciting information did he have to impart?'

A shadow of annoyance crossed her features when I told her, but she was smiling again within an instant. 'Exciting information, indeed,' she said.

'I am not mistaken, am I, madam? You had formed your design of bringing me here even before you had set eyes on me! I confess, I find that—er—curious.'

'I had set eyes on you, and I was interested in what I saw,' she informed me coolly. As my eyebrows rose, she told me she had seen me outside the church on a particular day last June. She had been one of the wedding guests when Miss Waring's sister had married Mr Helcott.

'You were there with the rest of Miss Johnson's girls.'

'I was,' I agreed, 'but I do not recall seeing you, madam.'

'How should you interest yourself in an old lady when there was a bride and bridesmaid

100

and a great deal of finery to stare at?' she enquired. 'And Miss Johnson too busy sighing over the happy couple to notice that one of her charges had something stuck in her throat and was about to choke to death? You noticed, did you not? I saw you pick up the child and turn her upside down and pummel her back until the obstacle shot out of her windpipe.'

'Daisy Sellors!' I exclaimed. 'Upon my soul, I had forgotten that.'

I confess, I was surprised that Lady Pascall had been impressed by what was, after all, only a matter of common sense and I regarded her in some puzzlement. 'Do you tell me you remarked me and determined to bring me here on the strength of a trifle such as that?'

Again, she looked amused. 'A trifle such as that can say a great deal about a person,' she informed me. 'But no, I am not as impulsive as that implies. I asked the rector's wife who you were and that casual enquiry brought me a great deal more information than I expected.'

I knew the rector's wife, and the greatest wonder about that lady was how she came to know so much when she herself never stopped talking long enough to receive her information.

'I have no need to ask what she told,' I said drily. 'My entire life history and her opinion of my character, manners and morals. Perhaps she also told you who my father is?'

'No, but she did say it was a shame that you

have only Miss Johnson to care what becomes of you. Do you know who your father is?'

'I do not, and neither does she, but conjecture very quickly becomes fact in a place like Stellham. I cannot believe her gossip influenced you into making schemes on my behalf.'

'My interest was aroused,' she said. Her voice held a note which I could not quite understand. She went on, 'What I learnt of your character taught me you were just the kind of young person I would like to have with me.'

'Indeed? Is that why you spent Christmas with the Warings?'

Her eyes danced. 'I always foist myself on the Warings at Christmas. This year, I also foisted Marcus on the Warings at Christmas, as I am certain you have guessed. It was naughty of me, I confess, but my reasons need not concern you.'

That was all she would say. Her explanation sounded very reasonable as she was talking: I could easily believe the circumstances might recommend me as a paid companion.

I wrote it down just as she told it. Upon reading however, it again struck me as odd, for I was not being used as a paid companion. My employment was a pretence, an excuse.

Lady Pascall had gone to great expense to set me up as a lady of fashion, and she wanted me to be known as her friend, rather than her employee. Certain I was that, in her attentions to me, there was a design which went beyond philanthropic good nature.

I was part of her scheme for thwarting the man named Bellamy and I wondered if I had been chosen because I had no family to protect me. Some feeling clutched at my throat. Was I a mere pawn in her scheme, someone expendable, someone she could use without having to account for herself?

'You play a dangerous game, madam.'

Over and over, snatches of that conversation came to haunt me and I was filled with a deep sense of foreboding. Her design was to thwart evil but, should matters go awry, how far would her liking for me prevail? She believed Bellamy had murdered her son, so I had to suppose her desire of thwarting the man would outweigh any other consideration.

I could not condemn her for that. I would help to bring the truth to light, if I could. If I could discover the child who needed protection I would do my utmost to ensure he got it. But, I thought, I should also be alert on my own behalf.

'Do not make yourself uneasy, Lady Pascall has a very sincere affection for you.'

Recalling what Sir Marcus had said, I felt a sudden rush of relief. He would not say so unless he had seen evidence of it, and he knew her better than I.

103

I had to accept she had some design, but I could not believe she was all calculation. She did have affection for me, for many of her speeches and gestures were impulsive and went beyond what a cold and scheming mind could devise.

Drowsily, I blew out my candles and settled down to sleep. I slept soundly, and I do not recall any dreams, yet, even in my sleep, my mind was mulling over these events, because, just before I was properly awake, I murmured, 'The wonder is that she remarked me at all.'

'Of course she remarked you!' The answering voice was also my own, impatient and a little scornful. 'She saw your likeness to that other lady, the one called Isabella!'

Startled into wakefulness, I sat up in bed, considering the idea. It was indeed possible that Lady Pascall had been struck by my likeness to that lady.

How could my likeness to Isabella have any part in her design? Sir Marcus thought ill of that lady and, if he was correct, I felt my resemblance to her would be unhelpful.

My conjectures brought me no rational explanation, though I returned to my writing and set down my suspicion. Reading through my journal a second time served only to increase my confusion.

I put it aside when Jane came in. Today, she advised a high-necked gown, green with a cream sash and long, close-fitting sleeves. 'And when you go out, miss, you should wear your full-length cloak with the fur muff, for it is bitter weather.'

It was. There was a freezing fog and, as I went downstairs, someone opened the front door and an icy draught floated up towards me. I tasted fog in the back of my throat, shivered, shook myself, and was then filled with a sudden sense of recklessness, such as I had never before experienced.

All my forebodings had vanished. Here I was, in a strange city, embarked upon some adventure. A crusade, shrouded in mystery, and I thought there would be danger, but there was a purpose to it. Some feeling rose within me and settled into place and I felt bold and strong, but also strange, as though I had discovered something about myself that I had not known before.

Life, I thought, was about to become interesting.

NINE

My days were spent in much the same way that other ladies spent their days in Bath. In company with Lady Pascall, I visited the Pump Room, the lending library, and the shops. There was dancing at the assembly rooms, there were concerts, there were invitations from Lady Pascall's friends.

We saw Sir Marcus often, in company; I danced with him, we had some pleasing exchanges but always I felt my disadvantages: he had a way of smiling at me, as though he would beguile me into a flirtation and I knew I could too easily be beguiled.

I heard nothing of consequence about the child who was in need of protection. I attempted, by making polite enquiries, to discover who he might be. Elderly ladies spoke proudly of grandchildren, mothers boasted of intelligent offspring, young ladies told of disgusting brothers, but I could not find the endangered heir.

I reached the conclusion that the child was not in Bath. If there truly was danger, it would make better sense to keep him hidden somewhere in the country, and it would be like Lady Pascall to make an arrangement for him.

Occasionally, my enquiries brought about awkwardness, when others countered with questions about myself which I was hard pressed to answer. One young man startled me by saying, 'Your father is a clergyman, as I understand?'

'I have no reason to think so,' I said drily and, upon seeing his surprise, I forestalled his next question by enquiring how he had come by that notion.

He was vague; he could not exactly say; he thought he heard someone say so. Another gentleman enquired which part of Gloucestershire I came from, which was more easily answered, but I was flustered when he asked if I knew a family called Goodwin in that neighbourhood.

'I have not had the pleasure of making their acquaintance, though I have heard my friend, Miss Waring, speak of them.'

By these means, subterfuge without falsehood, I avoided answering questions about my background, and when I spoke of my strategems to Lady Pascall, she was excessively diverted.

'But madam,' I said protestingly, 'I cannot continuously avoid the subject. Sooner or later, someone will ask a direct question. How am I to answer?'

'Your youth is sufficient answer for those who enquire about acquaintances: you are not long out of the schoolroom, you have not been about in society. You have already had the wit to make use of the Warings, you may do so again, and it is known you are acquainted with Marcus.'

'That *must* convince everybody of my respectability,' I said drily.

'Your respectability goes without saying,' she retorted. 'You are staying in my house, under my protection. Would I foist an impostor upon polite society?'

'Yes,' I said, 'you would.'

I knew I could speak so without serious

107

consequence but this time her reaction puzzled me. She did not laugh or offer any retort. Instead, she smiled and looked arch. When I asked again what I should say about my family, she told me she thought there would be very few questions on the subject.

I had no answer to that. As the days passed, we continued in our usual pursuits and when I was drawn into a friendship with three other young ladies, Lady Pascall encouraged me to leave her and accompany them on walks and visits to the shops. She said it was better for me to have friends of my own age than to be always accompanying her on morning visits to her elderly acquaintances.

I cannot disguise that, on the whole, it was agreeable to be accepted in polite society and I enjoyed wearing fine garments and going to assemblies and parties and concerts, though I was careful to remind myself, from time to time, that this was a charade and must one day come to an end.

Very soon I found myself a favourite with the gentlemen. I was amiable, though I took care not to encourage any of them, because I was very sensible of my true circumstances. Though I felt some consternation when it dawned on me that I was thought to be in possession of a handsome fortune.

'Why should people think so? Is it your doing, madam?'

'It is not,' said Lady Pascall. 'Do not make

yourself uneasy, however. It will do no harm.'

'It could be vexatious,' I warned her. 'Already, there are gentlemen paying court to me on the strength of it.'

Lady Pascall laughed. 'Who would have thought my idea of bringing you to Bath would give me so much entertainment?'

One day, I found an opportunity to confide my dilemma to Sir Marcus and asked if he would be so good as to offer the gentlemen a hint that I was by no means as wealthy as they supposed. He refused, saying they would not believe him.

'They will think I have my own design on you,' he informed me. 'Tell me, do you have a favourite among your suitors?'

'I do not,' I said. 'Even if I did, I could not encourage a gentleman who is deceived about my true circumstances.'

He opened his mouth to speak and evidently thought better of it. He was silent for a while and I thought he looked vexed. At length, he said, 'What does Lady Pascall say?'

'She thinks I should become engaged to all the gentlemen.'

He laughed. 'Yes, she would say that. I can offer you a better solution, should you make no objection.' He paused and I waited expectantly, but I was surprised when he went on with a wry look, 'Suitors are best discouraged when a lady appears to favour another. Could you bear to encourage my attentions?'

'I—er—I own I had not thought of that!'

I felt the heat in my cheeks and an absurd, fluttery feeling in my insides. Could I guard myself against his attractions, whilst all the time appearing to favour him?

I swallowed the ache in my throat and said, 'Such a scheme would answer my difficulty, but I can forsee how complications might arise, should you become attached to another lady. She would not understand . . .'

'I have yet to become attached to another lady,' he said coolly.

A feeling of recklessness flitted through me and I was tempted. A little dalliance would not come amiss. I could enjoy his attentions, so long as I did not lose sight of the reason for them.

'For the present,' he continued, 'we may both be easy. Let society observe an attachment between us and your unwanted suitors will take the hint and look elsewhere.'

He would pay attentions without having intentions. For me, such dalliance would be bitter-sweet. He would never have serious design on me. Yet he meant kindness: his design was to preserve me from complications which might arise.

'Come now, why the tears? Will my attentions be so abhorrent?'

'I beg your pardon,' I sniffled. 'I seem to be drawn deeper and deeper into deception. I

110

cannot be easy about it.'

In the days that followed, Sir Marcus played the ardent suitor and society observed our preference for each other. We danced together as often as was permitted, and between dances, he would be at my side. He would weave his way through the throng to join me as soon as I entered the pump room and, at dinner parties, he always contrived to sit by my side.

Encouraged by lights and laughter and music, my feeling of recklessness grew. When our eyes met and he smiled at me, I thought he could not smile so unless his feelings were engaged. Then, at a point of breathless happiness, I was plunged into despondency as I remembered this was a subterfuge. There was no doubt he was enjoying the flirtation: I thought he liked me but I knew that I had nothing to hope for. He was well born and he would not connect himself to a penniless nobody.

So I was guarded, enjoying his attentions in company, but taking care to resume a less encouraging manner when we were not. One day, all this would end and I knew that, for me, it would end in tears. It would be something, I thought, if we could part on amicable terms, with no suspicion on his part that my heart was breaking.

One evening, towards the end of February, we were at a ball given by Lady Morland, when

Lady Pascall stiffened and clutched my arm. 'Conrad Bellamy!' she breathed. 'Chloe, do you see him? That creature over there, in the salmon-pink waistcoat.'

I sought for a salmon-pink waistcoat and blinked in surprise when I found it. 'That is he? He does not look at all as I imagined.'

I beheld a man of around fifty years old, slightly built and not very tall. There seemed nothing purposeful about him. He moved in an aimless way, and he looked bewildered, giving the impression of an ineffective character, not at all the kind of ruthless creature who could contrive a horrible murder.

Lady Pascall told me not to be deceived because Bellamy was cleverer than he looked. He cultivated a feeble posture on purpose to mislead.

'Now pay attention, Chloe. If he remarks you, he will mistake you for Isabella Harcourt and he will pay very little heed to you on account of it. Should he speak to you, answer him, but do not enlighten him. Oh Marcus, thank Heaven you are here! Yes, I have remarked him; I had not known he was in Bath! Take Chloe away, dance with her, flirt with her, the less she is in my company the better!'

So I was led into the first set by Sir Marcus, who danced with me and flirted with me, according to her wishes. When the dance brought us close together, I spoke in a low tone. 'Lady Pascall told me how she suspects the man brought about her son's death. Do you think so, too?'

'What do you think?'

I took an opportunity to cast my eyes over Bellamy, the better to know him again. I noted the droop of his shoulders, the brown hair, thinning and streaked with grey, the loose mouth and the eyes, which blinked in mild surprise, as though he was not perfectly certain where he was or how he came to be here.

'He looks as though he could not swat a fly. However, I am perfectly willing to believe ill of any man who wears a salmon-pink waistcoat. Lady Pascall says he cultivates his feeble appearance. She also says . . .' I paused. 'She says he will mistake me for Isabella Harcourt. Is that why I have been brought to Bath? To be mistaken for Isabella Harcourt?'

'No,' he said shortly.

'No?'

'No, not at all.' His mouth softened and he smiled at me. 'Though I can easily comprehend how you might think so. Your likeness to her is fortuitous, however. It is better for all of us that Bellamy is deceived.'

'Indeed? I cannot feel he will be long deceived, since so many here know my name. A single enquiry will enlighten him.'

'If he thinks you are Isabella, he will make no enquiry. He knows her but, to him, she is of no consequence.'

The dance separated us. We circled the other dancers before coming together again and in that time I dismissed the notion I had taken from those words, the notion that if Isabella was of no consequence to Bellamy, I, for some reason, might be.

If Bellamy became interested in me, I thought, it would only be because I was patronized by Lady Pascall. I could easily comprehend how he would be interested in her doings. He must know she intended to bring about his downfall, if she could.

Reunited with my partner, I was instructed by that gentleman to simper and look arch. Deducing that we were observed by Bellamy, I exerted myself to comply. As I passed beneath his arm, I raised my face and batted my eyes at him.

Sir Marcus appeared to be struggling with some emotion. He controlled himself and said, 'The dance will end, very soon. I am instructed to restore you to Mrs Davenport. We expect Bellamy will presently go into the card-room, but you must remain with Mrs Davenport whilst he is in sight.'

I had seen Lady Pascall speak with Mrs Davenport and deduced she had somehow signalled her instruction to Sir Marcus. I said faintly, 'I feel I am taking part in one of Mrs Radcliffe's romances! Are these stratagems necessary?'

'Perhaps not, but we take precautions,

nevertheless. Who is your next partner?' I told him and he said he would remain by my side until the gentleman claimed me.

When we were talking with Mrs Davenport, I looked again at Bellamy. He was wandering in his aimless fashion, speaking to one, then another, until he happened upon Lady Pascall. Her features were expressionless, his were vague and I know not what passed between them. After a short exchange, he moved on.

His progress brought him to where we were sitting. He told Mrs Davenport he was delighted to see her again and asked after her health and she, in her turn, remarked she had not known he was in Bath and enquired how long he meant to remain.

'How long?' The question seemed to puzzle him. 'Do you know, I have not the smallest notion. A few days, I think. A few days, a very few days, at the most. I believe I have an invitation to go somewhere, I do not recall where precisely. Or why, for that matter. My man will know. I wonder how I came upon such an excellent creature as Travis? He has quite a head for detail; he always knows. Quite unlike myself, I fear.'

I might have been diverted by this speech, but I was not. I kept my eyes cast downwards as a modest young lady should. Perhaps this was not in accordance with the way Isabella would have behaved, but I could not help it.

I had caught sight of his hands, which hung

limply from ruffled cuffs. They were slender and white, with long tapering fingers, rather like those depicted in medieval drawings. They were striking, but I could not comprehend how they caused the horrible feeling which slithered through my insides.

Despite the assertions of Lady Pascall and Sir Marcus, I believe I had been inclined to dismiss Bellamy as a nonentity. But now, simply because I had seen his hands, I was consumed by a black terror, and I could not determine why.

Bellamy exchanged cold civilities with Sir Marcus, favoured me with a half bow and a 'Miss Harcourt,' and went away.

'I think—I think—I have seen him before.'

'What?' Sir Marcus stared. 'Can you be certain of this?'

'N-no. I cannot determine how it is, but there is something . . . I described my feelings. 'It was the sight of his hands . . . a vague memory, I cannot be more precise.'

Sir Marcus would have asked more but I was approached then, by my next partner. I shook off my uneasiness and turned my attention to the present and, whilst I was engaged in the dance, Bellamy went into the card-room.

The rest of the evening passed without alarms: Lady Pascall contrived, at supper, to ascertain that I was seated amidst a throng, out of Bellamy's sight. Later, she also contrived that we left without encountering him again.

It was late, but Sir Marcus returned with us to Laura Place. Lady Pascall, now acquainted with my reaction to Bellamy, quizzed me as to where and when I had seen the man before.

I could give no satisfactory answer.

'You would know you had seen him in Stellham, surely?' said Sir Marcus impatiently. Since we were not in company, he made no attempt to play the ardent suitor. 'Think, girl, for Heaven's sake, think!'

'I tell you, I cannot remember! I have not seen him in Stellham, or if I have, it was a long time ago, when I was but a child. In a village like ours, such a man would be noticed and ridiculed and talked about, yet never did his name strike any chord with me. It was just . . .' I shuddered. 'It was just the sight of his hands and I know not why I was so alarmed.'

They asked where I had gone beyond Stellham, and I could answer readily enough because, for me, excursions had been rarities. I spoke of how I had been invited to visit by schoolfriends, and I talked of one other occasion when we had been to Gloucester to look at the cathedral. 'I remember that day perfectly,' I said, when *they* began debating as to whether I had seen him there, 'and there were no alarms, nothing to account for this.'

'It is probably nothing at all to do with Conrad,' said Lady Pascall. Sir Marcus gave her an incredulous stare, but she swirled the wine in her glass, and looked into the ruby whirlpool as though seeking inspiration. 'I believe,' she said to me, 'the feelings you describe must result from some alarming experience, but I suspect they go back beyond your memory, to the time when you were an infant. Someone frightened you then, but how can we accuse Bellamy of that?'

Sir Marcus, after one quick look at her, turned to gaze into the fire, giving the matter his consideration. At last, he nodded. 'I am inclined to think you have hit upon the true explanation,' he told her. Then, to me, he added, 'Hands such as his are a trifle unusual but they are by no means unique.'

Lady Pascall put down her glass and smiled at me. 'We will not trouble ourselves. Be so good as to inform me should anything occur to you, but do not make yourself uneasy.'

'I wish you would take me into your confidence! You have some scheme to thwart the man and I would willingly assist you. But how can I when I know nothing of what is in your mind?'

Lady Pascall smiled her sweetest smile. 'Chloe, my love, I will not expose you to danger, if I can help it. I own, I had not expected to see Conrad in Bath. I cannot think why he has come here; it is most unlike him.'

'He said he was here for a few days only,' said Sir Marcus. 'I suggest, Chloe, that you

118

remain indoors until he departs. At this time of year, no one will wonder at a severe cold.'

'Already, I feel my temperature rising,' I said drily.

Lady Pascall chuckled. 'Are you afraid of infection, Marcus? I think you should visit often, to keep the invalid entertained.'

It became clear they were serious in wishing me to remain indoors for the duration of Bellamy's stay in Bath. When I protested that I was of no consequence and, in any case, the man had mistaken me for Isabella, Lady Pascall said that circumstance might alter.

'Bellamy has only to overhear someone call you by name to learn you are not Isabella,' explained Sir Marcus, 'and should he also learn that you are under Lady Pascall's protection, he will become—er—curious.'

'We do not wish him to become curious,' added Lady Pascall. 'Conrad curious is Conrad dangerous.'

I checked my protests. It would be churlish to begrudge a few days spent indoors after all Lady Pascall's kindness. Besides, I had said I would assist them: should I then cavil at giving the assistance they asked for?

'Very well,' I said, 'it shall be as you wish.'

I passed the time agreeably: so far I had written only short letters to Miss Johnson and my other friends, but now I had leisure to make up for my neglect. My new friends called to see me; I amused myself with books and I wrote up my journal.

Lady Pascall went out to visit the pump room, where she drank the waters, met her friends and heard all the news, but she remained at home to keep me company the rest of the time. Sir Marcus was a frequent visitor. He was agreeable, but since we were not in society, he did not play the ardent suitor.

One day, he spoke of Bellamy. 'He stays at The Pelican. I set my manservant to discover his intentions, if he could do so discreetly, and I understand he leaves Bath on Thursday.' He grinned at me. 'So, my dear, you may now begin to make your recovery. You will be well enough to see The Magnificent What's-his-name, after all.'

He was joking me by mention of a famous conjuror. Since I had never before seen a conjuror, Lady Pascall said she would take me, and she had prevailed on Sir Marcus to escort us.

'Bellamy is forgiven for coming to Bath,' I said, 'since my recovery comes about in time to see The Magnificent Marano.'

They teased me, saying I was not as grown up as I thought, because I looked forward to such childish entertainments.

'But we had nothing of that nature in Stellham,' I said. I turned to Lady Pascall. 'Would you rather not go, madam?'

'I would not miss it for the world,' she said.

When the talk returned to Bellamy, I learnt that Sir Marcus had his own grievance against the man.

'He did not murder my father,' he told me, 'but I am persuaded he hastened his death.'

Mistrusting Bellamy, the late Sir Charles Redgrave would not have ventured capital in any scheme of his, but he had been persuaded by another, not knowing Bellamy was involved. The fraud had not come to light until later.

I remembered Miss Waring saying a fortune had been lost through his father's gambling habits, and I had not questioned her assertion. Now I understood she had mistaken information.

'Was not Bellamy brought to book?' I asked. 'There are laws against fraudulent dealings, as I understand.'

'Indeed there are, but you know not how wily Bellamy can be,' retorted Sir Marcus. 'He knows the law, and he used his knowledge to prepare a scheme which would not implicate him.'

'Despite attempts made by the wisest and the best of men,' said Lady Pascall, 'there are discrepancies between law and justice.'

'I have no knowledge of law and my understanding is limited,' I admitted. I looked at Sir Marcus. 'Did you lose everything?'

To me, Sir Marcus did not appear to be distressed for money. But I had learnt the high born could be in debt for thousands and still contrive to keep up appearences.

'Not everything, no,' he said. 'We suffered a great loss, but it was not a complete reversal. I begrudge Bellamy his profit but, more than that, I detest him for the effect it had on my father.'

Lady Pascall and I sat in silent sympathy as Sir Marcus struggled with his feelings. 'My father sickened through blaming himself. He felt he should not have been so trusting; he thought he should have investigated the business more thoroughly. You cannot imagine how he tormented himself!'

'Slippery creatures like Bellamy,' said Lady Pascall, 'too often gain the advantage of honest and upright men. But it is painful to know that one has been taken in.'

I recalled how Lady Pascall pressed Sir Marcus to assist her by making the point that it was better to set right one injustice than none at all.

She was right, but it was not enough. I felt a sudden, overwhelming rage, and an urge to defeat Bellamy in all his doings.

TEN

He wore a bejewelled turban, did The Magnificent Marano, with long flowing robes and, on his feet, Turkish slippers. Candle flames burned from his fingertips; coloured silk scarves and brightly painted fans appeared from nowhere; cords, cut with scissors, were magically restored; interlinking rings flew apart; drooping paper flowers revived when water was poured upon them and, most wonderful of all, he produced living doves from the air. I, mystified and entranced, demanded of Lady Pascall and Sir Marcus, 'How did he do that?'

My wonderment changed to consternation when he announced he was going to cut a lady in half, but I was restrained from voicing a protest by Sir Marcus.

'Nonsensical girl! It is mere trickery. Clever trickery, I grant you, but trickery, nevertheless.'

Despite this assurance, I watched in some agitation when the two halves of the lady were separated. But she was restored in the end and seemed none the worse for her ordeal and, once again, I asked my companions, 'How did he do that?'

'We shall never know,' said Lady Pascall solemnly.

Sir Marcus looked amused and said, 'Conjurors have many secrets, many ingenious, hidden devices.'

I was intent on the next marvel and it was not until later that night, when I was in bed and half asleep, that his words struck a chord in my mind.

123

'Clever trickery . . . Ingenious hidden devices!'

I sat up, attentive now, because these words brought to mind another mystery, one that had haunted Lady Pascall for the past seventeen years. And it occurred to me that we might, at last, find a solution, should we consult with Mr Marano.

A man whose livelihood depended on practising deception would understand such things. I thought it not impossible that he would perceive the means by which Bellamy, whilst contriving to be elsewhere, had set a carriage on fire.

Could we put it to him? In the darkness, my fingers plucked nervously at my sheet, as I wondered how I could approach such an imposing gentleman. Lady Pascall might send for him—she had consequence in the world— but I, mindful of her distress when she last remembered that terrible event, was unwilling to remind her unless I was certain of a solution.

Sir Marcus could approach him, but I was reluctant to ask. He had laughed at me for admiring the conjuror's tricks and my spirits had plunged as his true opinion of me was revealed. In society, as we had agreed, he played the ardent suitor. He knew, however, that I was not the fine lady I looked and, in private, I remained as he had first seen me, a pert schoolroom miss, a lowly creature, dowdy and gauche.

I sighed as I settled down to sleep. I would risk his disdain, but only for Lady Pascall's sake. And, should he dismiss my idea as nonsensical, I myself would take measures to put the question before Mr Marano.

Having braced myself to bear ridicule with fortitude, I felt a little deflated when, meeting him in the pump room the next morning, Sir Marcus, after one look of astonishment, gave serious consideration to my notion.

'Have you spoken of this to Lady Pascall?' he asked, and nodded approvingly when I said I had not.

'The memories are distressing to her,' I said. 'If Mr Marano can be of assistance, then she must be told, but I would not have her distressed for nothing. He may refuse to assist us; he may be unable to assist us, I am very sensible of it! But I thought it a notion worth pursuing.'

'Certainly, it is,' said Sir Marcus, and he smiled, a smile of appreciation, which sent my spirits soaring. 'You are to be congratulated for thinking of it. I will send my man to learn where he is to be found and I will put the matter to him as soon as may be. Leave it with me, Chloe. I doubt he will refuse, not if I offer some financial reward.'

I confess, I had given no thought to paying the man for his trouble, but of course, Sir Marcus was right. 'I have a little money,' I said hesitantly, reflecting that I still had the greater part of the present from my Somebody. 'If he proves expensive, I can spare forty pounds.'

His eyes darkened and he drew in his breath. 'There is no necessity for that,' he said roughly. 'I am not without means.'

'I know, but—'

'Enough! You had the notion; I will bear the expense. Let us discover what the man can do for us.'

Lady Pascall joined us then and we were obliged to talk of other things. I did not see Sir Marcus again that day and it was not until the following day, which was a Sunday, that I learnt what was going forward.

We were strolling along the Grand Parade after morning service. Lady Pascall was talking to Mrs Davenport and Sir Marcus took the opportunity to draw me aside.

'I found your Mr Marano in lodgings on the Walcot Road,' he told me, and he looked amused as he went on, 'When he heard what I wanted, he was most indignant. "Sir, I do not use my arts for murder", he said, and it took some time to impress upon him that I wished to bring a murderer to justice, if I could. I think he remains suspicious, though.'

I confess I was diverted. 'He thought you a dangerous lunatic, no doubt. Once, I had that impression, myself.'

He gave an absent smile, but continued soberly, 'I was obliged to tell him the whole story: everything except Bellamy's name. Even so, he wishes to be certain I spoke truth. I own, I approve his caution.'

'Then he did not divulge how it could be done?'

'He did not know how it could be done. He said he would apply his mind to the matter, and he thought he could find out. Should he be sucessful, he will advise me of the fact.'

'That is obliging of him.'

'However,' said Sir Marcus, 'he wishes to assure himself that I am not a black-hearted villain, leading him to make disclosures for my own evil purpose. I told him he would not doubt if he saw Lady Pascall!'

'Indeed, he would not!' I said. 'What did he say to that?'

'That he would see Lady Pascall and make his disclosures to her. And since she is the person most concerned, I could not object. Which means, my dear, that I shall be obliged to bring him to Laura Place.'

'I see no difficulty there.'

'He is a theatrical, something of a vagabond, and though his manners are better than one might expect, he is not the kind of man Lady Pascall expects to receive in her drawing-room.'

'Is Lady Pascall so high in the instep? I think not. I doubt she will trouble herself at all, especially if he is so obliging as to assist her.'

'She does not expect him.'

'Well, you have only to send word when he is coming and I will undertake to explain it to her.'

I had no word the next day, or the day after, and I was beginning to despair when a servant brought me a brief note from Sir Marcus on Wednesday morning. He would present himself, with Mr Marano, in Laura Place at eleven o'clock.

We were at breakfast when the note arrived and, in high good humour, Lady Pascall quizzed me which of my suitors had sent it. I passed it to her, my mouth suddenly dry. Now, I was not certain I wanted to tell her how her son had been murdered.

'Marcus is bringing Marano to visit me?' she exclaimed, as she read the note. 'The conjuror? Is this your doing, Chloe?' She looked amused when I nodded and said, 'Why should Marcus bring him here?'

I faltered in the telling, because her features altered and she became rigid and very pale. 'Er—are you displeased with me, madam? You know I would not wish to give you pain . . .'

'I am just a foolish old woman.' Her voice was choked, and her hands fumbled for a handkerchief. 'For years, I have tried to discover how it was done. Now, I am afraid to know.'

'But you are certain it was murder, contrived by Bellamy?'

'I am,' she said, and then, to my

astonishment, she added, 'and so are you!'

She was right. Somehow, I had dismissed my reservations as to his guilt. All my rational considerations had been swept away by my hollow terror when I caught sight of his hands.

We stared at each other for a long time. She broke the spell, suddenly brisk and businesslike. 'We will receive Mr Marano in the small sitting-room,' she determined. 'We will be comfortable there and I shall tell Watson that I am not at home to other callers. Now, what refreshment should I provide? Sandwiches and plumcake, certainly, but will he wish for tea, or should I offer him some ale?'

She was occupying her mind with the social niceties to avoid thinking about what the conjuror would reveal. Servants were given instructions, the fire in the sitting-room was made up and when the clock struck eleven, with no sign of our visitors, her agitation increased and I sat beside her and advised her to take some valerian.

'You must calm yourself, madam,' I said. 'They have been a little delayed, that is all. They will come. You know Sir Marcus will not fail you.'

'Oh, Chloe!' Her hands grasped mine and there were tears in her eyes. 'Do you truly believe the man will have an answer for us?'

'He practises deception,' I said wryly, 'and he invents his own ingenious, hidden devices.

129

He does it to entertain, and not for unworthy aims. Sir Marcus told me how he was angry, very angry indeed, upon being requested to invent a device such as he proposed. He agreed to make the attempt only when told it would help to bring a murderer to justice. But he remains cautious, which is why Sir Marcus brings him to meet you.'

The doorbell rang and presently Sir Marcus was ushered into our presence, bringing with him a man of medium height and stocky build. He was bald-headed and wore a neat suit of broadcloth, and he bore no resemblance at all to the imposing figure I had seen performing miracles at the theatre.

'Upon my soul!' I exclaimed, forgetting my manners. 'Are you Mr Marano? How can you look so different on stage?'

'Nonsensical girl!' That was Sir Marcus. 'Would he go about the streets in his performance clothes? And his name is Mr Butler, Marano is merely for theatricals.'

'Oh!' I blushed for my want of manners. 'I beg your pardon!'

When Sir Marcus had performed the introductions, and the gentlemen were seated, Lady Pascall, who was struggling with her emotions, said tightly, 'I understand, sir, that you are going to tell me how my son was murdered?'

'I heard of your tragedy, My Lady,' he said gravely. 'I cannot tell you how shocked I was to

130

hear how your son died. And his wife, too!' He shook his head at the horror. 'Terrible, terrible! A ruthless villain indeed, and it is to be hoped he will come to justice. Well, madam, Sir Marcus asked if I could determine how such a murder was accomplished and I have, I fear, invented a diabolical machine.'

He stopped, looking a little uncertain as Lady Pascall sank, trembling, into a chair. 'Perhaps, My Lady, you would prefer not to hear about it?'

She gulped and swallowed and said faintly: 'No, no, I must know. Chloe, my dear . . .'

I went and knelt by her chair, placing an arm about her shoulders and clasping her hand tightly. Bracing herself, she contrived a smile and said, 'Indeed, it would have to be a diabolical machine, how could it be otherwise? Pray, sir, explain it, if you please.'

He began by explaining that his device would be situated under the body of the chaise and not, as had previously been suggested, under the coachman's box. 'Your villain would need to place it quickly into position, were he to do it without being remarked.'

'I have always assumed,' said Lady Pascall, 'that he stole into the coachhouse to work his mischief in the dead of night.'

'Indeed, madam, I believe he must have been about some mischief during the hours of darkness, but he would have only the light of a lantern to work by, and he could do no more than make a slight alteration to the carriage.'

'Indeed?'

'Suppose, madam, that all he did was attach two strips of iron to the underside of the carriage? That could be done easily and, were they painted to match the carriage, they would escape notice until he found his opportunity'

'I suppose so,' said Lady Pascall doubtfully, 'but I do not understand . . .'

Mr Marano produced from his pocket a strip of iron which he requested Sir Marcus to hold on the open palm of his hand. From another pocket, he produced another piece, which he held about six inches above the first. Instantly, the metal flew from Sir Marcus to attach itself to the other.

'How did you do that?' I exclaimed.

'This ore, madam, is magnetic,' explained Mr Marano. 'It will attract iron and hold it fast, as you see.'

'I have heard of such things, but I do not—'

'I propose, madam, that some device was made up inside a wooden box to which strong magnets were attached.'

Lady Pascall caught her breath. 'Now, I see! With his strips in place he could instantly secure it to the carriage!'

'And if the box was also painted to match the carriage, it would scarce be noticed, in the dusk, in the dark,' added Sir Marcus. He turned to Lady Pascall. 'Your son had been dining with the Bushmills, had he not? Upon my soul, the device could have been placed then, whilst they were dining within, and leave B— er—our villain—plenty of time to be elsewhere!'

Lady Pascall nodded, her lips tightly pressed together. I watched her carefully, but she had command of herself, so I turned to Mr Marano and asked, 'What of the device itself?'

The conjuror looked at Lady Pascall. She said, 'Tell me.'

He said: 'Clearly, madam, he used combustible materials, perhaps a mixture of gunpowder and oil-soaked rags, all stuffed into a bag of some sort. The difficulty was arranging for them to be ignited when he was elsewhere.'

'Could he attach a burning candle to the hand of a clock?' I asked, recalling how Lady Pascall had mentioned ideas put forward by other gentlemen. But Mr Marano shook his head.

'I think not. A candle might go out and your villain would be in trouble if his device failed and was later discovered. No, he would not take that risk, he would look for other means. I believe he arranged for a pistol to fire directly into the combustibles. The muzzle flash and the hot ball would begin the conflagration.'

There followed a clamour of exclamations and questions from all of us. 'How could he arrange for a pistol to fire itself?' The answer was diabolical, but startlingly simple.

With the pistol fixed into position, a cord attached to the trigger was passed upwards, over a hook, and the other end brought down and tied to a heavy weight which rested on sand. A nozzle at the bottom of the sand container, aligned with a hole in the box, would allow the sand to trickle away: as it did so, the weight would drop, drawing back the trigger, until it reached a point where it caused the pistol to fire.

Tears trickled down Lady Pascall's cheeks. 'So simple!' she breathed. 'Just like an hourglass. Oh, my poor Thomas!'

I was close to tears myself, but Sir Marcus was not yet satisfied. 'The sand would have been trickling away all the time the carriage was waiting,' he said. 'The pistol would have fired long before they were underway.'

'No, sir, I think he must have had a stopper of some kind, a cork, or a wad of cotton, to prevent that happening.'

Sir Marcus raised his brows. 'Which would fly out as soon as they entered their carriage?'

Mr Marano was unperturbed by this scepticism. 'It would be pulled out as soon as they set off, sir.'

He said a short length of thread, something strong such as fishing line, could be passed from the stopper to the nearest point on the carriage wheel. When the wheels began turning, the stopper would be pulled out and the device set in motion.

'Upon my soul, he could have timed it exactly!' Sir Marcus sucked in his breath. 'Well, we know our villain is clever: if he set his mind on it, he could devise such a scheme.'

Lady Pascall was sobbing. 'Oh, Thomas! Oh Laura! My poor, poor darlings!'

'I cannot say for certain it was done that way, My Lady,' said Mr Marano. 'The scoundrel might have found some other method, how can we tell?'

'It was done that way,' said Lady Pascall with decision. 'I know the man—I know him! He placed his device on their chaise, just as you have shown. I know him. He would have it all planned to the last detail. Before placing his device, he would disguise himself in livery, as a footman or some such, and he would have an answer ready for any enquiry as to what he was about. He would have a horse waiting nearby and some means of changing his attire. Long before anything occurred he would be with companions at the card table and he would stay with them until dawn so that none could accuse him.'

No one contradicted her. There was a grieving silence as she rocked herself backwards and forwards. 'The torment never ends,' she murmured softly. 'One never recovers, not really. But we will have justice yet. We shall prevail.'

No one could think of anything to say. At last, she pulled herself together and told Mr

135

Marano that she was very much obliged to him. She sent for refreshments and I, seeking to distract Lady Pascall from her grief, made enquiries of Mr Marano about his life as a conjuror.

I thought such a life must be exciting and I said so, but he looked rueful and said he spent an unconscionable amount of time packing and unpacking and being jolted along the roads from one show to another.

'Surely you have had some adventures?' I enquired.

He had once been chased by a performing bear, which had broken its chain and got free, but others had driven it back to its cage before it caught him. And once he had been bitten by a poisonous snake, and he described how he had to cut himself to suck out the venom.

'How could you bear it?' I asked, shuddering.

'I had to do that or die,' he told me solemnly. Then, perhaps recalling how we had been discussing other deaths, he brought a silver half-crown from his pocket, rubbing it to make it disappear and finding it again in my hair, swallowing it and then drawing it out of the plumcake and last of all, and most mystifying, he pushed a pencil right through the centre and when he withdrew it again the coin was intact.

'How did you do that?'

'You can do it,' he said, and gave me the

coin and the pencil and I tried, but I could not. 'Look,' he said, taking them back, 'watch me, it is really quite easy.'

He did it again and I tried again, but I could not do it. 'You are tricking me!'

The others were laughing and he brought out a deck of cards and tricked me several times more, but when the clock struck the half-hour, he stood up to take his leave.

Lady Pascall was looking decidedly more cheerful. She thanked him for coming, saying he had been of great service and went on to impress upon him that, should he have need of a friend, he had only to send her a message.

Sir Marcus left with Mr Marano and I regarded Lady Pascall uncertainly. 'Did I do right, madam? You did wish to understand how it was done, did you not?'

'Dearest Chloe!' She came forward to embrace me, then, stepping back, she took my face between her hands. 'You did exactly right! I own, I had no notion of consulting a conjuror. How clever of you to think of it!'

I blushed and disclaimed. 'Sir Marcus said Mr Marano used ingenious hidden devices,' I said. 'His words struck a chord in my mind, it was no more than that.'

'Upon my soul,' she exclaimed. 'I fear my wits have gone a-begging! Chloe, I should have offered your Marano some reward. I must despatch a servant—'

'Sir Marcus has the matter in hand,' I told

137

her, and when she was reassured on that point, her mind turned to the device Mr Marano had described.

'How simple it was,' she marvelled. 'I am really quite cross with myself for not perceiving it, years ago. I confess I imagined something far more complicated.'

'It seemed simple, as he explained it,' I agreed, 'but indeed, I think it most ingenious. But, madam,' I went on anxiously, 'can it avail us? Can we bring Bellamy to justice; can we prove he did all that?'

'Not immediately, no,' she said. 'I shall meet with obstacles, I have no doubt. But now, I will confound all those who said such a murder was impossible to contrive.'

She lapsed into silence. I said nothing until she showed signs of agitation. Then, I suggested we should go out to meet our friends in the pump room.

I knew she would not allow the matter to occupy her mind whilst we were in society. In the pump room, we were joined by a group of naval officers: they talked with great animation, clearly respecting her opinions and enjoying her wit.

Happy, because she was smiling and at ease, I went to the fountain to collect her glass of water and whilst I was there, Sir Marcus joined me. Once again, he congratulated me again on my notion of seeking the assistance of a conjuror.

'He said,' he told me, with a glimmer of amusement, 'Marano said he might use the device himself in one of his tricks. Not the dangerous part, you understand, but he thought the weight on sand could be used to bring about spectacular magic.'

'I want to know how he pushed the pencil through the coin,' I said. 'Do you know how he did it? Please tell me!'

He laughed and shook his head and began teasing me again and I made a few rejoinders and we were laughing together as I took the glass of water to Lady Pascall.

She took it and uttered a warning sound. 'Chloe! Look who is here. Behind you, across the room.'

I turned and found myself under the gaze of cold, blue eyes. Miss Helen Waring was regarding me with severe displeasure.

ELEVEN

Lady Pascall greeted Mr Waring with every appearance of pleasure. 'My dear friend, how delightful it is to see you again, and so soon! I had no notion you were coming to Bath. You must dine with us as soon as may be. Chloe, my dear, do we have an engagement this evening?'

'Yes, madam, we are to attend Mrs

Davenport's card party.' I paused. 'And there is a concert in the Upper Rooms tomorrow, we are to go with Lady Morland.'

'How vexatious! We cannot posssibly cry off. Well, we will expect you in Laura Place on Friday. Now, explain yourself, sir. Why did you not advise me of your coming?'

Mr Waring had felt out of sorts and Miss Waring thought the waters would prove beneficial. Their intention was only half-formed; they had made only the vaguest of enquiries when they were told of a house for hire on Charlotte Street.

'And Helen longed to see Chloe again, so we came without delay.'

There was nothing in Helen Waring's expression which suggested she longed to see me. The looks she directed at me held the icy blast of the Arctic.

Seeming not to notice, Mr Waring turned to me. 'How very pretty you look, my dear. I do not need to ask if you are in good health. I declare, anyone can see you are in bloom.'

I asked after his own health and enquired of Miss Johnson and my other friends in Stellham, and received kind messages. All the time I was conscious of Miss Waring's angry gaze and I wondered what had put her in such ill humour.

Sir Marcus, having joined in the civilities, excused himself to join other gentlemen. Mr Waring sat down with Lady Pascall and I was left to stroll around the pump room with Miss Waring.

'Well!' she exclaimed, when we were out of their hearing, 'I see how you have wheedled yourself into Lady Pascall's favour. You are to be congratulated on your swift rise in consequence, my dear. How clever you are to achieve so much, so soon.'

Her tone annoyed me, but I only said, 'I am at a loss to understand you, madam?'

'Oh, come now! Even if you forget what you are, I do not. How are you become so fine since I saw you last? I declare, one might mistake you for a lady of fashion rather than a paid companion.'

I caught my breath at this petulant speech, for she could have no notion, as yet, how far my wardrobe had improved. All she saw was what I stood up in, an amber walking dress under a dark brown pelisse, and a matching brown bonnet, velvet, with a gold feather curled around the brim. I felt it churlish indeed, for one who had so much, to begrudge me a little finery.

'I did mention, when I wrote to you, that Lady Pascall had been so obliging as to purchase fashionable attire for me,' I said, biting back my indignation. 'Indeed, she insisted upon it, and who am I to gainsay her? She does not wish to be accused of nip-cheese ways and she does not wish to be seen with a dowd! I am expected to accompany her wherever she goes, you know.'

'Aye, and you are known to society as her young friend, rather than as her paid companion! Is that her doing, too?'

'Yes, it is, as a matter of fact. Who told you?'

'Miss Johnson, of course. She is always so full of your letters, we hear of your doings at least twenty times over.'

I stifled a laugh. 'You have my sympathy.'

'This is all very well, Chloe, but you are getting above your station in life, and it is most improper!' Her voice took on the lecturing tone I had heard so many times before. 'Now you know,' she began kindly, 'that I am the last person in the world to begrudge you a little enjoyment, but I do most strongly advise you not to put yourself forward in such an unbecoming way.'

I raised my brows. 'Have you seen me putting myself forward in an unbecoming way?'

'Since you ask, yes I have, and I cannot imagine what Lady Pascall is about to encourage you! She must know you cannot hope for anything. Take my advice, my dear, and try to be a little more circumspect. At present, you are far too friendly and intimate with Sir Marcus!'

'Oh, Sir Marcus!' I laughed, which did not please Miss Waring. Now, I understood her ill humour. She considered the gentleman to be her own property.

Lady Pascall had asked me not to tell Miss Waring that Sir Marcus was with us in Bath and I had not, but I had mentioned him in my letters to Miss Johnson. I sighed. I should have realized that lady would pass on the information.

To own the truth, I had almost forgotten Miss Waring's design on the gentleman; now, I understood she had come to Bath with the scheme of furthering her ambition. Since Sir Marcus had told me that he had formed no attachment, I felt it would do no harm to pinch at her vanity.

'Sir Marcus makes himself agreeable to all the ladies,' I said lightly. 'I declare it is most entertaining to see how many have fallen for his charm. Well, he is an engaging creature, I grant you, but one should not take him seriously.'

Her mouth twisted. 'I have been in Bath no more than half a day, but the moment I enquired, I heard how Sir Marcus is most particular in his attentions to you. And you encourage him! You even went so far as to dance the waltz with him.'

My heart sank. She would have heard that, of course. Sir Marcus and I had been showing the world we were attached to each other. I had no scruple about pinching her vanity, but this went further. She must be deeply mortified to discover that a nobody, whom she

143

had been so gracious as to befriend, was now masquerading as a lady of fashion and receiving the attentions of the gentleman she had chosen for herself.

Miss Waring had never been a favourite with me, but I confess I felt for her. I did not immediately try to reassure her, however. I merely smiled and told her I had Lady Pascall's permission to waltz.

Sir Marcus had first invited me to waltz at a ball given by Lady Wilton. How he felt I know not but, I confess, I had been in a flutter to stand so close to him and to feel his arm about my waist. At the beginning, I had stumbled a little, but he, without exerting any pressure, had known how to guide me and in no time at all our steps matched.

I forgot the company, forgot Lady Pascall, forgot everything but my delight of moving in harmony with him. Haunting music fluted around the room; I caught a hint of perfume; his breath drifted across my cheek; and I felt a stirring of my blood, a flood of sensations like burning, liquid waves.

I lay awake a long time that night, reliving our waltz, stitching it into my memory with golden threads, keeping it safe for the future, something to be taken out and looked at now and again when I was returned to my own workaday world.

None of this did I confide to Miss Waring. To her, I said, 'Waltzing is not considered

144

improper here, you know. Only in country parts is it still frowned upon.'

'That is not the point!' she snapped, and I knew it was not. The point was, Sir Marcus was paying attention to me and she did not like it.

'Now Chloe, you know I am only telling you for your own good.' I looked at her incredulously, but she thought she was talking sense. 'I fear Sir Marcus is trifling with your affections. I beg you, do not allow your vanity to outweigh your good sense. He is a gentleman born and you have neither birth nor fortune to recommend you.'

'I know that and so does he,' I told her. Since this was insufficient to soothe her, I went on. 'He does not forget meeting me in Stellham.'

'Meeting you in Stellham? How did he meet you in Stellham? This is the first I have heard of it.'

I was nonplussed, recalling now that I had not told her of my first encounter with Sir Marcus. Happily, I remembered he had been in the room when I was introduced to Lady Pascall.

I reminded her of it and said, 'You introduced me yourself. The meeting was brief, but he recalls it perfectly because, as I understand, he was immediately struck by my resemblance to another lady of his acquaintance.'

'Indeed? And who might she be?'

'It does not signify. The point is, Sir Marcus knows my situation; he is not deceived. Here, he has business with Lady Pascall, and his attentions are no more than common politeness. I fear you have been listening too much to idle gossip, madam.'

'Stuff and nonsense! I have heard what is said and I have seen with my own eyes that you do nothing to discourage the talk. I declare I was quite shocked to see the two of you talking and laughing together in so intimate a fashion.'

My exertions to reassure her were having no effect; since I felt Sir Marcus had no great admiration for her anyway, I abandoned all attempts to explain to her satisfaction.

'Lady Pascall would have something to say if I refused to talk with him,' I said drily. 'As for laughing, I can scarce help myself, for he can be witty when he so chooses.'

'Oh, you are impossible! Do you never listen to advice? It does not do, in polite society, to become known as a flirt.'

'I believe Lady Pascall would advise me, should my conduct be as unbecoming as that implies,' I said coldly.

'It is perfectly clear she does not!' she retorted. 'She must know your conduct gives rise to the gossip! She knows you have duped polite society to think you a lady of consequence, but I know very well you are not!'

Her tone altered and there was a hint of malice in her voice as she went on, 'I confess, I fear for you. Society does not take kindly to being duped and you will find it disagreeable to have your true circumstances revealed. Invitations will no longer be forthcoming and all your new acquaintances will turn away.'

Unless I was very much mistaken, this speech held the threat of exposure. I regarded her calmly, knowing I had a powerful ally in Lady Pascall. 'How should my true circumstances be revealed?' I asked, 'Unless you determine to disclose them?'

Two spots of colour burned in her cheeks but she took refuge in high-minded propriety. 'You cannot expect me to engage myself in falsehood.'

'No, of course not,' I agreed amiably. 'You will have no occasion to mention the matter at all. I am persuaded,' I went on, 'you would not wish to incur Lady Pascall's displeasure. And,' I added triumphantly, 'Sir Marcus knows my situation, so your disclosures will do you no service with him.'

Her temper increased, but whatever she might have replied was lost, for Lady Pascall beckoned, saying she was ready to return home. She had made a firm engagement and the Warings were to dine with us on Friday.

'We must make it a large party,' she informed me later, when we were at home. 'I really cannot endure a whole evening with none but the Warings.' She sighed. 'George Waring is an estimable man, but never was his society enlivening. He was pompous as a young man and he is ponderous as he grows older. And his daugter is the most tiresome creature imaginable!'

Miss Waring was no favourite of mine, and I had not been at all pleased to see her but I was, in a perverse way, glad of her now because she had the effect of distracting Lady Pascall from the conjuror's revelations.

She said, 'The girl is here in pursuit of Sir Marcus, of course. I asked you not to tell her he was here, Chloe.'

'I did not, not in my letters to her, but I fear I made the mistake of mentioning him to Miss Johnson.'

'Oh, so that is how she learnt of it!' She paused and there was a decided twinkle in her eyes as she looked at me. 'I am persuaded Miss Waring is most displeased with you. I saw all her looks! How could you put her in such ill humour?'

'Why, I had nothing to say. She was displeased with me from the beginning,' I said. 'She tells me I am too fine for a paid companion. I am getting above my station in life; I am altogether too friendly and intimate with Sir Marcus; my conduct is most unbecoming and it does no good, in polite society, to become known as a flirt.'

'Insolent girl! I hope you gave her a

set down.'

'She was only telling me for my own good,' I explained. 'The situation is most improper and she cannot imagine what you are about to encourage me!'

Lady Pascall began to laugh, but she sobered when I told her of Miss Waring's veiled threats. 'I ventured to suggest,' I went on, 'that she would be unwise to displease you, madam, and also that she would do herself no service with Sir Marcus.'

'That should give her pause.'

'I know not how far my words made an impression on her. She considers me an inferior,' I said wryly, 'and she is not in the habit of listening to me. Also, she is angry. I suspect an angry Miss Waring could be troublesome indeed.'

'She is angry because Marcus is paying attention to you?' she enquired, and I nodded. 'Well, we must do what we can to give her thoughts another direction. How fortunate there are other personable young men in Bath!' She chuckled and mischief was in her eyes. 'I have often observed that regimentals make even the plainest young man look dashing. We must invite a few scarlet coats to our dinner party. When it becomes known that Miss Waring has a large fortune, she will not want admirers.'

I could not help laughing at this scheme, but I said, 'Could you take care to invite a

149

viscount, or an earl, or a duke? She is more likely to be tempted by future greatness.'

'Chloe! That is the most cynical speech I have ever heard you make.'

'Before I left Stellham,' I said, 'Miss Waring was willing to give up Sir Marcus in favour of a greater nobleman. She had it in mind to visit her sister in London where there would be many opportunities. What happened to that scheme, I wonder?'

'Mrs Helcott died,' Lady Pascall informed me. Then, as I looked startled, she said, 'Not her sister, not Jane! The older Mrs Helcott, her mother-in-law. But the Helcotts are in mourning and so Miss Waring's scheme is undone.'

'Oh, I see.'

'So she has come instead to Bath, to be a nuisance to us. Well, I will see what noble guests I can produce. Look in the *Bath Chronicle*, my dear, let us see who is available.'

Lord and Lady Morland were invited to impress Miss Waring. We found a titled gentleman who was not married and several single gentlemen who would inherit titles. We invited a colonel, a major, two captains and a lieutenent. Sir Marcus came and so did a number of plain Misters and Misses, the Misses being my own particular friends.

Sir Marcus paid attention to me, despite Miss Waring's displeasure. At table, the talk varied between trifling matters and affairs of the nation. The gentlemen thought it could not now be long before Napoleon was defeated.

From time to time, I glanced at Miss Waring. I knew she remained indignant about my rise in consequence, and I had seen a shrewish glance when Sir Marcus took the place beside me at dinner, but I thought her more subdued than she had been earlier. Perhaps Lady Pascall had spoken to her.

Upon her arrival in Laura Place, she had been quick to tell me, with chilly disapprobation, that some people were now saying I was related to Lady Pascall.

'Upon my soul, what will they think of next?' I exclaimed. 'I declare, some of the gossips could outdo Mrs Radcliffe in the stories they invent.'

'I am persuaded you began the rumour yourself!' she snapped.

'Would I dare? I know very well that Lady Pascall would not forgive such presumption. No, no, I assure you, the gossips thought of it all by themselves. I warned you, did I not, how idle tongues could rattle?'

She said nothing and I could not guess her thoughts. I took her to my other friends and introduced her as an old friend from Gloucestershire and she exerted herself to be agreeable.

Throughout the evening, she pleased the ladies and she won the admiration of two gentlemen. Sir Marcus was obliging enough to pay her a compliment and she was gratified when Lady Pascall begged her to entertain the company on the pianoforte.

The party continued with cards, trifling conversation, musical entertainment, and the gentlemen paying compliments to the ladies. Miss Waring received her share of attention, and this was a source of satisfaction to Lady Pascall.

'Mr Penrose was very taken with her,' she said later. 'He has no fortune, but he is handsome and he has determined to marry an heiress. Mr Gilbert will be a thorn in his side, for he has expectations of a barony, and may secure her affections without delay. Why are you looking at me like that, Chloe?'

'Do you think she could care for either of them?'

'No, but she might choose one of them. More to the point, they will occupy her time and keep her out of mischief.'

I felt it incumbent upon me to mention the mischief already brewing. 'Miss Waring tells me,' I said awkwardly, 'that the gossips have determined I am some relation of yours.'

Lady Pascall stiffened. 'Have they, indeed?'

'I assure you, madam, it was none of my doing. I cannot—'

'I do not accuse you, never think it. I own, it did not occur to me . . . perhaps I should have foreseen it, but I . . .'

'Will you refute the rumour, madam?'

'No, certainly not!' She laughed and rubbed her hands together. 'No one will speak to me of the matter, so how can I? Besides, it makes Miss Waring's threat of exposure look silly. No one will believe her.'

Miss Waring remained discreet, if not reconciled. In the following days I saw her in society and always we exchanged civilities. If she objected to Sir Marcus paying attentions to me, she pretended not to care. She was, in any case, taken up with her own admirers and she formed a set of her own friends. The intimacy between us was dissolving and I was not sorry.

We continued in our usual pursuits but Lady Pascall was restive and uneasy. 'One would think,' she said, striving for lightness, 'I would have learnt how to remain calm and patient, at my age. But I fear I never shall.'

She would not confide what was troubling her. Often she was visited by a gentleman named Mr Portman and she would send me away, saying they had private matters to discuss. Always, she emerged from these discussions more agitated than before.

I learnt that Mr Portman was a lawyer: I suspected she was demanding advice as to how she could move against Bellamy.

On the days when Lady Pascall did not go to the pump room, I went out to meet my friends. In the cold March air, few ventured into the Sydney Gardens, but we went there to escape

153

society. Unobserved by our elders, we could be less restrained: we would chatter, enjoying our youthful silliness, laughing and confiding.

Sometimes they chaffed me about Sir Marcus. 'I like him,' I confided truthfully, 'and Lady Pascall does not disapprove, but she says I am too young to be married, and I must wait to be quite certain I have formed a lasting attachment.'

In public, Sir Marcus had been so particular in his attentions that many were openly wondering why I was not already engaged, and this served as an explanation.

'I have often observed how our elders counsel young ladies to wait,' said one, and the others agreed and complained bitterly of how the older generation seemed intent on ruining their children's lives. 'They would have us wait for ever.'

One of my friends, Lucy Bricknell, invited us to a morning ball. 'It sounds very grand, does it not?' said Lucy, 'but it is only a dancing class for grown-ups, and we will learn all the fashionable new dances. We have sent an invitation to Sir Marcus, Chloe. Will you persuade him to accept?'

'I doubt he will yield to my persuasions,' I said. My friends laughed in disbelief, and I promised to mention it.

He went and the event was enjoyable, as informal occasions are. The Bricknells had a house on Great Pulteney Street, a very short distance from Laura Place, so I walked home and Sir Marcus escorted me.

I chattered idly as we went. We came to Laura Place, crossed the road, and when I reached the pavement I saw that Sir Marcus had stopped by the fountain and was looking up. 'What is it?'

An instant later, I was lifted off my feet and pinned with my back to the wall: I struggled, winded and indignant but with no breath to protest at this sudden attack.

Sir Marcus pressed himself against me. I wrenched an arm free and delivered a blow to his face, but before I could follow with another blow, I heard a rumbling sound from above, and a crash, and another and another, as slates slid down from the roof to shatter on the pavement where I had been standing.

Horrified, breathless and feeling weak and shaky, I have a confused memory of running footsteps, people shouting, other hands releasing me from Sir Marcus and a voice telling someone to run for a physician.

I heard my own voice assuring everyone I was unhurt.

'But, miss, you are covered in blood,' someone objected.

I wrenched my gaze away from the broken slates on the paving stones. My dazed eyes took in the fact that my glove, sleeve and shoulder were indeed covered with blood.

I regarded it without comprehension. 'Not

mine,' I said. Then I seemed to come awake. 'Oh, dear Heaven! Sir Marcus!'

I turned, and my insides gave a great twisting shudder. He was on the ground, half sitting, half lying. Cravat, shirt and waistcoat were stained scarlet with the blood he had spilt.

TWELVE

He heard my cry of alarm, looked up, and laughed. 'Do not make yourself uneasy,' he said. He laughed again. 'I apologize for looking seriously wounded when all I have is a nose-bleed.'

'Are you certain?'

'Quite the anticlimax, is it not? No, Watson, I do not want a key down my back.' This was to Lady Pascall's butler who had stepped outside upon hearing the commotion.

Lady Pascall was behind him. 'You had better come indoors, Marcus, and clean yourself,' she said. Her eyebrows rose when she saw the broken slates. 'Did they fall from my roof?'

Sir Marcus nodded grimly. 'Chloe was almost killed.'

Lady Pascall, suddenly forbidding, ordered me indoors. She told a servant to fetch Sir Marcus's man with a change of clothes and another was to arrange repair of the roof.

'I fear,' I heard Sir Marcus say, 'I fear I am injured, after all. My leg will not support me.'

They got him indoors, settled him on a sofa and fussed around him with hot water and all the time I was getting in the way as I tried to thank him for his prompt action, which had certainly saved me from serious injury, if not sudden death.

A physician arrived. I was sent upstairs to change out of my bloodstained garments and when I had done that, I sat down, feeling quite unequal to the stairs. I felt a shivering weakness, and my teeth began to chatter.

My maid placed another shawl on my shoulders. 'Shall I light the fire, miss?'

'N-no, I thank you. I will go downstairs again, just as soon as I . . .' I attempted a laugh. 'How foolish I am! I am perfectly sound, yet I cannot find my strength.'

'Shock often takes people that way, miss.' She paused. 'You should be downstairs, in the warmth.'

Jane assisted me on the stairs and when Lady Pascall saw me, she drew me towards the fire and ordered hot, sweet tea.

Sir Marcus had changed out of his bloodstained clothes. He was sitting with his feet up on the sofa, with one swollen and bandaged foot protruding from the blanket which covered his legs. If he felt any pain, he disguised it and he grinned when he saw me.

'Look at me, I am quite the wounded hero,' he announced. 'How are you feeling?'

'I had a moment of weakness but I feel better now. I was not hurt at all, thanks to your prompt action. I am very much in your debt, sir. How—how badly are you hurt?'

'It is nothing to cause alarm. I shall soon be restored.'

'Marcus has twisted his ankle and strained ligaments in his foot,' Lady Pascall told me. 'The doctor says he must rest a few days. I sent his manservant to fetch his belongings. He will remain here more comfortably than in the hotel.'

'I shall not impose on you for long, madam.'

'I do not consider it an imposition and neither, I am persuaded, does Chloe.'

'No, indeed. How did you know the slates were about to fall?'

'I saw someone on the roof dislodge them.' As my eyes widened, he added quickly, 'It must have been a chimney-sweep's boy, the careless creature. I am persuaded it was accidental.'

'Yes, of course. It was horribly frightening, though. Sir, I cannot begin to tell you how grateful I am—'

'Chloe,' he interrupted, 'you are not usually so tiresome. Please do not persist in being grateful, I find it irksome.'

'Very well, I shall say no more.' A spirit of mischief prompted me to continue in a sing-

158

song accent, 'I shall not mention the subject again. From now on, I shall be as silent as the grave. Not another word shall pass my lips.' As he covered his eyes with his hand, I added, 'But I am grateful.'

Perhaps we were light-headed after our escape from danger, but the banter continued. And simply because he was there, a little spring of happiness bubbled inside me, sparkling, rainbow-hued, a melting sensation of pure bliss.

An assembly was held in the upper rooms that night: we had intended to go, but Sir Marcus could not join us and Lady Pascall determined it would be much nicer to spend a cosy evening by the fireside, just the three of us together. So, after dinner, we settled ourselves comfortably, more interested in exchanging anecdotes than in bringing out the cards.

I was encouraged to talk of my life in Miss Johnson's boarding-school. 'I was happy there,' I said. 'I have heard some schools are dismal places, but Miss Johnson has kindness for her girls. We were cheerful; we were encouraged to assist each other and we were cosseted when we were unwell. I was fortunate indeed to be placed with Miss Johnson.'

Something passed between the other two. There were no words, only a coolly appraising look on his part and a faintly quizzical smile from her: then he looked away and nodded to himself, as though he had accepted some new point of view.

I fell silent, persuaded I had been talking too much and they were not interested. Then Sir Marcus, perverse creature that he is, looked at me with a gleam in his eye and asked if I had learnt anything useful whilst I was at school.

'Certainly, I did, we all did,' I retorted. 'We read from the Scriptures every day.'

Lady Pascall gave an appreciative chuckle. Sir Marcus raised a hand, acknowledging a neat riposte and, after flickering an eyelid at Lady Pascall, he retaliated with a quotation from the Scriptures.

' "Who is she that looketh forth as the morning, fair as the moon, clear as the sun, and terrible as an army with banners." '

His choice of quotation confused me, for it could be either complimentary or mocking and I could not determine what he meant by it. Though I could find no suitable rejoinder, I could identify the source.

'The Song of Solomon,' I said. 'I forget chapter and verse.'

'Dear me,' said Lady Pascall. 'I begin to suspect Miss Johnson has hidden depths. Did she advise you to read that?'

'She did not.' I paused to drink some wine and I saw another look pass between them. They had some understanding that I had not and I was piqued. I went on, 'Some of us felt

160

we did not receive proper instruction on that part of the Bible. We girls, being pious creatures,' I added primly, 'were determined to rectify the matter, so we studied in our own time. Though of course,' I went on, gazing at the ceiling, trying to look innocent, 'we were far too young to understand it.'

Two people inhaled their breath, held it, then burst forth with laughter; I endured a little raillery when they recovered. I was told, albeit good-humouredly, that in polite society, innocent young ladies, if they could not also be ignorant, should do their best to pretend they were.

Something changed in Sir Marcus after that. Towards me, there was a subtle shift in his attitude: I sensed it immediately, though I did not comprehend it. He contributed his share to the conversation, but there were times when he seemed to be engrossed in his own thoughts, and other times when he was uncommonly alert, as though the most trifling remark held some hidden significance.

When drowsiness overtook me I fought against it, unwilling to break up the evening, but Lady Pascall noticed, looked at the clock and declared it was later than she thought.

She sent me to bed. I know not how Sir Marcus climbed the stairs but, when I was propped against my pillows, I heard heavy thumping and muttered curses and Lady Pascall's laugh.

The next morning, when I went down to breakfast, Lady Pascall and Sir Marcus were before me and I had the impression that I had interrupted some discussion between them. They attempted to answer my pleasantries with civility, but there was a certain constraint, as though their minds were occupied with other matters. I confess, I felt uncomfortable and, when the meal was over, I was not reluctant to leave them. I went out to take exercise with my friends.

As we strolled along Great Pulteney Street, my friends reproached me for failing to attend last night's assembly. I described how that was a consequence of my adventure. The others exclaimed and told me it was fortunate that Sir Marcus had seen the danger.

'Yes, but he says it is wholly demeaning for the hero of the hour to be embarrassed by a nosebleed. I fear it was my fault: I hit him, because I did not know I was being rescued.'

They laughed and we continued our chatter. After half an hour, Mary Forbes drew to our attention a figure some distance behind us. 'Who is that man?' she enquired. 'Do you know him Lucy? Chloe? Sarah? I am persuaded he is following us!'

I stiffened and turned, at once alarmed by thoughts of Bellamy, but it was not he. He was a young man of some three-and-twenty years, tidy in his appearance but not fashionably dressed. His countenance was plain, but not displeasing.

I knew him not, and neither did my companions. Lucy was inclined to dismiss Mary's suspicions. 'I see no reason to suppose he is following us,' she said. 'We are in a public place; he can be here if he wants to be.'

'He followed us along Pulteney Street,' announced Mary. 'He was on the pavement opposite and I confess I paid him no particular attention. But since entering the gardens we have turned hither and thither and he has kept pace with us.'

Sarah, giggling, could think of only one reason why a man should follow four young women and began to wonder which of us he had formed an attachment to. Lucy said that was nonsense, but she looked uneasy. 'Can anyone imagine what he is about?'

I had an alarming suspicion about how he might be in league with Bellamy, but this was not a matter for confiding to my friends. Aloud, I voiced the nonsensical opinion that he was a French secret agent, sent by Napoleon to spy on us.

The notion entertained my friends. We amused ourselves by making up stories along that line. We laughed rather more than was seemly, and we took it in turns to observe him and inform the others what he was doing.

He kept us in sight, which made me feel uncomfortable. I told my friends I wished to go home and we left the gardens, and stepped out as briskly as possible. Our escort remained on the other side of the street, but he kept pace with us.

I was becoming frightened, and angry with myself for being frightened. 'I mislike this!' I said. 'Come, there are four of us, let us turn about and demand to know what he is doing.'

No man is equal to four determined young ladies with umbrellas. We turned about, crossed the road; we were upon him; we had him surrounded. By the time we had finished scolding, the poor man was mopping his brow.

'You know me, Miss Chloe,' he said reproachfully.

Upon closer scrutiny, I was obliged to acknowledge I did, though I was more accustomed to seeing him in livery. His name was Jenkins and he was one of our footmen.

'Why were you following us?' I demanded. 'Did Lady Pascall set you to spy upon me?'

'N-no miss. My Lady wished me to ascertain that no one else was spying on you, miss.'

'Indeed?' I confess that intelligence left me rather nonplussed. It needed no exertion on my part to comprehend how yesterday's accident had brought about this departure.

Jenkins assumed a blank-faced expression. 'My Lady told me to keep watch for anyone who might mean mischief.'

'And have you seen anyone who might mean mischief?'

'No, miss. My Lady said it was a precaution,

no more.'

I had nothing to say. To own the truth, I was embarrassed by the curious looks my friends were giving me. I said lightly, 'Perhaps Lady Pascall suspects me of having a secret assignation with a young man.'

I sent Jenkins home: by this time, my friends suspected intrigue and questioned me as to what was occurring. 'Does Lady Pascall believe you are in peril?'

'No, of course she does not; she believes I cannot possibly be sensible,' I grumbled. 'She is forever telling me that young ladies these days are allowed far too much licence. I do not believe the faradiddle Jenkins told. He was making it up. Lady Pascall sent him to spy on me. I was never more annoyed! Well, and we have uncovered her scheme and it serves her right. I shall complain,' I went on sulkily, 'but I know if I make a great to-do about it, she will simply threaten to send me back to Gloucestershire. It is not fair.'

My friends could easily believe it. They forgot their darker suspicions and were very much in sympathy with me. And later, I quite enjoyed telling Lady Pascall that I had been obliged to cast her in the role of tyranical guardian.

'I see,' she said. 'I beg you will not hesitate to malign my character whenever it suits your purpose.'

I was not mistaken in attributing her

suspicion of mischief to the previous day's accident. 'I fear I become alarmed too easily,' she admitted. 'But you will own I have cause.'

We received callers then, and I was unable to ask any more questions. But I did, later, chance to overhear Sir Marcus rather forcefully advising Lady Pascall that, in his opinion, Bellamy was no longer deceived into thinking I was Isabella.

'Marcus, you have told me so before. What would you have me do? You advised greater vigilance on my part; I took your advice, and look what happened! Poor Jenkins suffered an ordeal from which he may never recover and, moreover, my own reputation is in tatters!'

There was a thread of humour in her voice which suggested she was not displeased. Sir Marcus said something I did not hear and she said, 'Do not underestimate Chloe, Marcus. She has her own resources; I fancy she will prevail.'

'Madam!' Sir Marcus sounded exasperated. 'A girl of eighteen is no match for Bellamy! Send her back to her school, madam, keep her hidden. He has seen her here, and, if he knows she is not Isabella, then you can be certain he knows what you are about! I declare, a child could work it out!'

It would be a wiser child than I, I thought in bewilderment. If the well-born Isabella was of no consequence to Bellamy, how could I differ in that respect? It made no sense at all!

My confusion had kept me still, listening when I should not. I crept away, turned when I was halfway up the stairs and came down again, and this time I made more noise.

Lady Pascall did not send me back to Miss Johnson, but she did tell me I would have to bear with an unobtrusive escort until certain matters had been attended to.

'I am sorry for it, but it cannot be helped,' she said. 'Tell your friends I am spying upon you, if you wish, but do not let them persuade you to evade my man, Chloe, I beg you, because it is for your own safety. I could not bear to have anything happen to you.'

'Madam,' I said directly, 'am I in danger from Bellamy?'

'I did not expect to see him in Bath,' she said, 'but he came, and Marcus thinks we should be vigilant. Our precautions may be foolish but present folly is better than later regrets.'

So much for my earlier suspicion that she would sacrifice me to thwart the man! Her affection for me had brought her to this apprehension and I could not help being moved.

'But why should Bellamy have any unscrupulous design on me?'

'You are here,' she said fretfully. 'You are with me. It is my own doing but, should anything happen to you, I would be quite undone.'

I could only presume she meant that Bellamy would hurt me to hurt her. But I remained dissatisfied and I spoke in a challenging way. 'I look like Isabella.'

Lady Pascall merely looked tired. 'Not a happy circumstance, but it cannot be helped.'

A response which did not resolve my confusion.

We were engaged to attend a musical soirée that evening: Sir Marcus was obliged to remain at home but Lady Pascall had persuaded one of his gentleman friends to join him. We left them supplied with refreshments and engaged in piquet.

Upon our arrival, Lady Pascall's attention was claimed by Colonel Wheatly: he detached her from myself, seated her comfortably by the fire and clearly he was determined to spend the evening dancing attendance on her. I smiled faintly, wondering if I dared to suggest to her, later, that the colonel was trifling with her affections.

My thoughts were soon given another direction for the Warings were among the company that evening. I curtsied and spoke the usual civilities, but Miss Waring was flushed and so angry she could not bring herself to speak to me with civility.

'Insolent girl!' she snapped. 'I declare, I know not how you dare to show your face. Be warned, Miss Smith, I will not endure impertinence from any such as you!'

She flounced away, leaving me dumbfounded. I was a little vague with my other friends, as I wondered what had provoked her so. In an interval between recitals, I approached her with the design of finding out the cause of her displeasure, but she treated me to a haughty toss of the head and turned away.

Such conduct did not improve my humour. Inwardly calling her a beastly name, I determined to have no more ado with her.

I had other friends and so did she, so I did not approach her again and I might never have discovered why she was so put out, had not another young lady, her voice spiced with amusement, congratulated me on being very rude to Miss Waring.

'What nonsense is this? I have not been rude to her.'

'My dear Miss Smith, do not think I reproach you. I own, there have been many times when I longed to be rude to Miss Waring, myself.'

I felt I had been wrongly interpreted, but I was unable to say so because another recital was about to begin. Afterwards, a young man engaged me in discussion, pleasing me well enough to make me forget Miss Waring's silliness, and he remained attentive throughout the evening.

Lady Pascall remained smiling and gracious whilst we were in company but when we were in the carriage, she gave a sigh. 'I am too old to be gallivanting about so much,' she said. 'I find it trying to my nerves.'

I thought she was more tried by her other preoccupations, but I did not say so. Instead, I said, 'I am perfectly happy to remain quietly indoors of an evening, madam.'

In the darkness, I heard her chuckle. 'What an odd creature you are, Chloe! Do you dislike assemblies and parties?'

'I like them very well, as you know. But you should not indulge me at the expense of your nerves. Half the entertainments I enjoy would be more than sufficient.'

'Thoughtful child. But it will not do, you know. It is important to become known in polite society.'

'Is it?' I confess I was startled. 'I cannot imagine why.'

She stifled a yawn. 'I wish you recognized by people of rank.' She yawned again. 'Next year I shall take you to London. Would you like to be presented at court, Chloe?'

'Presented at court?' I felt my jaw drop and I was grateful for the darkness in the carriage. 'Me? Can you be serious?'

'I see no reason why not. I make no promises, mind. Much depends on how we are circumstanced.'

My thoughts whirled and alternating images of court grandeur and Miss Johnson's school passed through my mind. My confusion

170

increased as I thought vaguely of Bellamy and Lady Pascall and my likeness, Isabella, as though there was a connection to be made if only I could grasp some other, more elusive idea.

Whatever I was missing did not occur to me, and though I wrote up my journal and reviewed all that had occurred, I remained perplexed.

My friends and I did not go to the gardens the next day, because Sarah wished for some new gloves. The rest of us were perfectly happy to see what the shops in Milsom Street had to offer. We set off, speaking to such acquaintances as we encountered, and behaving with more propriety than we did when we were not observed. I looked around for Lady Pascall's man and saw him, but my friends did not notice him.

Sarah purchased her gloves, Lucy borrowed five shillings from me to purchase a length of muslin, and I indulged my fancy for a bottle of Rose Water scent. Mary demanded we should cross the street to look in a milliner's shop.

We admired the bonnets on display in the shop window, and we agreed that a confection of satin and velvet would become Mary admirably. We urged her to go in and try it on.

When we entered the shop there was one other lady, with her back turned to us. She held a looking-glass as she tried on a bonnet and I gasped and froze into immobility, anchored to the ground like a fixed, nerveless sculpture.

Reflected in the looking-glass, I saw a face identical to my own.

She took off the bonnet and set it down carelessly. The shop-keeper looked up and saw me and her look of astonishment was enough to make the lady turn around.

Her eyes widened and her lips parted. We stared at each other, neither of us speaking. What my friends were doing, I know not. I felt as though we two were in a separate space, and the rest of the world had receded into a void. I could see none but Isabella.

I had, upon learning of her existence, allowed my fancy to imagine such a meeting and perhaps I was, as a consequence, a little better prepared than she was. Nevertheless, the reality was overwhelming, quite unlike anything I had imagined.

Twins, I suppose, are accustomed to their siblings. I was used to seeing my own reflection, and I had thought that seeing Isabella for the first time would be the same as confronting myself in a looking-glass, but it was not.

It was an eerie feeling to meet with a stranger who, though dressed differently, in colours I would not choose, looked exactly like myself. My chest felt tight, my heart was thudding and a sound like the roaring sea pounded through my senses.

172

Isabella was the first to find her voice. 'Are you—are you a ghost?' she asked faintly.

'N-no' I drew in a breath, steadied myself and dropped a curtsy. I said, 'I—er—I think—I believe—you must be Isabella Harcourt.'

There was a chair by the shop counter for the use of customers. Isabella sank into it, and gazed at me for some time. At last, she said, 'So you know me, do you? Yes, I am Isabella Harcourt, but who, in the name of Heaven, are you?'

'My name is Chloe Sm—'

'*Chloe!*' Isabella was on her feet, her voice shrieking my name. 'Upon my soul! You are *Chloe?*'

I felt my jaw drop. Then, as I gaped without comprehension, Isabella went on, more to herself than to me, 'Yes! Yes, of course you are, you must be, how could it be otherwise? You must be Chloe, there can be no other explanation!'

I stared in dumbfounded silence. Isabella resumed her seat, drew in a deep breath, and said, 'Well! I cannot tell you how often we have wondered what became of you!'

THIRTEEN

Whilst I remained dumbfounded and speechless, my companions made their presence felt. They surged forward, all talking at once, exclaiming and asking insistent questions, none of which I could answer.

Isabella recovered her composure sooner than I did. 'Chloe and I are cousins,' she told my friends. 'Our mothers were identical twins and that, of course, is why we look so very much alike.'

Whilst I was absorbing this information and searching for threads to connect it with what I already knew of my own history, my friends began to remonstrate with me.

'What a dark horse you are, Chloe!' That was Sarah. 'Why did you not speak of this; why did you never mention it?'

'I knew nothing.'

'What?' I had spoken in a mumble, but Isabella had sharp ears. 'But you know me,' she protested, 'you know who I am.'

'Y-yes, I had heard of you, I knew of your existence, but only because someone mistook me for you.'

'Indeed? Pray, who might that have been?'

'Sir Marcus—Marcus Redgrave.'

'Oh Marcus,' said Isabella dismissively, 'that old bore.'

'He is not old!' I exclaimed indignantly. Neither was he, in my opinion, a bore, but I was too confused to mention this.

'Well, for all the starched notions he has, he might as well be in his dotage,' said Isabella. 'He was born old, that one!' And whilst I was blinking at this strange opinion, she gave a sudden squeal of laughter and I saw a hint of the waywardness I had heard about. 'So he mistook you for me? Upon my soul, that would have been something to watch.'

She looked at me, a gleam of speculation in her eyes and her smile held a certain relish. 'Chloe, my dear cousin, we will have some fun together, you and I.'

It was clear she meant we could impersonate each other.

'I fancy there will be confusion enough without any contrivance of ours,' I said. I recalled Miss Waring's ill humour and now I knew Isabella was responsible, but I did not say so. 'You cannot have been long in Bath, surely?'

'No, we arrived on Wednesday but had I known you were here we would have come much sooner,' she said. 'Oh, Chloe, I am so glad I have found you! Now, you must tell me everything that has happened to you since you disappeared!'

'Since I disappeared?' Once again I was all confusion, and for a moment I had wild thoughts of yet another lady, someone hidden, who also resembled me. 'I have no recollection of disappearing!

Isabella laughed again, but her reply was lost as the shop door opened to let in a gentleman. 'Have you completed your purchases, Isabella? What an age you take, to be sure. Come, your mama will be uneasy—' He caught sight of me, looked again and gasped in astonishment. 'Upon my soul!' His gaze went backwards and forwards from Isabella to myself.

'Papa, it is Chloe!' Isabella was on her feet, tugging at his sleeve. 'It is Cousin Chloe, Papa. I have found my lost cousin. I have found Chloe!'

The gentleman was blinking. 'Chloe . . .' he murmured, vaguely.

'Yes, Papa. Is it not amazing?'

He continued staring at me. I recollected my manners and dropped a curtsy. 'Sir William Harcourt?'

He started, drew in a deep breath, collected himself and bowed. 'At your service, madam.' He gave a shaky laugh. 'Well, this is a surprise! Upon my soul, I know not what to say! Chloe! Well, well, well!'

He shook his head, repeating my name. 'Chloe! Our little Chloe!' And then, absurdly, 'How you have grown!'

'Papa, Chloe is much the same age as me, of course she has grown. How fortunate that we look so much alike or we might not have

176

known each other.'

Sir William shook his head and looked at me. 'But Chloe, where have you been hiding these many years? I confess, we feared for you. I scarce dared to hope that you lived! And here you are, large as life, and the image of your dear mother. Well, Isabella, this is a day of wonders, is it not?'

'Indeed it is, Papa, and I cannot wait to see Mama's expression when we tell her. No, wait, I have the most splendid notion! Chloe, you must come with us to see Mama. Yes, you must, I insist upon it! She will be overjoyed, after all, she is your aunt, you know. We must go home directly, Papa, and take Chloe with us. We have not an instant to lose!'

'Isabella, Isabella, you are too precipitate.' Sir William recollected himself.' He turned to me. 'You are our Chloe?'

'Chloe is my name, sir, but I know not—I am confused—'

'You must be our Chloe, looking as you do, so much like Isabella, of course you must. I declare my wits have gone a-begging. Well, we must take our time, and come to know each other properly. We have much to discuss, much to understand.'

'Chloe can tell us all about it, Papa. We must take her home, I want to show her to Mama!'

'Isabella, take thought, if you please.' Sir William spoke mildly and shook his head. 'You know your mama is not strong: we must explain gently and prepare her for such a meeting. It is all too much, I declare, I can scarce take it in, myself. But I believe,' he added, looking around, 'I believe that here, in the shop, we are very much in the way.'

Others had come into the shop and the proprietor, who had now given up any expectation of selling her wares to Isabella, was silently contriving to inch us away so she could serve her new customers. Already, my friends had taken the hint and were waiting outside on the pavement, peering through the window to catch glimpses of what was going forward.

Sir William ushered us outside. And there, in the noise of the traffic, with my friends crowding around us on the pavements and being jostled by passers-by, we were further inconvenienced by a fall of rain.

'I declare, this is quite impossible!' exclaimed Sir William. 'We can settle nothing, not here, not now. Well, my dear,' he turned to me with an apologetic smile, 'impatient as I am to hear your story, I fear we must part for the moment. We have much to discuss, but it can wait. You are alive and in good health, which is a cause for great rejoicing, indeed it is! Now, if you will be so good as to give me your direction, I will acquaint your aunt with all that has occurred and I am persuaded she will call upon you as soon as may be.'

I swallowed and said, 'I will be very happy to make her acquaintance, sir. I am staying in Laura Place, with Lady Pascall.'

'Indeed?' Sir William seemed taken aback by this intelligence and Isabella gave a great whoop of laughter, causing passers-by to turn and stare at us. Her father reproved her and returned his attention to me. 'Lady Pascall, you say? Yes, yes, of course. My compliments to the lady and tell her she may expect a visit from your aunt Rosalind very soon.'

Isabelle had both hands clamped over her mouth and tears of mirth were streaming down her face. I regarded her in bewilderment. She was utterly overcome and unable to speak.

Sir William procured a sedan chair to take me to Laura Place, seeming not to understand I was with my friends.

When I turned to them, Sarah, full of questions, wanted to know everything about what had occurred. Mary checked her.

'Chloe can make us acquainted with the particulars some other time.'

Lucy urged me to take the chair. 'We will do well enough with our umbrellas, but you need to sit down, Chloe, because you look as pale as a ghost!'

Indeed, I felt quite faint with the confusions of what I had learnt that morning and I was not unwilling to be carried home.

Somehow, I contrived to make a civil leave-taking of my new-found relations, saying

179

I looked forward to becoming better acquainted. I got into the sedan and, as I was carried away, I slumped in a most unladylike fashion, exhausted, and quite unable to bring my thoughts to consider what had passed.

Like Isabella, I began to laugh. I was not amused, but neither was I hysterical, although I have to believe my laughter was a consequence of all that had occurred. I cannot say what I was feeling; I cannot even say whether I felt pleasure or pain. I knew only that I was in turmoil, and if I had not laughed, I would have cried.

I laughed helplessly, in a quiet, gasping way, my chest heaving, tears pouring down my face, and as I shook and shuddered, the scenes with Isabella and Sir William played through my mind, and I heard again the things they had said.

I had disappeared, according to Isabella, but she could not possibly remember that occurrence, she must have have gained her information through hearsay.

I knew this without thinking about it, because she was close to my own age. All I could recall of my life before Miss Johnson, was a neat little cottage where I lived with my nurse, Emma Gooding. Where I truly belonged I knew not, but I knew I must have been an infant when I was removed.

I had disappeared, I had been lost for many years, even presumed dead! I had been snatched away from my family, from those who might have loved me, left with a nurse and later with none but Miss Johnson and the friendships I made for myself.

And my Somebody.

My Somebody! A hidden, shadowy figure who provided for me, who placed me in good hands, who had been so far interested as to demand reports of me from Miss Johnson, but who communicated only through an attorney and who had left me to grow up alone.

My Somebody was responsible, I thought, but the knowledge did not bring comprehension. Then another vague notion formed in my mind and the pattern of all that had occurred shifted and twisted and exploded into a new certainty.

Lady Pascall knew my Somebody. Of course she did! There could be no other explanation for the way I had been brought to Bath, clothed in fine raiment and introduced to polite society.

Always, when challenged by my perplexities, Lady Pascall had accounted for herself and sometimes, when scrutinized, her explanations had seemed unsatisfactory. I could not accuse her of descending to outright falsehood. That she had concealed information, however, was a charge I could lay before her.

Never was I intended to be a paid companion: I was to be brought out and taught to regard myself as a lady of consequence. She had brought me to Bath for this purpose, certainly with the knowledge and consent of my Somebody, perhaps even at his request.

She knew my Somebody. She had been acting on her secret knowledge of who I was and where I came from: yet even this did not account for all that had occurred.

She knew I had relations within polite society. Today, these relations told me how I disappeared and they had been perturbed about it. Moreover, they had, upon a chance meeting, and despite their astonishment, freely acknowledged me as their kindred and had done so with every appearance of pleasure. Clearly, they had no thought of disowning me.

I now discarded my previous suppositions about my birth and my Somebody. I hesitated to be absolutely certain, but I began to suspect that I was, in fact, well born.

Helen Waring and Lady Pascall . . . Emma Gooding and Miss Johnson . . . As I was carried towards Laura Place, my thoughts flitted hither and thither, and only the thread I had woven between Lady Pascall and my Somebody remained intact.

My Somebody had me taken from where I belonged and raised in humble circumstances. I had accepted those circumstances, neither wishing nor expecting anything better than what I could achieve for myself. Now, I found myself drawn into polite society. Since my Somebody had once determined I should be removed and hidden away, why was I now being restored?

My bemused mind could make nothing of it.

The chair carriers brought me to Laura Place and set me down outside the front door. As I paid them, the door was opened by Watson and within the hall I could see a man talking urgently to Lady Pascall.

I had, in all my other perplexities, forgotten she was having me followed. This man had waited outside the milliner's shop, but he had seen me with Isabella when we left and, when I took the chair, he had run ahead to report to Lady Pascall. I saw at once that I had no need to make her acquainted with what had occurred.

I stumbled indoors and said in a high-pitched voice, 'Madam, Sir William Harcourt sends his compliments and asks me to tell you we may expect a visit from my aunt Rosalind very soon.'

I began to laugh again and this time I felt hysteria rise in my throat. I shook and had to lean against the wall for support and tears ran down my cheeks as I fought for control.

A stinging slap across my cheek sobered me. I looked up at Sir Marcus in astonishment, as two fat tears rolled down my cheeks. Then his hand jerked the strings under my chin and my bonnet was removed and tossed carelessly aside as he gathered me into his arms, making soothing noises.

I cried and mangled his cravat and, as if from a long way away, I heard Lady Pascall's voice, anxious and concerned. 'Marcus, I know not what to do.'

'Get her some brandy and take some yourself.'

He half guided, half carried me into the small sitting-room and settled me on a sofa: he sat beside me and, because I was still crying, he pulled me into his arms, holding my head against his shoulder, stroking my hair and making soothing, rhythmic noises.

Presently, he said, 'Drink this.'

He held a brandy glass against my lips and tilted the liquid into my mouth. I swallowed and choked as the raw spirit stung my throat. Then I said, tearfully, 'Lady Pascall knows my Somebody. Oh yes, she does!' I went on, as though he had denied it. 'She knows him, I know she does.'

'I am your Somebody.'

Her voice was muted, a mere thread of sound, but her repetition splintered my reality.

'I am your Somebody.'

I lifted my face from his shoulder to stare at her. She looked most unlike herself: she was seated in an armchair, huddled and awkward, like a badly stuffed rag doll. She was not looking at me. Her gaze was fixed on a box she held between her hands, a wooden box, highly polished and inlaid with mother-of-pearl.

I struggled for speech, but my throat had

closed and I was unable to form a single word. I could only stare.

Sir Marcus laid a hand on my shoulder and said kindly, 'This was not how we intended to tell you, Chloe. We meant to break it to you gently.'

She looked up then, taking a swift, appraising glance at him, before her gaze fastened on me. 'Marcus said I should have told you the truth right from the beginning,' she said. 'Perhaps he was right. But you remind me so much—I never felt myself equal to it.'

Still, I could not speak.

Sir Marcus said, 'Tell her now.'

She did not answer directly. Again she looked at the box she was holding. Then, with difficulty, she got to her feet and brought it to me. 'Take it,' she said.

I looked enquiringly at Sir Marcus, but he said nothing. 'Take it,' repeated Lady Pascall. 'It is yours, after all.'

I took it, gazing silently at the intricate pattern of flowers and vines on the lid, all worked in mother-of-pearl. Lady Pascall resumed her seat. 'Open it,' she said. 'Look inside.'

The interior was lined with blue velvet. Nestling within were two objects, each wrapped in tissue paper. I looked up, glancing from Lady Pascall to Sir Marcus and back again and then I returned my attention to the

185

box, gently lifting out one of the tissue-wrapped objects.

It was a miniature portrait, and it had that clear translucence which comes from painting on ivory. It portrayed the head and shoulders of a lady and I was filled with joy as I beheld the sweetness of her expression, and I smiled.

'Mama!'

The word came from nowhere. I had spoken quite without thinking, without knowing, impelled by feeling, not reason.

There was a breathless silence. I gasped as I realized what I had said, and looked again from Lady Pascall to Sir Marcus. Neither of them contradicted.

Trembling, I looked at the portrait again. She wore her hair powdered and piled high, elaborately curled, in the fashion of the time. Jewels gleamed in her throat and ears. Her gown, what was shown of it, appeared to be silk.

I remarked these particulars but paid no attention. I had eyes only for her face. I gazed and gazed and I saw that reason might have brought me to the truth, eventually. Her features were like my own, though I doubt I could ever achieve the sweetness of her expression.

I looked up at last and spoke to Lady Pascall. 'My mother.'

'As you say.'

I looked again. I might have sat there for

the rest of my life, just gazing at the portrait, but beside me, Sir Marcus stirred. Gently but firmly, he took it from me and indicated the other tissue-wrapped portrait, still in the box.

I lifted it, unwrapped it, and looked at the gentleman it portrayed. Like the lady, he wore the fashion of his day, and there was something familiar about his features.

'Papa?'

I was less certain, but it seemed a reasonable assumption.

'Yes, that is your papa.'

I smiled at my papa. It was a good face, I thought. A strong face with eyes that looked at one directly, a high forehead, straight nose and a firm mouth and chin. It was not a woman's face, but I had seen a woman who wore a softened version of those features, and not so very long ago.

I looked up and saw that face again, in the flesh. A woman's face, which now bore the lines of age.

Lady Pascall herself. My Somebody, my grandmother.

FOURTEEN

'I had to keep you safe,' she said.

I said nothing but I stared at her accusingly, and there was a hint of impatience in her voice as she went on, 'How long do you think Bellamy would have allowed you to go on living had I not kept you hidden? You know what happened to your parents.'

'What happened to my parents? Oh no, oh no, oh no!'

I wailed as I realized what she meant. The two who had been so horribly murdered were these whose portraits I held in my hand, my parents. 'Not Mama! Not Papa! I cannot bear it!'

Again I was crushed in a strong pair of arms, as I shuddered at the nightmare horror. I had felt pain even when I believed I was hearing of strangers: now those strangers had faces; they were my parents and, though they were beyond the reach of my recollection, I had feeling for them.

I shuddered and wept and moaned and Sir Marcus held me. 'It was a long time ago, Chloe. They are not suffering now. They are looking down on you from Heaven and they will be grieved to see you so upset. Come, my dear, calm yourself.'

When the storm abated, he took the glass which still held some brandy and again he tipped fiery liquid into my mouth.

Lady Pascall said something I did not hear and Sir Marcus replied, 'What did you expect? It has been too much! Shock, upon shock, upon shock. The poor child is about all done in. Do you have a sleeping draught? She should go to bed.'

'No!' I sat up, scrubbing my face with the handkerchief Sir Marcus provided. I looked at my grandmother. 'I want to hear the rest.'

'There is little more to tell.'

She was white and strained and Sir Marcus poured brandy for her. She drank, gathered herself, and began to explain.

I was sixteen months old when my parents were killed and only six weeks older when Bellamy made an attempt on my life. My grandmother, convinced that Bellamy was a danger to me, had charged my nurse, Emma Gooding, to be especially vigilant on my behalf. Emma had surprised him in the act of smothering me with a pillow. He pretended he had been arranging pillows to make me comfortable, but she was not convinced.

'Bellamy,' said my grandmother drily, 'is not a man to concern himself with the comfort of an infant. That night, Emma smuggled you out of the house and contrived, somehow, to bring you to Derby, where I was living at the time. She said that however vigilant she was, sooner or later, Bellamy would succeed. She said we must keep you hidden, for it was not safe for you to remain with me. My part, she said, was to provide for you, and I knew she was right. I cannot tell you how it pained me to part with you, but my fear for your life left me with no alternative.'

'But why should Bellamy want to murder

me?'

'You stand in his way,' said Sir Marcus. 'He took control of Oakwood Pascall, but only until you come of age, for you are the rightful heiress. Unfortunately, he is also your legal guardian, which gave him opportunity to harm you. Your grandmother made attempts to have you brought into her guardianship, but nothing would convince the judges that he was dangerous.'

I recalled the only time I had ever seen Bellamy, how he appeared weak and ineffectual and I could comprehend how none would judge him as murderer of my parents or any threat to me.

Lady Pascall had discovered she could not work within the law. 'Bellamy is a man, after all,' she said drily, 'as were the judges. None of them felt a female could be at all competent in managing an estate. And I was considered beyond reason, because I accused him of murdering Thomas and Laura. They said my wits had been overturned by grief and shock. And they had! Had I not been so distraught I would have been wise enough to work against him stealthily.'

'Which you did, in the end,' said Sir Marcus.

I looked at Lady Pascall. 'Well, go on. You sent me to Gloucestershire with Emma.'

'I did. And,' she added with a sudden flash of her usual spirit, 'I accused Bellamy of making away with you and Emma, as well as

Thomas and Laura. No injustice, either, because he did try! And because I was busily accusing him, nobody had the smallest notion I had you safe.'

'Now that was clever,' said Sir Marcus appreciatively. 'Though I never understood why you chose to place Chloe in Gloucestershire. Why there, near the Warings of all people?'

He had asked a question which I had not thought of, and when he saw my startled look, he added, 'Perhaps you do not realize, Chloe, but your home, the Oakwood Pascall estate is in Derbyshire, neighbour to my own.'

'Oh? I did not know that. I have never been to Derbyshire.'

'Yes you have, you were born there,' said Lady Pascall. 'However, Gloucestershire is well removed from Derbyshire and old ladies, without occasioning surprise, come to live in Bath. I could be but one day's journey away from you. Better still, there was no reason why anyone would think of looking for you there. Bellamy did look for you, Chloe. He suspected me and he had me watched. He wanted me to lead him to you.'

'Were you—did you—' I shook my head in helpless confusion. 'I have forgotten what I wanted to ask.'

'Lady Pascall moved here so that she could be by your side within hours, should the need arise,' explained Sir Marcus. 'Never were you

191

forgotten, Chloe.'

I dabbed at my eyes as Lady Pascall went on, 'There are many excellent physicians in Bath. Had you suffered from illness, you would have had the best attention, I assure you.'

'I have always enjoyed good health, madam.'

'Indeed you have, and I cannot tell you how thankful I am,' she replied. 'But there are too many diseases, too many children die, and I was anxious for you, always.'

Her words evoked a memory: soon after I entered Miss Johnson's school, a mysterious benefactor had sent a doctor, who explained we were fortunate girls indeed, because we were all going to be spared the scourge of smallpox. None of us felt we were fortunate to be given innoculations and three of the girls were unwell for a few days as a consequence but, as Miss Johnson told us, we were protected from something worse.

'Yes, I did that,' she admitted, as I spoke of it. 'Whatever I could think of to do, that I did. From the Warings, of course, I learnt of Miss Johnson's little school, where I could be certain you would be kindly treated and where, when I visited their house, I could take a peek at you.' Her smile was slightly self derisive. 'I awarded myself that indulgence from time to time, although you never knew. And that is why,' she added, with a defiant look at Sir

Marcus, 'I kept up a friendship with George Waring, tiresome as he is, because it gave me an excuse to go there!'

'Mmm.' I felt I had a hundred questions, but I could form none of them. I looked at the portraits of my parents and found I was crying again, without knowing exactly why.

'You are exhausted,' said Sir Marcus. 'It has all been too much. You must rest, Chloe. You will feel better when you have slept.'

A servant was sent to make a fire in my room and hot bricks for my bed and I carefully wrapped the portraits in their tissue papers and placed them gently in the box. I looked at Lady Pascall. 'May I keep them by me for a while?'

'They are yours, my darling, you may keep them for ever.'

I got to my feet, swayed unsteadily, collected myself, then, obeying some impulse I could not account for, I stepped across to where my grandmother sat and planted an awkward kiss on her cheek. She caught my hand, held it between her own, and looked up at me with a wavering smile.

'Chloe, I do so love you!'

It was enough. I sobbed and said, 'I can think of no other I would rather have for a grandmother.'

Sir Marcus assisted me to climb the stairs and handed me over to my maid. When she had helped me to undress, I sank thankfully into bed and fell asleep.

It was dark when I woke, but a branch of candles was lit and Lady Pascall was seated by the fire. She came to me when she saw I was awake. 'How are you feeling, now?'

'To own the truth, I feel very strange indeed,' I said. 'So much I have learnt! I fear I am not yet accustomed.'

She nodded. 'You need time. Emma always told you you were a lady, did not she?'

'I do not perfectly recall.' I sat up and drew my knees up to my chin as I searched my memory for such scraps as I could recover. 'I do remember her reproving me with "A lady does not pull faces", and "A lady does not slouch", and "A lady does not fidget". And, of course, the curate was paid to teach me my lessons, much to my indignation, because I wanted to run wild with the village children. The signs were there, I suppose, but they were too subtle for a child to comprehend.'

'Well, Miss Pascall, you are a lady and you have to remember you must not pull faces, or slouch, or fidget.'

'Indeed, I must always conduct myself with the utmost propriety, especially in church!'

We laughed together, then she said abruptly, 'I had no notion the Harcourts had come to Bath; their arrival has not been announced in the *Chronicle*. Had I known, I would have seen to it that you were better prepared. How did you come upon Isabella?'

I told her all that had occurred, but when she asked what I thought of my cousin, I had little to say. 'I confess, I was too taken aback by what I heard to form an opinion of her.'

Lady Pascall did not pursue the subject. 'Your aunt Rosalind called whilst you were sleeping,' she said wryly. 'I permitted her to take a peek at you, but I would not let her wake you. They are to dine with us, all three, so you may become acquainted.'

'Are they here now?'

'No, no, they will return later. After Rosalind had exhausted herself, Sir William persuaded her to return home and lie down. Well, at least you were spared the worst of her dramatics! Such recriminations she brought down on me! I had meanly spirited you away; I had deprived her of the solace of her dear sister's child; I have been unbelievably wicked and cruel! I kept you safe from Bellamy, I told her, but she said I should have told her you were safe. Ha! Her and the rest of the world! She would not keep her silence, that one.'

I looked at my grandmother. 'You do not like my aunt?'

'I—oh! I should make allowances for her. She was quite inconsolable when your mama died, and she changed. I do not know what it is—some say there is a bond between twins which others cannot comprehend. Certainly, Rosalind knew straight away that something dreadful had happened to Laura. Sir William told me she knew instantly, and she was feverish and distraught long before any news reached her.'

'Sir William did mention that she was not strong.'

'She has never recovered from Laura's death. Well, neither have I, not really. I loved your mama as though she was my own daughter, and still I grieve for her as I do for Thomas. I did not, however, attempt to take my own life, as Rosalind did. One has to endure; one has others to consider. But Rosalind . . .'

'So you did not tell her you had me safe?'

'Never think I kept silent to be unkind! Had she pulled herself together, had I felt I could depend on her to be sensible, I would have told her everything.'

'It seems a little harsh to keep her in ignorance.'

'You are the only relation I have left in the world; I would not risk your life for her sake. Rosalind had her own daughter, after all, and she had her husband and the prospect of having more children.'

These words startled me. 'More children? Have I other cousins besides Isabella?'

'No, no. She suffered a miscarriage, brought about, I am persuaded, by her foolish attempt to take her own life.'

'Another grief,' I said sadly. 'Poor Aunt Rosalind.'

'One must feel some sympathy,' agreed Lady Pascall, 'but I warn you not to expect too much of your aunt, Chloe, for she is too full of her woes! She will treat you as she treats Isabella, alternating indulgence with indifference.'

This was a little disconcerting: Aunt Rosalind was, after all, twin sister to my mama, and I had hoped to find in her some resemblance of a mother. Because they were twins, alike in all respects, I was now unhappily aware that my own mother might have behaved in exactly the same way, had the situation been reversed.

I would prefer to think, I wanted to feel, that my mother would have found the strength to endure, as Grandmother had.

'I believe she would,' she said, when I told her what I was thinking. 'They were not alike in all respects, any more than you are like Isabella! They looked alike, but Laura had more character than her sister. Certainly, your papa liked her better. Thomas once told me Rosalind was no more than a pale copy of your mama.'

Lady Pascall was prejudiced in Mama's favour, of course, but so was I. Since I could not know for certain, and since it could do no harm, I chose to believe what I wanted to believe.

Before she left she brought down from the mantelpiece a flat jeweller's box, opening it to reveal a necklace, a string of pearls and coral, with ear-rings to match.

'These belonged to your mama,' she said. 'Now they are yours. Wear them tonight.'

I wore them with a dark-blue gown which had a criss-cross pattern of pink satin across the bodice and sleeves. When I went downstairs, I found Sir Marcus alone in the drawing-room.

'Miss Pascall!' He bowed and there was a gleam of humour in his eyes. 'I trust you are well rested?'

I said I was, and looked at him rather shyly as I thanked him for his kindness, earlier. 'I fear I behaved very foolishly, not at all like my usual self.'

'You had much to distress you. How are you feeling now?'

'I feel very odd indeed. I have yet to become accustomed to everything I have learnt.'

'I will confess to feelings of confusion myself, when Lady Pascall first confided her story. I was of the opinion that she should tell you everything straight away.'

I had deduced that Sir Marcus knew my grandmother's secrets before I left Stellham. 'Why did you not tell me yourself?'

'It was for her to explain; I could not undertake it. She meant to guide you towards the truth in a gradual way.'

I smiled. 'I thought I was an impostor.'

'No impostor,' he said. 'You are a lady of

consequence, Chloe. You have more consequence, even, than Miss Waring.'

That struck me as excessively diverting and I dissolved into giggles. 'How mortified she would be to hear you say so!'

My giggles stopped abruptly, for a new idea had formed in my mind. Miss Waring, having designs on Sir Marcus on her own account, had been indignant to discover he was paying attention to me and had warned me that I could hope for nothing.

I had believed it, when I thought myself a nobody. I had believed it, I had spoken sternly to myself and if I could not keep my feelings under control, I had been determined to control my behaviour and give no sign that I wished for what I could not have.

Now my heart turned over, and spasms of delight came crowding thick, taking me by storm. My blood sang, my breath quickened as, bruised by ecstasy, a flower of desire unfurled within me.

I was well born, daughter of a baronet, granddaughter to Lady Pascall herself. In terms of consequence I was equal to Sir Marcus.

Should he, by some miracle, come to wish for a match between us, my birth was no obstacle.

FIFTEEN

'Where is she? Where is my niece? Where is my dear sister's child?'

The voice, reaching us from beyond the drawing-room, could only be my aunt Rosalind. I stood up, my insides lurching, my mouth dry, as I braced myself for this first encounter.

She came in without removing her outdoor clothes and, as I dropped a curtsy, she surged forward to embrace me. 'Chloe! My dear, dear child! I cannot tell you what great happiness it is to see you safe and well! Let me look at you! Oh, it is as though my dear sister herself had been restored to me! This is a day of wonders, indeed.'

Her gloves dropped to the floor as she dabbed her eyes with her handkerchief, waved a vinaigrette under her nostrils, and added faintly, 'I declare, I am quite overcome!'

As she sank into a chair, I restored her gloves, curtsied again and said inadequately, 'I am very happy to make your acquaintance, madam.'

'Such formality!' she sighed. 'But of course, dear child, you cannot possibly remember your aunt, how could I expect it?'

'I am very sorry to say I do not, madam. I do not recall Mama, either, and I quite depend on

200

you to tell me everything about her. I am persuaded you have many stories to relate.'

This time, I had said exactly the right thing. Her eyes lit up and she exclaimed, 'Indeed, I have! Dearest Chloe, you cannot imagine how I shall enjoy recalling those happy days. How naughty we were, sometimes! For we were so much alike, you know, and we caused a great deal of confusion amongst our friends. "Like two peas in a pod", my dear father used to say. "Like two peas in a pod". Ah, those were happy times, indeed!'

'I have often heard you speak of them, Mama.' Isabella flashed a smile at me. 'Indeed, how often have I wished a twin of my own, never thinking I might find one in my cousin. Chloe, would it not be diverting to appear together, side by side, at the next assembly? We must do it; we shall have our hair dressed in exactly the same way, and we must purchase new gowns, both alike. How people will stare!'

Isabella appeared to relish the notion. Sir Marcus, who had been talking to Sir William, turned to intervene. 'I doubt you will persuade Chloe to wear garments so strewn about with ribbon bows as you appear to favour,' he said, in some disapprobation.

Never before had I known him remark feminine apparel, and I was surprised. Though I confess I agreed with him. Isabella wore a yellow figured muslin which would have been much prettier were it not adorned from waist to hem with a double row of blue ribbon bows.

Isabella tossed her head. 'How stuffy you are, Marcus! This is quite the latest fashion in London, I do assure you.'

'The dressmaker told you so herself, I collect?'

This was Lady Pascall at her driest and I hid a smile. Isabella seemed not to comprehend the irony because she only said, 'Yes, as a matter of fact, she did.'

'I thought so.' Then, whilst Isabella was thinking about it, she turned to my aunt. 'Rosalind, my dear, you have quite forgotten to remove your pelisse. Allow Marcus to assist you.'

Whilst he did so, I studied my aunt. She was pale and very slender, too slender for good health, and she wore a gown of lilac silk trimmed with vast quantities of lace. Her hair had once been dark but was now streaked with grey beneath her rose-point cap and, in her features, I could find only a vague similarity to that dear face I had seen painted on ivory. I could not feel the joy I felt upon beholding Mama's picture.

With a shock, I saw she wore mousetails in place of her own eyebrows, a fashion with some ladies. I could not like it and I had to control a shudder of revulsion on finding my mother's twin had adopted this conceit.

At table, my aunt, sometimes tearful and sometimes smiling wistfully, recalled some stories about my mother. I listened eagerly, but I fear I was disappointed by her rambling discourse, and her habit of sprinkling her talk with well-worn phrases did little to illuminate her descriptions.

Sir William enquired how I had lived, and Isabella made schemes for how, together, we would astonish society.

Sir William was talking to Sir Marcus. 'I own,' he said, 'I cannot like Conrad Bellamy and I know his conduct is not always right. I can easily comprehend how you distrust him. But I have to say, madam,' he turned to Lady Pascall, 'that I cannot perceive your accusations as rational. Certainly, he took advantage of our tragedy but I doubt he contrived it. I doubt he has the stomach for murder.'

'He is an oaf,' said Isabella uncompromisingly. 'Have you met him Chloe? Then you know what I mean. He bumbles around like a jackanapes.'

'Certainly, he gives that appearance,' I said, 'but I—'

'Appearances can be deceptive,' interrupted Lady Pascall. 'You have seen him, but you know nothing of his character.'

I stared at her in astonishment, but I saw a warning in her eyes: I had been about to mention how I had been terrified by the sight of Bellamy's hands, and how I had since learnt my instincts were right. Instead, I remained silent as Sir William repeated that Bellamy would not resort to murder.

Aunt Rosalind agreed. 'It was an accident, not murder, that took my dear sister from me,' she declared. Rousing herself to indignation, she went on, 'It was quite unnecessary for you, madam, to spirit dear Chloe away and keep her hidden from us. Had you wished it, I would have been perfectly happy to take in my niece, to raise her along with Isabella.'

Later, I heard what my grandmother thought of this idea but then she said only, 'If you recall, my dear, you were most unwell, at the time. I could not place that charge on you.'

No one tried to convince my aunt that Bellamy had contrived murder: I presume Lady Pascall had, by previous experience, discovered she would not believe it. And I was frowned at, clearly forbidden, in the presence of my aunt, to enlighten Sir William how such a murder was possible.

When we ladies withdrew from table, Isabella returned to her scheme of appearing side by side with me at the next assembly. The notion pleased my aunt and Lady Pascall agreed to it.

'Though it will not do to dress yourselves alike,' she said. Isabella protested, but she continued, 'It is pretty for children but childish tricks are not becoming in young ladies.'

My grandmother had perceived the only means of silencing argument from Isabella.

Not wishing to be thought childish, she allowed the judgement to stand and turned her attention to considering which colours would look pretty together.

'I have a pink satin ball gown,' she told me. 'It is quite my favourite and I should like to wear it. Do you have anything that will look well against pink satin?'

Lady Pascall recommended my turquoise silk. 'The one with silver embroidery, Chloe.'

'Yes . . . That might be pretty,' conceded Isabella.

She turned her attention to headdress, telling her mother she must purchase new feathers and all through that evening we were engaged in conversation of such trifling nature.

Later, when they had gone, there was an easing of manner among the three of us left. We sat by the fire, taking wine, and my grandmother quizzed me as to how I liked my relations.

To own the truth, I had been feeling disappointment, but I only said, 'I thought Sir William a pleasing gentleman, but I have not yet determined how I feel about my aunt and cousin.'

My grandmother knew me too well. 'Yes you have, you have them marked as trifling and silly,' she announced. 'And I will not say you are mistaken.'

'I cannot comprehend why you agreed to Isabella's scheme, madam,' I said. 'There will be a little sensation, to be sure, but I see no advantage.'

'Enough sensation for your true name and consequence to become well known,' she said. 'It is time for us to abandon Miss Smith. The world must learn that you are Miss Pascall.'

'The world and Conrad Bellamy,' I observed, giving voice to a thought that no one had yet spoken. 'It seems a little rash to announce that here I am, just waiting to be murdered.'

There was a startled silence. I regarded the other two with feelings I cannot quite describe. I was quite calm, not at all afraid. After all, I had known Bellamy was a danger to me, even before I understood why. Yet it was my business, my life was in danger, and I resented the way I was being managed.

'Depend upon Chloe to reach the heart of the matter.' Sir Marcus gave a strained smile. 'I have been putting it about that, should anything happen to you, then terrible retribution will follow. By which, I hope, your safety will be better secured. Because, my dear, if I am not mistaken, Bellamy already knows very well who you are.'

I nodded, recalling a moment when I might have been killed. 'The slates?'

'As you say. We are looking for the ruffian who set them falling, for Bellamy would not attempt a rooftop adventure: he bribed a man to do that. We have certain papers in our

206

possession, enough, with his evidence, to persuade the law to act against him.' He gave a wry smile. 'We would prefer the law to deal with him, if that is possible.'

'The law should have dealt with him years ago,' said Lady Pascall, sourly.

'Chloe.' To my suprise, Sir Marcus came and knelt by my chair, taking my hands between his. 'We cannot disguise there is danger for you, whatever precautions we take. It is unfortunate that Bellamy came to Bath, for he does not, as a rule, spend time here. Will you consent to return to Miss Johnson? You will be safe there and, I own, I would be easier in my mind.'

'I do not wish to return to Miss Johnson.' I spoke absently, more intent on the way his dark hair fell over his brow and seeing, in the soft glow of the candles, how his features were tense and his eyes shadowed with concern.

'I do not wish to return to Miss Johnson,' I repeated.

'You will be safe there,' he urged.

'I do not intend to run away. If Bellamy wishes to murder me, then let him try.' I smiled at my grandmother. 'I believe we should make it easy for him.'

Sir Marcus was instantly on his feet. 'Chloe, are you mad?'

My grandmother shook her head. 'I see your design. You think we might tempt Bellamy to act unwisely. No, my dear. Such a scheme could too easily go awry. I cannot allow it.'

'But I could carry a pistol.'

'You will only spare Bellamy the trouble of murdering you!'

That was Sir Marcus. 'I know very little about firearms,' I admitted, 'but I could learn; you could teach me. It cannot be difficult, after all. You just point and pull the trigger.'

I used every persuasion at my command, but my grandmother would not be swayed and she was supported by Sir Marcus.

'I have not protected you so long to put your life at risk now,' she said. 'I am having Bellamy watched; I learn of his doings. At present he is but a short journey from here. I believe he means to return to Bath, but I shall learn when he comes and keep you hidden, as I did before.'

'But madam,' I protested, 'we could go on like that for years! It will not serve to undo Bellamy.'

'Well, we may be doubly fortunate,' said Sir Marcus drily. 'He might murder Isabella by mistake!'

Lady Pascall laughed and I confess I could not help smiling, but I only said, 'You cannot mean that!'

He did not. They were trying to persuade the law to act. Emma Gooding had signed an affidavit, telling how she had seen him attempt to smother me. This was not enough for, though no one would doubt Emma's sincerity, it would be said she was mistaken. Even Mr Marano's explanation of how the carriage was set alight gave us no means of proving Bellamy's guilt.

Sir Marcus had informed Sir William, when left alone in the dining-room, what we learnt from Mr Marano.

'He was very much astonished but he does not wish Rosalind to know. He says, and I agree with him, there is nothing to be gained by making her accept that her sister was murdered.'

'Even if she did, she would be no help whatsoever,' said Lady Pascall.

'Sir William, on the other hand, is now persuaded and he is willing to lend assistance. With his support, we may prevail.'

At the end of that remarkable day, when I retired for the night, I found myself so filled with complicated emotions that I could not settle to sleep.

I took out the portraits, gazing at my parents and through my tears they shimmered and stirred and I had the strange fancy they were whispering to me. I closed my eyes and, placing their portraits against my ears, I listened intently.

'Know that we love you, Chloe, and fear not. We are with you always: we are watching over you; we will protect you from evil. You are our beloved child; no harm will come to you.'

I believed them. The melting voices slipped through my thoughts and I wept for love and grief. When at last I slept, they came to me in my dreams: I heard their laughter, felt their caresses, and loving words soothed away my fusses and frets. Perhaps a few fragments were drawn from my earliest memory because I saw how they moved, how Mama arranged her gown upon seating herself, how Papa warmed his hands before the fire and how he took out his pocket watch to read the time.

I awoke, still feeling unlike myself, not yet accustomed to the notion that I was part of a family, no longer Miss Smith but Miss Pascall.

No longer a nobody, but a lady of consequence.

Strangely, this was difficult to accept. I was divided, conducting an argument with myself, one part insisting it was true whilst another part (which sounded for all the world like Helen Waring) told me sternly that it was stuff and nonsense and I had better squash that presumption straight away because it did no good at all to entertain such fanciful notions.

I looked at my portraits again and I will swear I saw Papa wink at me. I was smiling as I went downstairs for breakfast.

Sir Marcus was not there: Lady Pascall told me that he had ventured out of doors to take exercise for the first time since his ankle was injured.

I was instantly conscience stricken. 'Oh,

heavens!' I exclaimed. 'I had forgotten his injuries and never once enquired! What will he think of me?'

'That your mind was much occupied with other matters,' she said. 'Do not make yourself uneasy, Chloe. He is mended and wants only a little exercise to ease away the stiffness.'

He joined us twenty minutes later in a state of ill-humour. 'Isabella!' he exclaimed in disgust. 'She has known Chloe but one day and already she is about her mischief. I swear, I will strangle the wretch, so help me, I will!'

Lady Pascall raised her brows. 'What has she done?'

'Three times!' he said. 'Three times have I been stopped by gentlemen of my acquaintance, all taking it upon themselves to warn me about Chloe. I was told she is a lady of doubtful origins, who has insinuated herself into your favour and persuaded you to impose her on polite society. The gossips are repeating the story all over town. They say they have it on good authority!'

'I expect they have,' I said, 'but I think we cannot lay that charge on Isabella.'

He stared at me, and demanded, 'Who, besides Isabella, would speak such ill-natured falsehood?'

'I think it was Miss Waring,' I said. 'And certainly it was ill-natured, but not falsehood, not to her mind.'

'Miss Waring? Why would she begin such a

211

rumour?'

'She has been offended with us ever since she first came to Bath,' said Lady Pascall. 'She thinks Chloe has no place in polite society and she resents the way you, Marcus, have been paying attention to her. Yes, Chloe, I think you are right.'

'I have no great opinion of Miss Waring, but she has been in Bath these several weeks. Why did she not speak out before?'

'She had not then met with Isabella.'

They listened, half indignant, half amused, as I related what I knew. 'She mistook Isabella for me and Isabella was rude. She was piqued, so she determined to have revenge.'

'I knew Isabella had a hand in it!'

'Well, never mind that. We must determine what is to be done. What did you tell your acquaintances, Marcus?'

'That it was ill-natured falsehood, that Chloe's background was impeccable, that I was very well acquainted with all her relations, and I would be obliged if they would take pains to scotch the rumour.'

'Very well, that will do for the present. We need not concern ourselves with whatever nonsense the gossips are spreading about, for they will be utterly confounded when the girls show themselves at the assembly'

My grandmother chuckled. 'It will give me great pleasure to see the expression on Helen Waring's face.'

SIXTEEN

'I declare, the two of you together look as pretty as a picture,' said Aunt Rosalind.

In this opinion, my aunt and my grandmother were united. Even Sir Marcus expressed approbation and Sir William surveyed us with a smile and said it reminded him of the old days, when Mama and my aunt were young and carefree.

Isabella was persuaded to abandon her feather headdress and wear a jewelled ribbon. For me, Grandmother had produced a chased silver band, set with turquoise to match my gown.

We left Laura Place in separate chaises, Isabella with her parents and I with Sir Marcus and Grandmother. We were early arrivals at the assembly rooms, in spite of Isabella's expressed wish to be late and make a grand entrance.

Sir Marcus told her she would not suggest such a thing were she at all acquainted with Bath assemblies. 'You may depend upon it,' he said, 'with the press of people around, a grand entrance would be impossible. You would have to squeeze your way in and squeeze your way about the room.'

Isabella grimaced. 'Is it really so uncomfortable, Chloe?'

'Private balls are much nicer than public assemblies,' I said, and I wondered why Sir Marcus found that diverting.

My grandmother gave me a swift smile. 'For now, a public assembly will serve our purpose very well.' She returned her attention to Isabella. 'Be content to astonish the earliest arrivals for, I assure you, that will get you talked about.'

I did not enjoy, as Isabella did, the idea of creating a sensation and I confess to a nervous ache in my throat as we were conveyed to the assembly rooms.

In the Octagon Room we arranged ourselves, Isabella and I side by side, Sir Marcus lending his arm to me, Sir William leading my cousin, and my aunt and my grandmother following.

Some fifty people were before us, not enough to please Isabella. We caused a bustle and stir, and won admiration, but the sensation was less than she wished for.

The news had been put about beforehand. My friends, who had witnessed our first encounter, had talked about it. Older ladies recalled those events that occurred in my infancy and, because I had been brought into society by Lady Pascall, their speculations taught them the truth.

I was separated from Isabella, talking with my friends, when Miss Waring arrived. I watched her greet some acquaintances and I

214

was still watching her when she saw Isabella fluttering her eyelashes at a group of young men. Among them was one who belonged to her own set of admirers.

Miss Waring had taken Isabella for me. I was amused to see her lips tighten and an angry flush colour her face and neck. She rose and began moving purposefully towards my cousin with, I presumed, the design of causing trouble and embarrassment.

She was about to bring embarrassment on herself and I could not let her do it. Once, she had been as kind as she knew how and I had been welcomed at Stellham House.

Some remnant of friendship moved me to intercept Miss Waring. I caught her arm and turned her to face me.

Ignoring her angry exclamation, I smiled with every appearance of pleasure. 'I am so happy to see you here, Helen. I have been wishing to introduce you to my cousin. Now, where has she got to? Ah, there she is. I declare, it is almost like seeing myself in a looking-glass. Our mothers were identical twins, you know.'

Her mouth was working and her eyes were wide with amazement. Clearly, she could not answer, so I moved closer and tucked her arm into mine, and spoke so that none but she could hear.

'Here are matters more complicated than you or I could have dreamt of when we were in

Gloucestershire. My Somebody has turned out to be Lady Pascall. She is also,' I added with some emphasis, 'my grandmother.'

'Indeed?' Miss Waring had found her voice, which was frigid and scornful. 'Does she know that?'

'She has known it since the day I was born. I fancy you will hear the story soon enough. Allow me to introduce my cousin.'

I made introductions, and saw recognition dawn on Isabella. 'You are the lady who accosted me in the pump room the other day,' she said, and her voice made it known she did not recall the occasion with pleasure. 'Ah! Now I understand!' A hint of malice curled Isabella's smile. 'You mistook me for Chloe.'

'It is a common mistake,' said Sir Marcus who came in time to forestall any indiscretion Isabella might utter. 'I fear you two will cause confusion all your lives, each being mistaken for the other. No blame can be attached to Miss Waring.'

The lady was not gratified by his intervention. She turned to me. 'You should have told me there were two of you!'

'How could Chloe tell what she did not know?' He regarded her with a quirk of his eyebrows, then turned to me. 'Your grandmother wishes to speak with you, Chloe.'

I excused myself, and went to join Lady Pascall, who wanted to know why I had saved Helen Waring from herself. 'She will not thank

216

you for it,' she told me. 'Already she has made herself look foolish by her ill-natured attempt to expose you. She will not forgive you for that.'

'It does not signify,' I said. I took a seat and went on, 'I do not begrudge her that small service, or even her ingratitude. After all, she has been grossly misled.'

I did, however, begrudge her when the dancing began, for she was engaged by Sir Marcus, when I expected to be dancing with him myself. I stifled my disappointment, believing he did it to soothe her ruffled feelings. I accepted another partner and consoled myself with the reflection that he would certainly engage me for the next two dances.

He did not. He danced with other ladies and he danced with Isabella and, though I did not lack partners, I confess I was hurt by his neglect. The evening was well advanced before he approached me and I was, by that time, out of charity with him.

I allowed him to lead me into the set, though I displayed less enthusiasm than usual. I was tempted to give voice to the acid remarks which sprang to mind, but my better sense told me it would do me no service to appear sulky and childish.

So I said nothing, and he made no attempt to open a conversation. When I ventured a peep at his countenance, I saw he wore a stony expression, which frightened me a little.

'Has something occurred to vex you, sir? I declare, never have I seen you look so grim.'

'Should it signify how I look?'

'If your vexation is my doing, then I wish to know it.'

Something flickered in his eyes and there was a brief alteration in his expression, but it disappeared so swiftly I had not time to read it. His voice was cold as he said, 'I beg you will not trouble yourself with my vexations, Miss Pascall. They are no concern of yours.'

His tone and the formal use of my name was, after all that had occurred, like a blow in the face. I gave utterance to the only reproof in my power.

'I am Miss Pascall, now, am I? You were quite happy to be calling me Chloe, not so very long ago.'

'An unwarranted liberty on my part,' he said stiffly. 'I beg your pardon.'

'What on earth has got into you?' I demanded.

His mouth tightened and he made no attempt to answer. I was angry, for I had done nothing to deserve this. Knowing he would see, I shrugged my shoulders as the dance separated us.

We continued the dance in silence and perhaps it was as well he had reminded me who I was. The impostor, the lowly Chloe Smith, would have been crushed by such high-handed disdain: Miss Pascall could carry it off with dignity.

I maintained my outward dignity at all events, though I was deeply pained by this alteration of his manner. I was relieved when the dance ended and I returned to my grandmother.

I wanted to leave, but I would not give Sir Marcus the satisfaction of knowing his ill-humour had distressed me, so I danced again and took pains to appear animated. Afterwards, I joined my aunt and cousin, asking Isabella how she was enjoying the evening and it was she who grimaced, not I.

'Are these assemblies always such a squeeze? My toes have been trodden on a dozen times!'

'I confess, I find the noise quite intolerable,' said Aunt Rosalind. 'For your sakes I have endured it, my dears, because I would not spoil your enjoyment for all the world, but I would willingly leave early, if you have had enough.'

Isabella, declaring she was crippled for life, was willing to leave. My grandmother agreed and a gentleman acquaintance obligingly fetched Sir William from the card-room.

Sir Marcus was informed of our departure. That gentleman, who was about to dance with another lady, chose to remain at the assembly.

'I declare, all these country dances are quite tedious,' said Isabella, as we waited for our cloaks. 'Do they never waltz? Upon my soul, Chloe, what are you crying for?'

A few tears had escaped me, despite my attempts to blink them back. I shook my head, unable to speak and unwilling to reveal my distress to Isabella. My grandmother attributed my tears to all the events of the past two days. I was overtired and overwrought and I should be in bed.

Mutely, I followed her to our chaise. I was relieved to retire before Sir Marcus returned, relieved to be alone and give way to the shuddering grief that twisted my insides. Heart-wringing thoughts, blade-sharp, slashed my dreams and mocked my recent hopes of a closer bond. I released a flood of angry tears and eventually fell into an exhausted sleep.

When I woke, calmer after my sleep, I knew the alteration in Sir Marcus could not occur without cause. I puzzled over it, and a review of my own conduct brought no enlightenment.

Sir Marcus was not one to bite his tongue: I recalled how I overheard him telling Grandmother his opinion of her schemes and I knew that, had I done anything he found objectionable, he would express his views in a forceful manner.

Such frankness does not comfort, but he was understood. This change in his demeanour was by no means understandable, and it accorded ill with what I had previously observed in him.

I recalled his appreciation when I had the idea of consulting Mr Marano, and I recollected the swift action he had taken on my behalf when danger threatened. I remembered how, only the other day, he had soothed me when I was confused and distraught and, most of all, I remembered the concern in his eyes when he spoke of keeping me safe from Bellamy.

I had, I confess, been more affected than I should have been over his attentions to me. We had agreed upon a subterfuge to discourage my suitors because, believing myself an impostor, I had scruples about attaching any gentleman.

Even then, I had known I was in danger of becoming too attached to him, but he had no thought that I might. Unlike most gentlemen, who thought themselves irresistable when they favoured a lady, Sir Marcus seemed unaware of his charm.

I felt his attraction: no longer certain of my own motives, I wondered if I had agreed to the subterfuge so that, when we were in society, I could enjoy his attentions.

In private, I had been carefully restrained, partly for my own sake, but also because I felt he would be appalled and embarrassed to learn how I had tumbled headlong into love with him. I allowed myself the satisfaction of a sharp retort once in a while, but I kept my feelings hidden.

221

Only when I learnt the truth about my birth, only then, had I ventured to hope. A short-lived hope, indeed!

I understood him, now. The change in his manner was directed against any such presumption. My throat ached in my despair, but I resolved to keep my dignity. I would tell Sir Marcus he need no longer trouble himself on my behalf.

I had opportunity to inform him of it at breakfast, because Grandmother had to leave the table to settle some dispute among the servants. Before that, he had joined us at table without enthusiasm or appetite, and made only brief answers to our civilities.

When Grandmother left the room, I looked at him directly. I said, 'I understand the purpose behind the alteration in your manner, sir. You have determined there is no longer any need for our subterfuge. Well, you are quite right, though I must say, I feel it would have been more civil to speak plainly, rather than subject me to a display of ill-humour—and in public—as you did last night.'

Something flashed in his eyes when I was halfway through this speech, but when I finished his expression was unreadable. His voice, when he spoke, held a hint of irony. 'How fortunate you are so quick of understanding.'

This gave me the uneasy feeling that I had not, after all, understood anything. Having no answer, I watched him uncertainly. He was flushed, but I could not determine whether his colour was due to anger or embarrassment. I was thankful when my grandmother returned to the table, describing with exasperation the falling-out she had been obliged to settle.

That day was Sunday and when we attended morning service, I confess my mind was less on religious observance than on the peculiar behaviour of Sir Marcus. I sent up prayers for better understanding, but none was forthcoming.

That day, I avoided him as much as possible. When he was there, my grandmother gave no sign that she noticed anything amiss but when we were alone she asked why we had quarrelled.

'Indeed, I wish I knew,' I said frankly.

I stumbled a little as I told of our subterfuge and of my own conjectures.

'Last night he was acting so strangely, as though we were no longer friends! I cannot think I did anything to vex him and I can only presume he wished an end to the subterfuge.'

My grandmother seemed vexed on her own account and she said, 'Plain speaking on his part would have settled that matter without acrimony.'

'Yes, and I told him so. But I can think of no other reason for his conduct.'

We talked it over again, then Grandmother went on to talk of something else. If she made any attempt to question Sir Marcus on the subject, I could not find out what she learnt.

The following day, Sir Marcus left Laura Place and returned to his hotel, saying he was recovered from his injury and he would impose on us no longer.

The friendship between us was now at an end. Once, I had prepared myself for that: I knew I would be distressed but I had determined to keep a cheerful countenance, not revealing my pain. I had, however, always believed it would occur amicably. I had not expected this cold animosity.

Our days resumed their usual pattern. I would accompany Lady Pascall to the pump room and our evenings were spent at parties or concerts or assemblies.

When we encountered Sir Marcus we were treated with just enough civility so as not to occasion remark. He paid attentions to other ladies and it was clear he was a favourite with them. I saw just how foolish my own short-lived hopes had been. With so many to choose from, why would he wish for me?

I often saw my aunt and Isabella and the likeness between my cousin and myself was helpful in distracting the attention of society away from the coolness between myself and Sir Marcus.

Early in April, other events of greater import occupied everyone's mind for a few days, for the news reached us that Paris had been taken and Napoleon was, at last, defeated.

All over the town, houses were decked with laurel. Transparencies and coloured candles were lit in windows, the church bells rang and people from all walks of life poured into the streets, dancing and singing, all celebrating the end of twenty years of struggle.

I was caught up in the rejoicing, how could I help it? These wars had been going on since before I was born, and never before had I seen jublilation affecting the whole populace. It went on for days, the triumph and joy, and there were occasional tears as we recollected how many had fallen.

We heard that Napoleon had abdicated and been exiled to the island of Elba. We heard that the Russian Czar was to visit London and there were to be lavish victory celebrations in the capital. Travel to the continent was permitted again, and several gentlemen expressed an intention of visiting France to see the country for themselves.

In those days, it seemed churlish even to consider my own personal grief. But, at night, in the dark, I could not help reflecting that the occasion would be even more joyous for me had I been able to share the celebrations with Sir Marcus.

Gradually, everybody settled down once more to normality. For some reason, I felt my own loss even more acutely when the general rejoicing had died down. When I was alone, I gave way to despondency, though I tried to keep a cheerful countenance in company.

I began to comprehend there were implications in my new-found identity which I had not yet thought of. Since learning of it, my mind had been much occupied by learning of the past. Although I had realized I must now expect a future very different from the one I had envisaged, that future had seemed a distant one. I thought that, for some time to come, I would go on in much the same way as before.

Now, I saw how my present circumstances were altered: there was a subtle difference in the way people behaved towards me. The haughty ones, who had been condescending to an unknown Miss Smith only because she was protected by Lady Pascall, now treated me with more affability and pressed invitations upon me. My friends, on the other hand, had become a little hesitant: when making plans, instead of stating their own wishes, they first enquired what I would like to do.

They had, however, noticed that all was not well. One day, when we four were taking a stroll, Lucy rather delicately mentioned the matter.

'I would not ask, Chloe, but you have not been quite yourself for some time now, and I cannot feel you are so changed because you have discovered your family. It has to do with

Sir Marcus, am I right?'

'He seems to have taken against me,' I said forlornly, 'but I cannot find out why.'

My friends knew nothing of our subterfuge and I did not mention it, feeling it was too complicated to explain. I told how the alteration had begun at the assembly and asked if they had observed anything in my conduct which would explain it.

They had not; they were bewildered. They promised to inform me if they heard anything which might account for it.

There came a day when Lucy and I set out without the others, Sarah being unwell and Mary having other matters to attend to.

There had been rain earlier and we thought there might be more rain to come. Nevertheless, we both felt the need for exercise, so we took umbrellas and went out. As we walked together, Lucy said she had heard some talk.

'The gossips are saying that Sir Marcus knew you were Lady Pascall's granddaughter before you knew it yourself,' she said.

'For once,' I said, 'the gossips have it right. He knew, but he could not tell: it was Grandmother's secret, not his.'

In society, opinions on my grandmother's stratagems varied, but it was known she had hidden me away for safety.

The gossips, Lucy said, had been busy. 'Someone has put it about that Sir Marcus is distressed for money. It seems his father gambled away a good portion of his inheritance.'

'I have heard that story,' I said. 'It is not perfectly true. His father made an unwise investment and lost money. His circumstances were reduced, but Sir Marcus is not a pauper. What has this to do with me?'

Sir Marcus had, according to the gossips, taken advantage of his secret knowledge to engage my affections. His design had been to marry my fortune.

'Indeed?' I said drily. 'If that is his design, he has a strange way of achieving it.'

'I do not believe he had any design of that nature,' said Lucy. 'He is altogether too straightforward to contemplate such a scheme. But he might have been confronted by those opinions. Would it account for his withdrawal, do you think?'

'Certainly, it would account for his ill-humour,' I said. I felt some indignation on his behalf. 'I cannot determine—I must give this some thought.'

Sir Marcus might have heard whispers and they might bring him to put an end to our subterfuge, but why should he blame me? As Grandmother said, it could have been ended without acrimony.

I recalled, uneasily, that he had danced with Miss Waring. I had expected him to engage me to dance afterwards but he had not. Was that because she had said something to injure me in his opinion?

Since that assembly, Miss Waring had avoided me as much as possible. I had not wondered at it. She had patronized me and lectured me so it was not surprising she should feel some degree of embarrassment at the way things had turned out.

Certainly, she had come to Bath meaning to pursue Sir Marcus and she had been angry to learn he was paying attention to me. She would be even more angry, now, to learn that my birth made me as eligible as herself.

I had wounded her vanity and Isabella had done likewise. Isabella had been rude to her and later compounded that offence by flirting with one of her admirers. Putting all this together, Miss Waring might well determine to cause a rift between myself and Sir Marcus.

Started in this train of thought, I had no difficulty in guessing how she would snatch at half-truth and stretch it into something ugly. Had she congratulated him on taking the trouble to engage my affections before I discovered I was not, after all, a penniless little nobody? Had she implied that I had been insufferably smug, thinking I had made a conquest?

I was still pondering when Lucy pointed out that it was raining again. Raising our umbrellas we turned homewards, quickening our steps as the rain increased to a downpour.

Arriving at her house, Lucy invited me to take shelter indoors, but that would have left Lady Pascall's man (she was still having me followed) standing outside in the rain. I was not so used to my new status that I could bring myself to treat servants with callous indifference.

Still pondering over Sir Marcus, I hurried towards Laura Place. Entering the house, I was unprepared to find myself accosted by my grandmother, Aunt Rosalind and Sir William.

All were anxious, all demanding to know if I had seen anything of Isabella.

'Not today, not yet,' I said. 'We are to meet later.'

I felt a cold chill of apprehension when they told me my cousin had been missing for longer than three hours.

SEVENTEEN

'Isabella would go out,' said Aunt Rosalind fretfully. 'Nothing would do but she must purchase a new fan! I begged her not to take long, for we had an engagement to keep, and she promised she would return within the half-hour!'

My aunt and Sir William were annoyed when Isabella had not returned as promised. They surmised she had taken shelter from a fall of rain. When the rain ceased, they expected her but still she did not return. Their annoyance increased. After an hour, Sir William had determined on going out to look for her.

'You cannot imagine my anxiety!' My aunt was twisting a handkerchief around her fingers. 'I sent a note to cry off from our engagement, of course. It was another hour before Sir William returned and he had not found her.'

Sir William had drawn from the shopkeeper the information that a lady answering Isabella's description had purchased a fan and, upon observing the rain, had summoned a sedan chair.

'I questioned some of the chair carriers,' said Sir William, 'and none had carried Isabella. But most were about their business around the town, so I could not speak to them all. Then I went home, thinking I had missed her and she was there.'

She was not and my aunt became alarmed upon hearing what Sir William had to tell. He, fearing that she would work herself into a fever, had the happy notion of bringing her to Laura Place, saying he thought Isabella might have come to see me.

'She might have returned home, by now,' I suggested, 'only to find you away.'

Sir William had provided for that. 'I left a note telling Isabella to follow us here, directly.'

'And she has not come!' wailed Aunt Rosalind. 'Oh, what has happened to her? What has happened to my baby?'

I began to have some very uncomfortable ideas. We laughed when Sir Marcus expressed a hope that Bellamy would murder Isabella by mistake. Now it did not seem so diverting. She could have been taken for me. I thought how easy it would be for Bellamy to position his henchmen with a sedan chair, just waiting to carry off an unsuspecting passenger.

Despite my alarm, I hesitated to mention the possibility for fear of completely oversetting Aunt Rosalind. Whilst we did not know for certain, it would be cruel to suggest that Isabella had been abducted, possibly murdered.

My grandmother was attempting to soothe my aunt. 'Do not make yourself uneasy, Rosalind,' she said. 'Marcus is looking for her. He will find her, you may depend upon it.'

Sir Marcus, I heard later, had told servants to search different quarters of the town; he went to the pump room and received negative answers to his enquiries. When the servants reported failure he, too, suspected the sedan chair.

Like Sir William, he questioned the chair carriers: those men knew each other and would notice strangers plying a chair. And indeed, they had observed newcomers. It was assumed they had been recently employed in the trade, though one pair had been most indignant with them. 'They came on our pitch, where they had no right to be!'

They would have come to blows with the Johnny-come-lately pair had not they been occupied with a passenger. As it was, they muttered darkly about what was in store for them later.

'Never mind that!' Sir Marcus cut them short, demanding to know if the newcomers were carrying a lady: the men said not, the chair was unoccupied. But it had been waiting on Milsom Street, not far from the shop Isabella had patronized.

Convinced this was Bellamy's work, Sir Marcus sent the servants to glean what intelligence they could. Then he heard of an empty sedan chair, abandoned in a narrow dark alley. When he got to the place, a trio of ragamuffin children were using it for their games and, bribed with sixpences, they told how they had seen a fine lady carried from the chair to a chaise-and-four, all the time making a great to-do about it.

Just as Sir William formed an intention to look for Isabella again, Sir Marcus came to Laura Place. After telling us what had occurred, he turned directly to Lady Pascall. 'I need a good horse, madam,' he said. 'I am going after them.'

Aunt Rosalind had fallen into a swoon. I attended to her with hartshorn and looked up.

'It has been some hours since they took her,' I said fearfully. 'Will you be in time?'

'I had better be,' he said grimly. Perhaps seeing something in my expression, he smiled at me, his animosity forgotten in this emergency. 'I know their direction,' he said. 'Look after your aunt and try not to worry.'

'The first I will do,' I said. 'The second is impossible. Isabella was taken for me, was she not?'

'Bellamy will soon discover the mistake, I imagine.'

Sir William determined to go with Sir Marcus. Lady Pascall ordered the horses saddled and whilst that was being done, Sir William sent a servant running to fetch his riding boots.

Aunt Rosalind stirred and began to weep. She demanded the gentlemen should rescue Isabella; she said they had not an instant to lose and she begged them not to leave her side.

'The case is not altogether desperate, Rosalind,' said my grandmother. 'I have men watching Bellamy and we know where he will take her. Marcus, you know my men and I expect you will meet them. They will assist you in whatever is necessary.'

He nodded. 'Look after Rosalind. She should remain with you until we return.'

After they went, my aunt began to apportion blame: it was her fault for not insisting that Isabella remain at home: it was Isabella's fault, for wishing to purchase a trumpery fan: it was my fault for resembling Isabella so exactly.

'Bellamy is to blame, no other,' said my grandmother. 'Perhaps now, Rosalind, you will believe in his wickedness. He is altogether—' She stopped, for it would not do, at that moment, to convince my aunt that her sister had been murdered.

For the next hour, despite our own misgivings, we attempted to soothe my aunt. At last, my grandmother suggested she should take a sleeping draught and lie down.

'How can you suggest such a thing? Have you no heart? How can I possibly sleep whilst my daughter is in such peril?'

'Marcus will rescue her,' said Grandmother. 'Though I fear we will be many hours waiting. The time will pass more quickly if you sleep. We will wake you as soon as we have news.'

I added my own urgings, saying that my aunt would do well to rest now, so that she would be stronger when Isabella came back. 'For I am persuaded that, when she returns, she will need all your support, madam.'

We continued our urgings and at last she consented. We gave her a sleeping draught and sat with her until she fell asleep.

I looked at my grandmother, seeing in her the traces of strain. 'Perhaps you, too, should rest, madam.'

She shook her head. When we went downstairs, she ordered tea and bread and butter and we both felt better after we had taken something.

She shook her head over the way Isabella had been abducted. 'I had you guarded against any such attempt, but I confess I had no thought of guarding Isabella.'

'What do you suppose Bellamy will do when he discovers he has the wrong cousin?' I asked.

'He may not discover it,' she said. 'Isabella may determine not to enlighten him. He has but slight acquaintance with her. How will he know you apart?'

I could not answer. I hoped Isabella would tell Bellamy who she was, for I had a hollow dread of what would befall her if she did not. Grandmother did not speak the fearful word but I knew that murder was a strong possibility.

'How will I endure my own life, if it is purchased at the expense of Isabella's?'

'The evil is not your doing!' said my grandmother sharply. 'Place the blame on Bellamy where it belongs, Chloe.'

'I cannot but feel we should have foreseen this,' I said fretfully.

Grandmother might have seen something in my expression for she said softly, 'It is difficult to avoid self-reproach at times of anxiety, but it does no good. Do not look at me like that, Chloe. I have taken other measures. I told you,

236

I have men watching Bellamy: I am persuaded Isabella will be rescued.'

'I hope you are right. You know where Bellamy is?'

'He has taken a house in Bristol.'

'Oh! Not so far away, then?'

'No. When he came to Bath, I determined I would keep myself informed of his whereabouts and when I heard of his sojourn there, I knew he was about his scheming. Which is why,' she added triumphantly, 'I have men spying on him!'

I stared. 'Do you tell me Sir Marcus has his direction?'

She nodded. 'He will rescue her. She will be returned by six o'clock.'

I said nothing: she knew that Bellamy would have time to murder Isabella before Sir Marcus reached her.

I glanced at the clock on the mantelpiece. It was half past two. After what seemed like an hour I looked again to discover that only ten minutes had passed.

How were we to endure the anguish of waiting for hours? We could settle to nothing; clenched tight in the fist of time we could scarce bear to breathe, our minds clamouring for news.

We lapsed into silence. I tried to read and could not. I tried to occupy myself with needlework and could not. I fidgeted when dark horrors overtook me, sometimes getting up to peer through the window, even though I knew they could not return for hours.

Aunt Rosalind woke soon after five o'clock. We gave her tea, placed shawls around her shoulders and assured her it would not be long before we had news. She said nothing. She sat with one hand against her throat, hunched, shivering, staring at nothing, her thin body rigid with anxiety.

My grandmother ordered a scuttle of coals to be left by the hearth. 'There is a sharp wind blowing,' she observed. 'We must keep the room warm for they will be cold when they come.'

Time dragged. At half past five, I went to the window, looking out, listening, and every time I heard hoofbeats I stiffened in hope and every time I was disappointed.

They did not arrive by six o'clock. They had not arrived at quarter past, nor half past. Just when I thought I could bear no more, Sir Marcus returned alone, at seven o'clock.

He was tired but he raised a smile and spoke directly to my aunt. 'She is safe; she is well; she is with her father.'

How long I had been holding my breath I know not, but at these words I began panting, drawing air in huge gulps. Mists gathered before my eyes and I shook my head to clear them.

Aunt Rosalind swooned again. I revived her with hartshorn, and my grandmother drew Sir

Marcus towards the fireplace and set servants bustling to bring sustenance.

Aunt Rosalind stirred. 'Where is my daughter?'

After putting a few miles between themselves and Bellamy, Sir William determined that he and Isabella would put up at an inn whilst Sir Marcus came on to bring us the news.

'We got her away without difficulty, but she was chilled to the bone, far too cold to continue the journey,' he told us. 'And they had taken away her boots.' He grinned. 'A wise precaution, since she had no scruples about kicking anyone who came close enough.'

In her stockinged feet, Isabella had ridden pillion behind her father until they came to Keynsham. There, they had intended to hire a conveyance but this plan was changed because my cousin, who had been imprisoned in a cold place, was in need of warmth and rest. Which was why Sir Marcus had seen them comfortably settled in the inn and left them there.

'I must go to them!' said Aunt Rosalind, sitting up. 'I must set out, this instant.'

'No, Rosalind, you shall not,' said my grandmother gently. 'Tomorrow you must take your chaise to fetch them but for tonight they are well enough. Marcus, I am impatient to hear your story, but first you must take some refreshment.'

A footman had pulled off his boots and he stretched his feet eagerly to the blaze. My grandmother had a table set up and dinner was brought in, soup and a sirloin of beef and a goose and turkey pie. We persuaded Aunt Rosalind to take some food and found we were hungry also, now the waiting was over.

I expected Aunt Rosalind to be plying him with questions, but her assurance of Isabella's safety seemed to be enough. She was deep in thought and was content to wait for the particulars. We ate in silence, allowing relief to melt through the strain of the last few hours.

When the covers were removed, Grandmother said, 'Now, Marcus, you shall keep us in suspense no longer! I wish to know what has been occurring. Did you meet with my men?'

He nodded. 'They thought Bellamy had Chloe. They determined, between them, that Gilbert should ride to inform you, madam, and that Jacob should keep watch. We met with Gilbert on the way and he took us directly to the place.'

'And what of Bellamy, did you see him?'

'Had we done so, I would have taken him and given him up to the constabulary. But no, he was not there. He had left Isabella guarded by his two ruffians. We burst into the house and tied them up and left them in the cellar where Isabella was imprisoned. She, by the way, was wholly astonished when her father turned up to release her.'

For the first time in many hours, I saw my grandmother smile. 'Indeed, I imagine she would be.'

'Is Bellamy a fool?' I exclaimed. 'Surely he knew someone would attempt a rescue?'

'No, how could he?' That was my grandmother. 'He thought himself very well concealed in a city, where all were too busy to be noticing his doings. He had no notion my men were watching him, no suspicion that we knew where to find him. He thought himself safe.'

'I see.'

I thought Lady Pascall's men must have been most ingenious to keep Bellamy under observation without arousing his suspicions, but it was not until much later that I learnt of the many ruses and disguises they adopted. Taking turns, they swept crossings in the street, they acted as delivery boys, news-vendors and muffin men.

'And Isabella is well? Bellamy has not harmed her?'

'That was not his first design,' said Sir Marcus. 'Bear in mind that he thought he had you, Chloe. Isabella, as I understand, flung many insults at him, but she did not disabuse him of that idea. Bellamy had determined to make you convince the world that Lady Pascall was mad!'

'*What?*'

'You were to write it down, just as he dictated. You were desirous of escape from her, to which end you had sought his protection. He is your legal guardian, after all. He had not abducted you, Chloe, nothing like that, he had rescued you from a mad old woman.'

'Upon my soul! what did Isabella say to that?'

'I had better not repeat it, she was very rude to him.'

'I am very happy to hear it,' said Grandmother drily. 'Well, I can easily comprehend the rest. He meant to work on Chloe until she wrote to his direction. I would be undone and he would then have the charge of her, none to deny him.'

'Did he really think he could prevail on me to write such nonsense?' I asked indignantly. 'Upon my soul, I hope I am made of sterner stuff than that!'

'Isabella was imprisoned in the dark, in a very damp, very cold cellar,' said Sir Marcus. 'She was chilled to the bone when we rescued her. Bellamy thought he had only to bide his time until the cold wore down her resistance.'

I was silent and dismayed. I like to think I would resist against such circumstances. And so I might, for a time, but I cannot honestly say I could do so indefinitely. I would have given in, even knowing I was meant to suffer a fatal accident!

I would have given in, with intention of making an escape later, and exposing him as villain. And he, I thought dismally, would know I had such a scheme! I would not escape, for he would see to it that I found no opportunity.

I said bleakly, 'He is clever, is he not? Such a pity he does not use his wits to better purpose. Is there no end to his villainy?'

Aunt Rosalind had not spoken during these exchanges. There was a quality in her silence which puzzled me, and I glanced at her from time to time, but I had been eager to learn what Sir Marcus had to tell and paid her only slight attention.

Now she spoke, in quite a different tone to any I had yet heard from her, and I shivered at the sound. 'Bellamy murdered my sister.'

There was something dark, deep and ice-cold in her voice which astonished me. My grandmother heard it too, and her eyes widened. 'Your sister and my son. Chloe's parents.'

'Yes. He murdered them, I am certain of it, now.' She looked at Lady Pascall. 'Do you know how it was done?'

'We do, but Rosalind, dear, are you sure you wish to hear about it?'

A strange smile twisted her lips. 'I am perfectly sure that I do *not* wish to hear about it.' she said. 'But you must tell me, nevertheless.'

There were no hysterics, she was calm and purposeful, and a little frightening. We all blinked, fascinated by this extraordinary change. It was as though the torment she had endured these last hours had wrenched her into a new shape, hard, cold and unrecognizable.

'Later,' she said, 'we must all consult together to determine what is to be done. First, I would hear how he contrived it, if you please.'

So we told her of Mr Marano and how he explained the murder of my parents. My aunt sobbed, and so did I, and so did my grandmother. It was left to Sir Marcus to complete the tale.

'No one can be certain it was done exactly as Marano said. But the man has shown that such a murder is not only possible, but remarkably easy! And who would believe that, at the time?'

'Oh Laura! Oh, my dear, beloved sister!' My aunt shook with spasms of renewed grief and I knelt by her chair, held her and comforted her. When the worst was over, she dried her eyes and looked at my grandmother.

'I would not believe it,' she murmured. 'I could scarce bear to believe Laura had died by accident. Had I known she was murdered and by that—that *jackanapes!* I would have gone mad! Indeed, I believe I did go mad, for a time. Well, madam, we will have justice, or vengeance! Bellamy made his greatest mistake when he abducted my daughter.'

'Yes,' said my grandmother, still bemused by the alteration in my aunt. 'I can see that he did. What do you propose to do, Rosalind?'

'First, I must recover my husband and my daughter,' she said.

I was immediately diverted by my own imaginings of how those two would adjust to the change in Aunt Rosalind and, I confess, I had doubts as to how long her resolution would last. Occupied with these thoughts, I missed what she said next.

'I have been saying as much to Lady Pascall for the past six weeks, madam,' said Sir Marcus. 'At present, Bellamy knows where Chloe is and I cannot be easy about it. She should be hidden until we have secured her safety. She should return to Miss Johnson's school; Bellamy will not look for her there. You will like to see Miss Johnson again, will you not, Chloe?'

'I would, but I do not wish to be bundled out of the way. I am not afraid of Bellamy.'

'Well, you should be!' retorted Sir Marcus.

These words brought to mind the animosity which had lain between us these last two weeks and I raised my chin, determined he should not see how I was pained.

Aunt Rosalind supported Sir Marcus. 'You cannot remain alone in Bath and I have grave reservations about your safety should we take you with us to London.'

'London?'

'We go to London as soon as may be,' she said. She reminded my grandmother that her cousin was a High Court judge, (she called him Arthur) Mr Justice Brady. They would visit him and, when he heard the whole, he would set all the power of the law against Bellamy.

'He made a mistake when he abducted Isabella. And when Arthur learns what he did to Laura, he will be relentless! Wriggle as he might, Bellamy will not escape us now.'

Grandmother considered this. 'We can put it about that we go for the victory celebrations,' she said. 'And none to know that Chloe is not of our party. What of Isabella? She must go with us, of course, her testimony is necessary, but there is danger for her, too. With your permission, Rosalind, I will have Isabella guarded until we have Bellamy by the heels.'

They settled the particulars. Tomorrow, Aunt Rosalind would take her chaise to collect Sir William and Isabella. Also tomorrow, I would take Lady Pascall's chaise to Stellham. Sir Marcus would escort me and return with the carriage to Bath.

'Madam,' I appealed to Lady Pascall, 'must I go to Stellham? Much as I would like to see Miss Johnson again, I feel I should go with you to London. Surely I will be safe from Bellamy there? How can he know where we are gone?'

'He has only to spend a night in Bath to

discover that,' said Grandmother. 'The gossips will tell him and he will follow us, you may depend upon it. We cannot anticipate all his scheming, Chloe, as we have discovered. No, it is better you are hidden away. You will be safe with Miss Johnson and I,' she added with finality, 'will be easier in my mind.'

After that, I could not, in all conscience, refuse. I was to be excluded from their party but I would, at least, be escorted to Stellham by Sir Marcus.

There was advantage in that, for the journey would take several hours, giving me time and opportunity to discover what had brought about his animosity.

EIGHTEEN

'Whenever Lady Rufford went into the country, miss, she would take the finest of her ball gowns.'

My maid, Jane Farley, frequently spoke of her former mistress, often quoting her as a shining example of how a lady ought to be dressed, or how a lady ought to behave. Now, she lamented my lack of riding dress.

'But Jane, I have never ridden horseback in my life. I am not going to stay at a great country seat, you know. There will be no morning rides and no balls and parties, either.

I need only a few gowns and a serviceable cloak.'

Jane was to accompany me to Gloucestershire, and I hid a smile as I realized she had no notion of what awaited her when we arrived at our destination. Meanwhile, she insisted I should be prepared for invitations.

'You must have at least one special gown, miss, for it would be of all things the most dreadful should you be obliged to refuse on account of having nothing suitable to wear.'

She was clearly distressed, so I consented to her packing five muslin gowns instead of the three I had intended, and a ball gown besides, the turquoise I wore at the assembly.

'Very well, miss.' Satisfied with this, she also assembled a headdress, long gloves, satin slippers, silk stockings, a pelerine and a velvet evening cloak. I giggled, imagining how Miss Johnson would look if she saw me attired in such finery.

At breakfast, Aunt Rosalind was dressed for her journey. She had remained with us overnight, having sent servants to fetch what she needed. She appeared just as calm and resolute as she had the previous evening.

'I have sent for my chaise and I shall be off within half an hour,' she announced. 'And you, Chloe, will be on your way to Gloucestershire before we return. I fear it will be some time before we meet again. Have you any messages for Isabella?'

I asked her to tell my cousin that I hoped she was none the worse for her adventure and I said I would write to her.

Grandmother asked how I was prepared for my own journey. She smiled when I told how Jane regarded the excursion. 'I believe Jane wishes I was going to London,' I said. 'She thinks I should be there for the victory celebrations.'

'Meaning she would like to be there herself,' said my grandmother. 'She may have her wish, if fortune favours us. I shall send for you when Bellamy is no longer at large.'

My aunt had pricked up her ears when I spoke of my lack of riding dress. 'What is this? You have never ridden horseback? Upon my soul, your education has been sadly neglected!'

'Not at all, madam, I have ridden on the back of a pig.'

'A saddleback, no doubt,' said Grandmother drily. 'Do not look at me like that, Rosalind, Chloe is joking you.'

'Indeed?' Whatever changes had occurred in my aunt, they had not brought her to understand humour. 'It seems to me, madam, that even if you did find it necessary to keep Chloe hidden, you could have given her a lady's education!'

'And where should I have sent her?' enquired my grandmother. 'To one of the fine private seminaries in town? It was not a risk I was prepared to take. No, Rosalind, she was safer with Miss Johnson, whatever you think. Chloe does not want for sense or courage, and these are qualities of better value than trifling accomplishments.'

'Well, she must take advantage of her time in the country to learn to ride. Ah! Here is my carriage. I beg you will excuse me, madam. I shall leave you now.'

She embraced me, shook hands with my grandmother, called for her outdoor clothes and we followed her outside to see her off. She was the sole occupant of the chaise, but I was surprised to see there were footmen behind, occupying the rumble seat.

When she had gone, I remarked upon it. 'She goes but ten miles at the most,' I said. 'Why would she need servants on such a short journey?'

'They are there to rescue her should her carriage catch fire,' said my grandmother. 'They have axes, under their seat. After what happened to Laura, she goes nowhere without them.'

My aunt was gone and we were free to discuss her. As we returned to the breakfast-room, I said, 'I cannot tell you how astonished I was to witness the alteration. How can it be possible? Has she been acting a part all these years?'

'It cannot be so simple! No, I think not. I know that what happened to Laura overset her mind to some degree. I own, I feared that her anxiety over Isabella's predicament would make her worse, but it seems to have had the opposite effect.'

'I suppose it might,' I said. 'After all, Isabella was rescued, whilst Mama . . .' I faltered, swallowed and asked, 'Has my aunt returned to the way she was before?'

'No, she has not, I declare it is the strangest occurrence! Whilst Laura lived, Rosalind was a pretty little butterfly, not as clever as your mama, but she was amiable and kind. After Laura died, she seemed to lose all common sense. But now . . .' My grandmother shook her head in perplexity. 'Never have I known her like this. I declare, I am at a loss.'

'Her way of thinking was changed,' I said. 'I saw it, I watched it happening, though I confess I did not comprehend.'

I sat with my elbows on the table, my chin propped in my hand, musing over the matter. 'She believed my parents died by accident, and nothing to be done about it,' I said. 'Everybody said so, Sir William even insisted upon it. Only yesterday, and then only when she knew Isabella had been saved from Bellamy, then she truly understood what had happened. Now there is a murderer to be brought to justice and she has something to do. *Now* she feels her power.'

'So you think Rosalind has turned into an avenging angel?' I nodded and Grandmother said wryly, 'Well, never did I imagine that

251

would happen! However, since Isabella has escaped with a story to tell, the law will be obliged to act, at last.'

'Guard my cousin well, madam. Bellamy knows she is a danger to him.'

'I will, we all will, you may depend upon it. Now, my dear, you will be setting off very soon, and you will need some money to take with you.' She took a roll of bills from a drawer and placed it in my hand. 'If you run short, write to me and I will send more.'

The briefest glance told me there must be at least a hundred pounds. 'Madam, how am I to spend all this in Stellham? Here, in Bath, I have spent little more than ten pounds! I still have most of the money my Somebody—er— the money you gave me, before I came here.'

'Frugal Miss Smith!' She lifted her gaze to the ceiling. 'How am I going to teach you to be extravagant?'

I smiled at her. 'What was left for me to purchase after all your extravagance when you first determined I must be tricked out in finery?'

A bustle from without taught us the carriage had been brought round and Jane was busily supervising the safe bestowal of my belongings.

I stood to embrace my grandmother. 'Oh, how I wish I did not have to leave you. I shall miss you abominably!'

She sobbed and said she could scarce bear to part with me. We hugged each other, shed tears and promised to write. Jane brought in my cloak and bonnet and I put them on.

Sir Marcus arrived, remarking that the skies threatened rain. 'I fear we will have a wet journey.'

He was right. There was no question of Jane travelling on the rumble seat: we had to have her with us, in the chaise. I sighed. In her presence, Sir Marcus would be civil, but I would have no opportunity to resolve our differences.

And so it proved. Jane sat primly between us and, after Grandmother had waved us off, he remarked upon the rain and hoped our journey would not be inconvenienced by roads turned into quagmires. He debated which would be the best route. He thought we should arrive before dinnertime and he hoped Miss Johnson would not be too put out, for there had been no time to announce our visit.

I ventured my opinion that Miss Johnson would be delighted to receive us. With my suspicion of Miss Waring occupying my mind, I remarked that, since we had left that lady in Bath, I would not be obliged to visit Stellham House, or put myself at her disposal, or endure her embarrassing attempts to find husbands for me.

This was all I could say in front of Jane and I could not properly watch his expression. I was, however, rather pleased with myself for finding an excuse to mention Miss Waring and

I was alert for anything uncommon in his reaction.

So I heard his sharp indrawn breath and observed a brief stiffening in his posture. There was a noticeable pause before he answered and when he did, I thought he deliberately made his voice sound light. 'How many husbands did she find for you?'

'Four, altogether,' I said. 'It was all nonsense! I confess, I found her meddling very tiresome indeed, but she would not desist. When Miss Waring gets an idea into her head, she cannot be distracted. She would look about her and determine which gentleman must fall in love with me that week.'

He did not answer this, but I had seen enough to confirm my conjectures that somehow, Helen Waring had made mischief. Only Jane's presence prevented me from opening up the subject.

After a long pause, Sir Marcus spoke again. 'Since you disliked Miss Waring's meddling so much, why did you not distance yourself from her?'

'How could I?' I asked. There had been a hint of condemnation in his tone and I was nettled. 'I had Miss Johnson to consider. For her, any falling out with the Warings would be disastrous.'

'Would it? How so?'

'Oh, come now!' I was exasperated. 'They are the local gentry; they could, if they chose, make her life difficult. Surely you can comprehend that?'

He said nothing. I changed the subject and the rest of the journey was accomplished with inconsequential talk and occasional silences.

To Jane, Sir Marcus and I must have appeared easy together, but I was very sensible of discord between us, and his present manner was odiously polite with none of the teasing and banter we had previously enjoyed. It did nothing to improve my temper and I was obliged to suppress a number of sharp retorts.

The afternoon was well advanced before we arrived in Stellham. Miss Johnson was surprised but welcoming and ushered us into her parlour to take tea. I had written often, so she knew of the twists and turns my life had taken, though she confessed she found it hard to think of me as a great lady.

'And here you are, fine as fivepence! How the fashions become you, my dear. My girls will be quite envious. But you have not told me what brings you here so precipitately?'

'We had a fright yesterday, madam.'

That was Sir Marcus, who went on to tell how Bellamy had abducted Isabella, mistaking her for me. Miss Johnson shook her head, exclaiming over the wickedness in the world, but asserting her faith that good would triumph over evil.

'After all, we have overthrown the Corsican Ogre and I expect this man Bellamy will be 'dealt with, as was Bonaparte.'

'He will be dealt with, madam, do not doubt it. But we cannot prevent what we cannot anticipate, and Bellamy has more tricks than a monkey. Which is why Lady Pascall wishes her here, where she is safe. He knows nothing of this place.'

'I am only too happy to receive Chloe, but sir, though I am sorry for it, I cannot offer to put you up for the night. In a school full of girls, it would be most improper! And our local inn is no better than an alehouse, not at all suitable for a gentleman. Such a pity Stellham House is shut up. Mr Waring would receive you, but he is not at home. Ah! Now I have it! The rector will accommodate you, I will send a message to the parsonage . . .'

'Madam, I beg you will not put yourself or the rector to such trouble. When the horses are rested, I shall be off.'

Miss Johnson was horrified. 'You cannot possibly return to Bath tonight!'

'I can go a good piece of the way.' He smiled at her. 'There is a tolerable inn at Malmsbury, and I shall spend the night there and accomplish the rest tomorrow.'

'Sir Marcus and the others are to go on to London, madam.'

'All this journeying! I declare, the very thought of it makes me dizzy. Well, sir, at least I can offer you dinner before you set out again.'

She determined that we would not dine in the refectory with the children (this being unsuitable to Sir Marcus's dignity) but privately, in her parlour. Then (forgetting my dignity) she sent me with a message to Cook.

When I had delivered the message, I went into the schoolroom to renew my acquaintance with the girls and spent an hour talking about the assemblies and concerts in Bath.

I was not required to sleep in the dormitories. Instead, I had been given one of the guest-rooms, usually reserved for visiting parents. Nevertheless, Jane was scandalized.

'I told them, miss, I told them!' She was almost in tears. 'This is not suitable for Miss Pascall. There is no carpet, miss, nothing but this threadbare runner and as for the furniture, I declare it came out of the ark!' She saw I was laughing and delivered the final blow. 'And not a featherbed to be had, miss, the mattress is stuffed with horsehair!'

'Jane, it is of no consequence, I am quite accustomed to such. Now I beg you not to set everybody at odds! I am sure I shall be perfectly comfortable.'

She sniffed. 'Well, at least the place is clean, we may be thankful for that.'

She had bullied someone into bringing coals for a fire and said she would have the sheets aired before bedtime. 'For I expect to find they are damp.'

'I would be very surprised indeed if they

257

were. Jane, I lived here for eleven years and was very kindly treated, even if I did not have the luxuries I have recently enjoyed. Please understand these people are my friends and I do not wish you to be upsetting them.'

'Very well, miss, if you say so. Though I cannot imagine what My Lady was about, to place you here.'

'She had her reasons. What of yourself, Jane, where have they put you?'

She had the next room and was less indignant on her own account than she was on mine. 'I shall be close at hand, miss, should you need me.'

She had procured hot water for washing and brought fine soap and towels from Bath and insisted I changed my gown before dinner. She arranged my hair, and would have decorated it with feathers, but I determined on plain combs and nothing fancy.

'Here, it will do no good to flaunt my finery or to adopt airs and graces,' I said. 'It would only give offence.'

So I wore a muslin with blue flowers embroidered on the bodice, a gown which looked pretty but not extravagant.

When I returned to the parlour, Sir Marcus stood as I entered and offered me a bow which seemed to have some embarrassment in it, perhaps because he considered himself not properly dressed. He still wore his travelling garments, though he had washed, shaved and changed his neckcloth.

Miss Johnson had changed in honour of the occasion: she wore an old-fashioned gown of dark-green silk with lace at the collar and cuffs, and she had on her best rose-point cap. She was nervous in case the repast was not equal to the expectations of a high-born gentleman.

How it had been contrived, I know not, but the table was laden with delicacies. There was soup, a roast chicken, a veal and ham pie, with vegetables and mushroom fritters, not to mention a lemon tart and a pineapple which, in Stellham, could only have been procured from the Warings' succession houses.

She would have been distressed by teasing, so I checked the impulse to tell her, in jest, there should have been a salmon poached in wine and a breaded turbot.

Over dinner, we recounted the events of the past few months. When she enquired of the Warings, I gave her a kind but wholly fictitious message from them, and I did not miss the sardonic lift of Sir Marcus's eyebrows.

'It was the good reports she had of you from Mr Waring that determined Lady Pascall to place me in your charge,' I said. 'She could not have done better. Always, I was happy here.'

'And to think she has turned out to be your grandmother,' said Miss Johnson. 'My dear, I cannot tell you how shocked I was to learn what happened to your parents. I declare, I can scarce bear to imagine it.'

'Indeed, it pains me to think of it, madam. Lady Pascall gave me miniature portraits of my parents. I have them with me. You must allow me to show them to you later.'

The meal over, Sir Marcus sent for the chaise and took leave of us. We went outside to see him off and I was surprised when, before climbing into the carriage, he took my hand and kissed it and bade me to have a care for myself.

'Oh! But I—' I faltered a little at this unexpected courtesy. 'I shall be perfectly safe here, you know. May I beg you will have care for Lady Pascall? There are times when she overtaxes herself and never will she admit it.'

He said he would and looked from me to Miss Johnson and back again, as though he wanted to say something more but could not. Once again, I thought there was an air of embarrassment about him. I wondered what had caused it, for it was not usual with him.

His constraint was not apparent to Miss Johnson. She charged him with assurances to Lady Pascall that she would take good care of me, and asked him to pass on messages of goodwill to the Warings, should he happen upon them.

He agreed to it and, after a little fidgeting, he took out his pocket watch and said it was time he was away. The postillion mounted the leader and they moved off.

I returned with Miss Johnson to her parlour. She chattered happily about Sir Marcus whilst I wondered what had brought about his constraint.

I had thought he would have spoken freely had not Miss Johnson been present. Not until later did it occur to me that it might have been the other way about, that my presence had prevented him speaking freely to Miss Johnson.

Whichever it was, I could not guess what was in his mind and I put the question aside when it was time for evening prayers.

The next day I settled into the pattern of my former life: I accompanied the children on a walk, helped them with their needlework and renewed my acquaintance with the village people.

On the second day, I had a letter from my grandmother. She told me their journey to London was delayed, because Isabella had a feverish cold, brought about by her adventure. The physician thought she would recover within a few days.

Grandmother also suspected Bellamy was in Bath. Her men reported that he had left Bristol and headed in that direction. Discreet enquiries had taught her he was not staying at any of the fashionable hotels, or moving in society. She had not seen him, but she had been alert for signs and she was certain the house in Laura Place was being watched.

'I cannot tell you how thankful I am that you are safe in Stellham,' she wrote. 'Clearly, Bellamy realized I had a hand in rescuing Isabella, and now he is pursuing you more vigorously than before. Thank Heaven, he will not find you in Bath!'

No one knew whether Bellamy realized he had abducted the wrong cousin, but certainly he understood his escaped captive was now dangerous. Whilst Isabella was laid up she was safe from him and they had determined that, as soon as she was well, they would steal quietly away to London without telling anyone they were going. Indeed, my grandmother had already determined upon the subterfuge of having her chaise collect her from the pump room instead of beginning her journey from Laura Place.

I read all this with a feeling of dismay. Would Bellamy be deceived by my grandmother's subterfuge? Or would he, knowing she was his enemy, take some measure against her?

I wrote to her express, begging her to have care for her own safety and, in particular, to be certain that her chaise was inspected for hidden devices before she set foot in it. I told her I could not support myself should anything happen to her.

In Stellham, I was obliged to smooth over a few little offences, caused mainly by Jane's insistence that I should have a fire in my room and hot water for washing. Cook sniffed and remarked how I was grown so fine I would soon be charging half-a-crown when they wanted to speak to me.

I smiled. 'For you, dear Cook, I will make a reduction and charge a mere one shilling and sixpence. But mind, it is only because I know you.'

'You still have your saucy tongue, then? And do not dare snatch my tarts! Here, if you have nothing better to do, you can start beating up some batter. What made you bring that starched-up baggage with you?'

'My grandmother, Lady Pascall, engaged her,' I said. I reached for an apron, broke eggs into flour and began to whisk, smiling mischievously at her startled glance. 'She thinks I need a maid such as Jane to remind me to be a lady.'

She watched me pour milk into the mixture. 'Perhaps you do.'

'A lady,' I said loftily, 'may be easy in any company and make any company easy. That is a mark of true gentility.'

'Aye, no doubt, but she would not like to see you helping in the kitchens. I should not have asked, but I forgot . . .'

'I will not tell, if you do not.'

I asked her if she could arrange, at my expense, a special victory celebration tea for all the girls, and she agreed to it, planning pies and jellies and cakes. Later, I consulted Miss

Johnson about my notion of purchasing some fireworks.

We discussed it with the rector and the idea grew larger. A party was arranged for the village too, and a fiddler for dancing and the fireworks would be set off after dark.

A day was decided upon and arrangements were made. I purchased a cask of ale for the men and procured lemons and sugar for lemonade and changed some of my bills for a quantity of silver half-crowns to give to the children at the close of the party.

As it became known that the treat was planned, the pleasure was greater than the most illustrious ball could raise in Bath society. Once or twice, I felt tears prickling my eyes at their excitement and I gave thanks for the change of fortune which allowed me to treat all my friends in this way.

The treat took place, and I heard later the day was a great success, but I was destined to miss it.

On the appointed day, very early in the morning, Sir Marcus appeared. He had ridden through the night, exhausting himself and his poor horse, and when he arrived he was white with urgency.

'Tell your maid to pack up, Chloe, we must leave this place immediately. We have not an instant to lose!'

'Why, sir? Whatever is the matter?'

He told me that Bellamy, advised by my

264

dear friend Helen Waring, now knew exactly where to look for me.

NINETEEN

'How could she betray me in such a way?' I exclaimed. 'I own, I had not thought her as spiteful as that!'

'She has her own view,' said Sir Marcus. 'Bellamy is your legal guardian and he has the right of decision in your affairs. She has taken up a high-minded notion of moral duty and has not the smallest intention of departing from it.'

This was not the first time I had come across Helen Waring's peculiar notions of propriety. 'She listens to the gossips, so of course she knows much more about it than Lady Pascall!' I said bitterly.

'We cannot undo Miss Waring's mischief,' he said, 'but I can get you away before Bellamy reaches you. Go, Chloe, tell your maid to pack, we must leave immediately. I will take you to Derbyshire; I have friends there, they will keep you safe.'

He had stopped on the way to hire a post-chaise and a team of fresh horses. It was to be here within the half-hour, to convey us to Derbyshire.

'I must warn Miss Johnson,' he said, 'for

Bellamy will come here. I hesitate to ask her to speak falsehood, but do you think we can persuade her to misdirect him?'

I had an idea, one so outrageous and so naughty, I could not resist. 'I will speak to Miss Johnson,' I said. 'I can teach her to deceive without a word of falsehood.'

He gave me a blank look. 'How can she do that?' he asked.

'Leave it to me. You had better have a care for your horse, the poor creature is exhausted.' I directed him to a farmer who would stable the beast.

Miss Johnson grew white with alarm the moment she heard my news. 'Oh, Chloe, that man, he will come here, will he not? What am I to do? What am I to say to him? For it pains me to say so, but never have I been clever at dissembling.'

'Dear madam,' I said affectionately, 'you need do no more than tell him I am nowhere to be found—which will be true when we are gone—and show him a letter I left for you. Tell him you are thankful he has come, because you cannot leave the children and you have been in a puzzle to know what to do.'

I moved to her writing desk and, with her permission, took out pen and ink and paper.

Dear Miss Johnson (I wrote)
By the time your eyes alight on this letter, I shall be many miles distant. This will come

as a shock to you and I beg you will understand that only my present difficult situation has persuaded me to act in a manner which is repugnant to me. I am, however, persuaded the only way my dear Marcus and I can be together is to take the dreadful step of eloping to Gretna Green...

'Chloe!' she gasped, looking over my shoulder, 'you cannot mean it?'

'No, of course I do not! I am sending Bellamy on a wild-goose chase. He will make a long and tedious journey all the way to Scotland, and all for nothing.'

My smile faded as Miss Johnson hit upon the difficulty. 'Chloe dear, do not forget you, too, are travelling northwards. He may catch you before you reach Derbyshire.'

'We can travel eastwards until we pick up a different route. By the time we reach Derbyshire, Bellamy will be miles ahead.'

I returned to my letter, finished it, and sprinkled a few drops of water on it, telling Miss Johnson to say the paper appeared to be marked by my tears.

Then we were all hurry and confusion, for when the post-chaise arrived at the gates, Sir Marcus was impatient to leave straight away. Whilst our belongings were bestowed within, Miss Johnson pressed a mug of spruce beer upon him and Cook came out with a hamper of food.

I suggested to Sir Marcus we should go in a north-easterly direction, towards Banbury, from whence we could make the journey through Northampton, Leicester and Nottingham. I said Bellamy would expect us to take a more direct northwards route, and he would first go towards Coventry and Birmingham.

'Avoiding him in such a way will add a few miles to our journey,' I admitted, 'but we shall be easier for not having to look over our shoulders.'

Because Sir Marcus was tired and alarmed on my behalf, he thought this was a sensible notion. He imagined Bellamy in hot pursuit and did not enquire why the man should follow us northwards if he had no knowledge of our destination.

We took leave of Miss Johnson. As we set off, I asked about his friends in Derbyshire and was told their name was Carson, a retired colonel and his wife. 'We will reach them tomorrow.'

'Will they be dismayed to have a stranger foisted on them?'

'They will be delighted. They knew your parents.'

As we travelled, we were jolted a great deal, the hired chaise not being as well-sprung as Lady Pascall's carriage. Sir Marcus was tired and we had little conversation. I heard only that Isabella was recovered from her cold and tomorrow, they began their journey to London.

When we stopped for the night, I heard more. Bellamy had not announced his presence in the *Bath Chronicle* but they suspected he was there and, in the end, they found him, staying in lodgings in a part not usually frequented by polite society.

'He had been there three days before we had news of him,' said Sir Marcus. 'He had men watching us and we set our men to watch them! I know not by which means he came to learn of Miss Waring, but he scraped an acquaintance with her, and in no time at all he knew where to look for you.'

'How did you know she had told him?'

'Mr Waring heard of it and became uneasy. He told your grandmother who dispatched me to remove you from Stellham.'

'Oh! I may be thankful I have one friend in that family.'

Sir Marcus grimaced. 'He was all excuses for his daughter. Dear Helen truly believed she was acting in your best interest, she thought it only proper . . . You know what she is like.'

'Self-righteous and malicious at the same time,' I said. 'Well, you would expect her father to defend her.'

We lapsed into silence, and my mind became occupied with the other mischief

269

which Miss Waring had caused. Sir Marcus had set aside his animosity during the emergencies which had arisen and perhaps, now she had exposed her true nature, he would take less account of whatever she had said.

Hopeful that our differences were resolved and anxious to promote accord between us, I searched for a subject which we could discuss without embarrassment.

'One matter has never been explained,' I said at last. 'How is Bellamy my guardian? Are we related? I seem to recall Lady Pascall saying he was a cousin of her husband.'

'A cousin of your grandfather,' Sir Marcus reminded me. 'A half-cousin, rather! *His* grandfather made a second marriage late in life, an old man's fancy for a chit young enough to be his daughter. A result of that union was that your grandfather had an aunt younger than himself. Bellamy is her son.'

'Heavens! That makes him a half-cousin three times removed. Did not Papa have closer relations?'

'Too many of the Pascall children died in infancy,' said Sir Marcus soberly.

I was silent, recalling how my grandmother had spoken of her fears for me. *'There are too many diseases: too many children die, and I was anxious for you, always.'*

'Is he married?' I asked. 'Does he have offspring? Someone to inherit the estate, should he succeed in murdering me?'

'He may have entertained hopes of such at one time,' said Sir Marcus daily, 'but they were not fulfilled. His wife died, childless. He could marry again, I suppose, if he can find a female to have him. Why do you ask, Chloe?'

'Since he has no offspring, why is he not content to let me inherit the estate after him?'

Sir Marcus stared at me. 'Chloe,' he said at last, 'you are being very foolish. He cannot make such an arrangement; the estate is yours, whilst you live. To gain possession, he must inherit from you.'

'Oh! But he controls everything.'

'He controls the estate, but he cannot touch your fortune. Moreover, his control ends when you are five-and-twenty. Should you marry before you reach that age, Bellamy loses his authority even sooner, because your husband will claim your property. Now, what is the matter? Why are you looking at me like that?'

'Upon my soul!' I sat up, staring at him as I realized I had set Miss Johnson to deliver Bellamy a more telling blow than I thought. 'He *will* pursue us, will he not?'

I felt my cheeks go hot and I regarded Sir Marcus in some apprehension. 'I fear I have done something rather silly.'

'Have you indeed? Then you had better tell me about it.'

I swallowed and said baldly, 'Bellamy thinks you and I are eloping to Gretna Green.'

'*What?*'

Sir Marcus was flushed, staring in his turn, and I could not tell how he felt about it. For my part, I felt very foolish indeed. I told how I gave Miss Johnson a note to show Bellamy and gabbled an explanation of how I meant to send Bellamy on a wild-goose chase, all the way to Scotland.

'Th-that is why I suggested we travelled roundabout, instead of going directly northwards, because I thought Bellamy would follow that route,' I said. I faltered a little at his fixed expression. 'Are you—are you very angry with me?'

Sir Marcus drew in a deep breath and called me a saucy baggage but not, apparently, in anger. 'You are more like Isabella than I thought.' I opened my mouth to speak again, but he silenced me with an upraised hand. 'No! Let me think!'

He was a long time thinking, and I watched in apprehension until I saw a smile pulling the corners of his mouth.

'I believe it will answer,' he said at last. 'Bellamy had no notion that I left Bath before him. He will see no need to hurry to Stellham; he will go when he is ready. Such a shock awaiting him, when he arrives! He will certainly believe we are headed for Scotland because, in England, you cannot be married without his consent.'

'Can I not? I confess, I never gave that a thought.'

'That is of no consequence, because he will see all the implications. He cannot afford to let you be married. He will pursue us, as you say. He will go directly northwards but he will enquire at turnpikes and post-houses and when he learns we have not been seen, he will retrace his route.'

I looked at him in dismay. 'Will he pick up our trail?'

'He will discover we are heading northwards on a roundabout route. He may follow us but, in his situation, I would chafe at the time wasted and determine to go back the way I had come, to travel directly and intercept us on the way. We can avoid him long enough to place you safely with the Carsons.'

'What will he do then?'

'He will continue northwards, I imagine, always presuming we are taking a devious route. He has a devious mind himself, so that way of thinking is natural to him. Yes, he will push on towards Scotland.'

I drew a deep breath and smiled. 'At least he will be out of harm's way for a while. What are your plans? What are you going to do when you have taken me to your friends?'

'I shall go directly to London to join the rest of our party. Isabella's story will confirm your grandmother's opinion and the law will set the militia to take him.'

'They will have their work cut out,' I said. 'He is a wily fox, though I doubt he can avoid pursuit for ever.'

'He could.' Sir Marcus frowned. 'I own I had not thought of it, but the wars are over, the continent is opened up again.'

'You mean he might flee the country?'

He nodded. 'Bellamy will easily perceive his best chance. I fear your grandmother will not have the justice she wishes.'

I stared in bewilderment, trying to accustomed myself to a new situation. The wars had being going on since before I was born. Never had I known the continent to offer refuge.

'Well, I cannot wish the wars to begin again,' I said. 'Indeed, I believe it would it be better for Bellamy to escape. We would be spared all the unpleasantness of a trial and—and—it is a hanging matter, after all.' I gulped. 'Grandmother surely would not wish—'

'Your grandmother is haunted still by the manner of your parents' death,' said Sir Marcus. 'She wishes him broken by the law, and why not? He knew the penalty before he became a murderer. Bellamy is an evil man, Chloe. He pursues his own ends without the smallest regard for others. Do not waste your sympathy on him.'

I choked on a sudden nightmare vision of my parents suffering the horrible death Bellamy had devised for them, and I wished I did not have such a vivid imagination. Again, I heard my grandmother's voice: *They would not let me see the remains.'*

Tears overwhelmed me. 'I am s-sorry,' I gasped. 'Every time I think of what happened to my parents I—I—'

He stood, as though to make a move towards me, but he checked himself and reached for his handkerchief instead, passing it to me rather awkwardly. 'You are knocked up by the journey. I will call your maid; you should retire now.'

I made no protest, though I spent the first part of the night feeling as though I was still bowling and bounding and swaying over the road. I slept in uneasy snatches, with dreams of Bellamy pursuing me with a firebrand. Not until the small hours did I sink into a profound sleep and Jane woke me at six, telling me Sir Marcus wished to be on the road within the hour.

I scrambled to make myself ready, took a hasty breakfast and spent another interminable day on the road. After passing Nottingham we turned north-west into Derbyshire.

We travelled along the local byways, avoiding the main roads in case we happened on Bellamy. Our chaise lurched and swayed over rutted tracks, our journey took us up hills and down, through towns and villages, over bridges and rivers, past woodland and sloping pastures and fields of green corn.

Sir Marcus told me to take out my

handkerchief. 'I want you to hide your face from anyone we pass, hereabouts.'

'Indeed? May I ask why?'

'You resemble your mother. I wish no one to make the connection, not here, so close to Oakwood Pascall.'

'Close to Oakwood Pascall?' I sat up. 'Will I see it?'

'You may catch sight of it between the trees. Soon, now. Look! Down there!'

He pointed into a valley and I saw, for a few brief moments, a large grey stone building with tall chimneys and slate roofs: I had a glimpse of conservatories and extensive grounds, then we were past our vantage point and it was gone.

'Can we stop for a better look? I scarce saw it.'

'No, I told you, I wish to pass unrecognized. You will have time to look, and explore, when we have Bellamy where he belongs. Cover your face, someone approaches.' So saying, he opened a newspaper, raising it so his countenance was invisible. I did as he asked, and brought my handkerchief to my eyes, as our chaise went past a gentleman on horseback.

'John Bestwick,' said Sir Marcus. 'A friend, though I place no reliance on him holding his tongue: just as well we travel in a hired chaise: he did not recognize me.'

I was tired of being cooped up in the chaise,

and cross with him because he refused to stop, and after hiding from the next passer-by, I said sulkily, 'Is all this cloak-and-dagger business necessary, do you think?'

'Perhaps not, but I would be ridiculous now rather than have later regrets. Look about you, Chloe, you see what Bellamy wishes, you see what is at stake? All the land, as far as you can see, belongs to you. It is at least twenty miles round.'

My jaw dropped. 'Upon my soul!'

I looked about, seeing great swathes of pasture with cattle and sheep and horses: more fields were planted with crops and, here and there, I caught glimpses of a river gleaming like silver ribbon: we passed a weathered church with a squat Norman tower where, according to Sir Marcus, I was christened.

There was much to delight but I, who had been raised in the country, found cause for perturbation, also. Timber had been cut down and when we passed farm buildings and cottages, there were signs of disorder, neglect and dilapidation.

I remarked upon the mismanagement, and received a wry smile from Sir Marcus. 'Spoken like a true Pascall,' he said. 'Aye, you know, do you not?'

'I have lived in the country and though I expected to find Derbyshire very different from what I am used to, this is different in the wrong way! Is it Bellamy's doing?'

'It is,' he said grimly. 'He has milked the estate for his own profit. I fear it will be a prodigious task to set it to rights.'

'And all this is mine,' I said. 'My property and my responsibility. How very strange it is. I confess, I now feel more like Chloe Smith than ever I did before! How can I possibly manage an estate? None of my experience has prepared me for this. What is to be done?'

'When the time comes, your grandmother will advise you.'

He made no offer to advise me himself and there was something in his tone which reminded me of his previous animosity. I felt a weight of misery settle in my insides, knowing I was of little consequence to him. He had joined with my grandmother because they both had the same enemy and all his endeavours on my behalf were part of his wish to defeat Bellamy on his own account.

I sniffled and said, 'What of your own estates? I seem to recall you saying we are neighbours.'

'We are, but our route does not take us that way. Redgrave Hall is to the west.'

'You appear to spend little time there,' I said, letting my disapproval show. 'How do you manage your estates from a distance?'

'My steward has my authority to act. Matters of greater import are dealt with by correspondence. But I have been absent longer than is my wont. It may have escaped

278

your notice, but I have been occupied with pressing matters of business elsewhere.'

He was aloof, sarcastic, not teasing. I sighed, knowing very well I had invited just such a response. I wriggled in my seat, uncomfortable and hot from being cooped up, feeling every lurch of the carriage. 'Will this journey never end? How much further is it?'

'Two miles past the windmill,' he said shortly.

'I do not see a windmill.'

'When we pass it, you will know we have two miles to go.'

He sounded testy and I was silent. Sulkily, I determined I did not like him. He was ill-humoured, sarcastic and unkind and I was a fool to wish for him. I ought to prefer someone else. I thought about other gentlemen of my acquaintance to determine which of them I liked better than Sir Marcus.

A reproving voice in my mind told me that he was tired of travelling, too. He, the voice reminded me, had ridden hard from Bath to Stellham before embarking on this journey.

'What is more,' Grandmother's voice became austere and reproachful, 'he must spend more days on the road, because he means to set out straightaway for London.'

'That is not my fault,' I protested.

'It is on your behalf. He does much and asks nothing in return. It pains me you should be so ungrateful, Chloe.'

279

Even in her absence, my grandmother's influence made itself felt. My irritation dissolved into remorse, as I saw the hint of strain about his mouth.

When we turned a corner the windmill could be seen, with the miller's cottage close by. It was set high on a rock-strewn hillside, stone built, in the shape of a thimble, with a white painted cap, fantail, and six huge white sails turning busily. A homely building, yet well proportioned, pleasing to the eye.

Staring, I became aware of some feeling of disquiet which I could not account for. I looked away, and an image of the mill near Stellham came to mind and I saw how it differed.

I looked again, and my eye did not deceive me. On the Stellham mill the sails were set high, beyond reach of a man on the ground. On this one, they cleared the ground by no more than two feet. To my astonishment, I saw the entrance was behind the sails, a design so foolish it raised my indignation. 'How can the miller enter without being struck down?'

'I believe there are two entrances,' Sir Marcus told me, 'one on each side.'

'Oh, I see.' That made better sense. 'Yes, of course, there must be. Then, whichever way the sails are positioned, one entrance is clear.' I paused. 'I cannot but feel there is danger there, nevertheless. Those sails could kill anyone careless enough to blunder into them.'

'Most have better care for their skins. Do not make yourself uneasy. No one has yet been slain by a windmill.'

The chaise took us past the mill and presently we found ourselves on good road and I remembered we had but two miles to go. I looked about me, seeing good pastures edged with dry-stone walls, and acres of woodland beyond.

Sir Marcus leaned out of the carriage to shout directions at the postillions and we crossed a bridge, skirted a paddock with mares and their foals and moved through an archway and along a gravel drive to the courtyard of a large, unpretentious manor house, with a stable block at the rear.

I felt nervous qualms at the prospect of being left with strangers and the feeling intensified as the lady and gentleman, noting our arrival, came outside to greet us.

They greeted my companion with every appearance of pleasure but when they saw me, there was puzzlement. 'Miss Harcourt,' the lady said. 'Well, this is a surprise, but you are welcome.'

'This lady is not Isabella Harcourt.' Sir Marcus grinned at their astonishment. 'Can you guess who she might be?'

I felt my cheeks go hot under their scrutiny. I curtsied and said simply, 'I am Chloe Pascall, madam.'

'Upon my soul!' When they had done

exclaiming, Sir Marcus said he hoped they would give me shelter until my affairs were settled.

Grooms were called for the horses and orders given for the postillions: we were ushered indoors and given wine whilst servants were sent to prepare for company at dinner.

I was still uncomfortable and apologized for foisting myself upon them. 'I beg you will allow me to make myself useful whilst I am here, madam.'

'My dear child!' exclaimed my hostess, 'we are delighted to have you with us. How long it has been since we saw you last! You were but a babe in arms. So your grandmother hid you away from Bellamy? I will not say she was mistaken.'

Sir Marcus was to remain overnight, since the horses needed rest. My bedchamber pleased my maid better than the one at Stellham. She laid out a green muslin with not a crease in it and I was thankful to wash away the dust of our journey and change into fresh clothes.

At dinner we told our hosts what had been occurring. When the talk turned to other matters, I fell silent, watching the Carsons to determine how well we would deal together. They were a kindly couple, well disposed to me, but their conversation was ponderous, not enlivened by humour.

They were in their fifties, placid, narrow in

their outlook, the lady inclining to corpulence. Of the two, I thought the colonel was the more active.

Later, Sir Marcus proposed we should take a walk. Having been cooped up in the carriage for two days, I was eager for the exercise. Our hosts joined us but after half a mile Mrs Carson declared herself tired and turned back with her husband, leaving us to walk on together.

We talked of the Carsons and he expressed satisfaction at the way matters were going. 'Bellamy cannot be in two places at once. He will go after us, not knowing our friends are moving against him. We may hope he will not discover his mistake until he reaches Scotland.'

'In that way,' I said, 'it could be said Miss Waring did me service in advising Bellamy where to look for me.'

'That was not her intention,' he said grimly. 'Never was Helen Waring a friend of yours, Chloe.'

'Once she was,' I said. 'When we both thought I was just little Chloe Smith, of no consequence to anybody. Then, she sought to secure my future prosperity.'

'By finding you a husband!' He spoke with disapprobation. 'She patronized you to enhance her self-esteem, and she meant to bully you into marriage!'

'She does not read herself so,' I said drily. 'She befriended me because she thought me friendless and she meant well, even though I did not greatly appreciate her exertions on my behalf. How do you know of it?'

'You mentioned it yourself,' he reminded me, 'as we travelled from Bath to Stellham. And later, Miss Johnson confirmed your version of the story.'

'My version of—?' I gaped at him. 'Is there another?'

He made no answer. His gaze was fixed on his fingernails and I saw the hot, painful colour rise in his cheeks. I recollected the alteration in his manner towards me and how I suspected Helen Waring of mischief.

'There *is* another version,' I said coldly. 'I see it all now! There is Miss Waring's version. That is why you were determined to quarrel, is it not? What did she tell you? That I was a shameless, husband-hunting little butterfly, intent on marrying for advancement?'

'She said something of that nature,' he admitted.

'And you believed her, since this was in accordance with all you knew of me!' I was shaking, furious with him for accepting her implications. 'Did it ever seem to you that I was on the catch for a husband? I thank you for your good opinion!'

'Most young ladies of limited means are on the catch for a husband,' he said dispassionately, 'and who shall blame them, when marriage is the only means of prospering? You knew less of yourself then, you thought yourself penniless!'

'Indeed I did, but you may believe I was not so friendless or so desperate as to throw myself at every gentleman who crossed my path. These accusations are most unjust! You knew very well I had scruples about attaching any gentleman whilst I thought myself an impostor.'

'You had no scruples about trifling with me!'

'T-trifling with you?' I spluttered indignantly. 'How can you suggest such a thing? When did I trifle with you?'

'All those weeks in Bath!' he said savagely. 'You were showing a preference for me in company, all encouragement and smiles, yet altering your demeanour the moment we were alone! What did you think? That my passions would drive me to the point of ravishment if you did not show me the cold shoulder?'

Cheeks burning, I stared at him in bewilderment. I had known he enjoyed the dalliance, but never had I believed his passions were aroused. I gulped and said faintly, 'I had no such thoughts! I-I thought we were p-pretending! We had an arrangement! You know we did! It was a subterfuge designed to discourage other suitors.'

He said nothing. In the pause that followed it occurred to me that his speeches indicated some hurt feelings, as though he truly believed I had been trifling with him. I confess I, too, had enjoyed the dalliance, even allowing myself brief moments to fancy it was real. Yet I had believed I should be on my guard and I had formed a habit of giving myself a sharp and painful reminder that I could hope for nothing.

'You knew I had scruples about attaching any gentleman when I thought myself an impostor,' I said sulkily. 'You suggested the subterfuge yourself! Never did I trifle with you!'

His lips thinned into a cold, humourless smile. 'Do you deny,' he said tightly, 'that you bandied my name about, boasted of your conquest?'

Great surges of anger twisted and shivered within me. 'What a vulgar creature you must think me,' I said hotly. I was now persuaded he regarded me as an ignorant, common girl. Since I had not always moved in polite society, he thought me lacking in conduct. I said, 'Certainly, I deny it! I was raised in humble circumstances, but I was taught how to conduct myself better than that! Did you have this from Miss Waring, too?'

'I heard it from a more reliable source,' he said coldly.

'Indeed?' I was growing increasingly bitter. 'Then perhaps you should ask your *reliable source* where the information came from! Because I heard, from a reliable source, that you knew, long before I did, that I was well born *and* the heiress to a fortune. There were some,' I added, with malicious emphasis, 'who thought it not at all astonishing that you should take advantage of your secret knowledge to flatter me and take pains to engage my affections!'

'Upon my soul!' His voice lost its cold aloofness and turned savage. 'And you believed it?'

'I did not,' I said loftily. 'I may hear gossip but I prefer to judge by my own observation. My error was in supposing you would do likewise. Well, now I know you have no better sense than Miss Waring!'

I felt tears prickle my eyes and I turned away, dispirited to learn he had no better opinion of me than what he had heard spoken by malicious tongues.

'Chloe . . .' His voice was uncertain, as though he would placate me, if he could, but I was too upset to listen to him.

'Oh, do not speak to me!' I snapped. 'I have heard a great deal of nonsense this last half-hour and I am in no humour to hear more! I wish to return to the house.'

I turned and walked away from him and though he caught up I refused to look at him. There was coolness between us throughout the evening, and when, the next day, he set off for London, the coolness remained.

TWENTY

I was growing restless. I had little to occupy my days and there were times, during the first week I spent with the Carsons, when I suspected Sir Marcus of some ill-humoured design in taking me to those particular friends.

They were kind, and I felt I owed them a debt of gratitude, but Mrs Carson was indolent and her husband talked mostly of crops and livestock. Conversation was repetitive, my humour met with incomprehension and I found their society tedious.

I expressed a wish to be useful. Mrs Carson allowed me to embroider an altar cloth, but no more. They moved little in society, and the visitors they received were like themselves.

I received letters and wrote replies. Miss Johnson wrote that Bellamy had visited, and she had been frightened by his fury when he saw what I had written. He believed my elopement.

My grandmother was delighted with that deception, her letter telling me how she had laughed upon learning of it. Less pleasing to her was the way the law was dragging its heels.

Isabella's letter gave an account of her abduction, telling me what he said and what she said. Surprisingly, of her suffering, she said only that she had taken a horrible cold.

Her letter gave an account of the public

288

excitement as the victory celebrations drew near. She was impatient to have me join them in London. When we appeared together side by side, we were sure to create a sensation.

My aunt Rosalind's letters repeated what the others told me and, from her, the only fresh intelligence was that Sir Marcus was in a state of ill-humour and pressing the law to act.

I thought a great deal about my quarrel with Sir Marcus. I sensed he had wished to make peace, but I had denied him opportunity. Now, recalling all his kindnesses, I felt some remorse. I realized belatedly how his information that I had 'boasted of my conquest', might indeed have come from a reliable source, had that source mistaken Isabella for me.

I do not accuse my cousin of wilful mischief. I doubt she even mentioned a name, but I could easily imagine her chattering blithely about a conquest, and anyone hearing that, might make the mistake of supposing I was speaking of him.

As for his accusation that I had trifled with him, there was a suggestion that I had caused him pain. I, on the other hand, had suspected him of simply enjoying a dalliance. So often had I reminded myself!—we had an arrangement, I was unequal, eventually we must part.

Though Sir Marcus had known my true identity, I could not believe he suggested the subterfuge for the cynical purpose the gossips proposed: had he a design to enrich himself by marriage, he would have taken what Miss Waring had to offer.

He proposed the subterfuge to spare me the importunings of unwanted suitors and the complications which might arise. Yet it was possible he had not been guarded against my smiles and encouragement and had allowed himself to forget we had an arrangement.

Hope surged within me, but also a certain caution, because I remembered how I had once before allowed myself to hope and how very soon afterwards those hopes had been dashed.

My reflections, I thought wryly, were pleasing to my vanity and to my dearest wishes. Here I was, foolishly supposing Sir Marcus had fallen as much in love with me as I had with him! It would not do to dwell too much upon that notion.

In the dull company of the Carsons, however, it was not easy to put it out of my mind. With little to distract my thoughts, my fancy played too often with my wishes. I remembered his smiles, and things he had said, and I caught myself making rather more of these than I should.

The Carsons owned a pianoforte. Seeking to occupy my mind, I asked Mrs Carson if she could teach me a little music.

'I doubt I shall ever become proficient,' I

said wryly, 'but I might learn enough to amuse myself.'

She agreed, and whilst I was labouring over the first exercises, wincing over wrong notes, I recalled my aunt's suggestion that I should learn to ride horseback. I had the happy notion of asking the colonel's advice.

The next morning, in a borrowed riding dress, I found myself many perilous feet above the ground on the back of an enormous mare called Sally. For all her size, the colonel explained, she was a gentle, patient creature, perfect for a beginner.

She shifted and I lurched and clung to the pommel, gasping at new sensations as I recovered my balance. The colonel taught me how to handle the reins and led her around the paddock at walking pace, and that day I did not venture more.

We persevered, Sally and the colonel and I, and within a week I became accustomed to the feel of a mount beneath me and I could stay on as we trotted round the paddock. After that, the colonel took his own mount and accompanied me on gentle rides in the country, past hawthorns, heavy scented with bloom and through meadows salt-sprinkled with daisies.

So I occupied my time. In her letters, Grandmother complained that with London in a fever of excitement over the celebrations, no one would exert themselves. Even the combined insistence of my grandmother, my aunt, Sir William and Sir Marcus was having little effect. 'Rest assured,' she wrote, 'it is only a matter of time. We shall, in the end, prevail.'

I had the uncomfortable feeling that time was running out. Bellamy was still at large, and clever enough to be making schemes of his own.

Sometimes, when I lay awake in a state of perturbation, I would ease my mind by allowing myself to dwell on Sir Marcus. In the dark, it was easy to convince myself that I had read him right, and my troubled spirits were comforted.

One day, when I had become used to cantering on horseback, I asked the colonel whether he thought I had progressed well enough to stir Sally into a full gallop. He said she was a lazy old thing and would not gallop for long, but he led our mounts in a new direction, where there was a smooth upwards-sloping stretch of turf and we urged the beasts to stretch themselves. For a few minutes I was wholly exhilarated by the pounding rhythm of the gallop, the wind in my face and the glorious sensation of speed.

I reined in, laughing with the sheer joy of the ride. The colonel looked on benignly and later, as we rode at a more sedate pace, he said horsemanship was in my blood and talked of teaching me how to jump.

'I will set up low fences in the paddock—'

he was saying as we skirted the windmill, but his speech was cut off with a sudden grunt and he slumped forward over the withers, clutching at his shoulder. His mount surged forward, startling Sally, who tossed her mane and whinnied with fright.

Her pace quickened and I pulled at the reins. Fortunately she responded, but my companion's horse had bolted. I watched in horror as the colonel slithered sideways and fell to the ground. His hand clutched at his shoulder and, when I reached him, I was astonished to see blood oozing through his fingers.

'I have been shot,' he gasped, as I dismounted. He dismissed my exclamations and waved feebly towards the windmill, the only building in sight. 'Get help, be quick now, get the miller.'

I pulled off his cravat and folded the muslin square into a pad to staunch his bleeding. I could not remount Sally, so I left her with him and ran towards the windmill.

I had not heard the shot which wounded the colonel, but I heard the next one. Indeed, I felt the bullet whistle past my cheek and saw a boulder shatter into fragments.

My heart twisted and blood hammered through my veins. This was no accidental shooting by a heedless fool. This was deliberate, this was my enemy! I had not seen Bellamy, but I knew he was here. He was here with murderous intent.

Sobbing, slithering and scrambling, I clawed my way up the rockstrewn hillside towards the mill, hoping he had only one pistol, hoping I could reach the miller, and safety, before he had a chance to reload. My hat fell off and rolled downhill and I did not stop to retrieve it. Panting with relief, I reached the summit and dashed through the open doorway.

Inside, the noise was deafening, a combination of sounds which made the head spin. The great upright shaft turned with a relentless rumble and, on the floor above, two pairs of grinding millstones competed to be heard against the noise made by the great spur wheel which drove them. Higher still, more machinery added to the din, cogwheels and shafts making each other turn, creaking and rumbling and, coming from outside, the sound of huge sails whipping through the air.

Not surprisingly, my call was unheard. On this, the ground floor, sacks were hitched to the chutes, catching flour and meal as it poured down from the grindstones.

Assuming the miller was above, feeding the hoppers, I struggled up the narrow stair which led to the next level.

No one was there. As I hesitated, a shadow appeared on the floor below and moved towards the stairs. One glimpse of a fine coat was enough to teach me it was not the miller, and my insides lurched. Bellamy was coming for me: I was trapped.

Stacked against the wall were sacks of grain, waiting for the hoppers. I seized one by the neck, dragged it along the floor and pushed it down the stairs with my foot, just in time to topple Bellamy as he mounted the stairs. His pistol was discharged again, this time into the sack. He fell, sprawled and winded on the floor below, the sack across his middle.

I had done him no injury because he heaved the sack aside. My heart pounded with terror: he had abandoned his foolish ineffective demeanour. His features were contorted, his mouth set in a grim line; his eyes were narrowed and his movements were purposeful. He was determined to finish me.

My instinct was to climb higher, but he, I realized, as I ran towards the second stair, would reload his pistol. Without thinking about it, I turned round, determined to fight Bellamy, to injure him if I could, and escape into the open.

Now he was back on the stairs, and I dragged a second sack forward to topple him again. He was quicker this time and he reached the level and kicked the sack aside.

He lunged and I snatched a fistful of loose grain from the hopper, which I flung into his face. It checked him, but only for a moment. He spoke, but his words were lost in the din, and my retort, 'Murderer!' was barely audible even to myself.

He lunged again, I dodged, and my foot hit another sack, one that had had most of its contents poured into the hopper. I lifted it easily, and swung it at Bellamy. Two stones of grain connected with his hip and sent him sideways, to lurch against the case housing the grinding stones.

I bolted for the stairs. I was halfway down when a shower of grain hit me. Bellamy had opened a sack over my head, and particles of corn stung like red-hot needles, lodging in my hair and my clothing and rolling under my feet. At the foot of the stairs, I fell over the grain-sack I had sent down.

He was there in an instant: he had picked up a sharp metal tool, a bil, used for cutting grooves in grinding stones, and he meant to use it on me.

I scrabbled away, kicking one of the flour sacks under the chutes and his first slash with the bil slit it open. Now the air was filled with a fog of flour, and more flour was pouring from the chute to the floor and rising again in a dust. Coughing, we continued our desperate battle.

I slithered in the flour and I could not regain my feet. Bellamy, coughing, eyes streaming and unable to see properly, slashed wildly with the bil. I scrambled on my back, propped up by the elbows, gasping for air and taking in flour, dodging his blows and kicking upwards, hoping my boots would catch him.

My heel connected and even above the noise of machinery I heard his yell. He was a mere shadow now in the flour-dust and I kicked again and scuttled sideways, like a crab.

I wanted to get outside, away from the choking dust and the dreadful clamour which went on and on, piercing my senses, numbing my body, making me slow and clumsy. Light glimmered, the open doorway tempted, and I struggled towards it.

The wrong doorway! Almost, I had thrust myself into the way of whirling sails! I sobbed, realizing I must cross the floor to find the safe way out, and Bellamy was in front of me, angry because I had hurt him and even more determined to kill me.

I sat, coughing, with my back to the wall beside that lethal doorway, as he came towards me brandishing the bil. I thought of the grief my fate would bring my grandmother and, somehow, I found the strength to fight on. I kicked again and again, but I was growing feeble and I knew this could not long continue. Then he was above me and the bil was raised to strike. I closed my eyes and turned my face away.

The blow was a long time coming. There must have been a scuffle, but I heard nothing above the grinding din of the mill. When I opened my eyes again, I could barely comprehend what I saw. Someone had come, and dragged Bellamy away.

297

Bellamy slashed the bil at his new opponent but a hand caught his wrist, forcing the weapon aside. Then an arm shot forward, a fist connected with his chin and Bellamy staggered backwards and disappeared through the doorway. I doubt he knew what hit him. The windmill sails never stopped whirling.

A strong pair of masculine hands caught me, raised me and lifted me unceremoniously over his shoulder and carried me outside. Instantly, the noise was muffled. I shook my head and gulped greedily at the blessed fresh air, coughing too much to protest as he lowered me to sit on a wall.

He, too, was coughing to clear his lungs; he recovered sooner than I did however, and as I coughed and wept and shuddered, his coat was placed around my shoulders, and a strong arm held me fast to him and a handkerchief wiped away a sticky mixture of flour and tears from my face.

'All is well now, my love. You are quite safe. You may be easy now.'

I hiccuped and sobbed and all the time the dear voice, rough with emotion, soothed and gentled me and called me his love, his dear one. He told me I was brave; he told me I was wonderful and he laughed and told me how funny I looked, all covered in flour. And when my tears stopped and I looked up into his face, his mouth came on mine and I felt him shudder as he gathered me into his arms.

'Eh up! What is to do, 'ere?'

A large dusty person was looking none too pleased to discover the pair of us behaving with such impropriety outside his mill.

I know nothing of what was said and done, after that. I was told I swooned when Marcus assisted me to my feet, and all I recall is finding myself lying on a rough settle within the miller's cottage, being pressed to drink something hot.

'Just you lie still, miss, give your nerves time to settle.'

The miller's wife treated me with rough kindness. 'Eh, there is some cleaning up to do, flour all ower t'mill! Bellamy is done for.'

'B—' My voice was husky, my throat dry with coughing and I swallowed some of the tea and tried again. 'Bellamy is dead?'

'Aye, miss. He got in the way of the sails.'

'Oh yes. Yes, I remember now! He—he tried to kill me!' I spoke through chattering teeth. 'I-I would be dead had not Sir Marcus— where is he? Where is Sir Marcus?'

'Gone to fetch Colonel Carson's gig, miss, to convey you—'

'Oh, how could I?' I clutched the woman's arm, appalled because I had forgotten the colonel's predicament. 'The colonel was shot! He has been lying wounded for some time, someone must help him. Please, you must—'

'Never fret, miss, the gentleman is safe. Ned Staples took him home on his cart. Drink your tea, miss.'

The tea was a rough brew made from previously used tea leaves, but it did much to refresh me. Whilst I drank, the woman went into another room and returned with brushes, for my hair and clothes. She would have brushed the flour from me as I sat, dirtying her cottage, but I insisted we went outside.

Two men came to carry Bellamy away. I looked at him, my broken enemy, and thought how strange it was, that a man I had seen once only, could have such a profound effect on my life. I felt nothing for him, but I had a sense, now, that all was well with my murdered parents.

Marcus came with the gig and helped me into it and I smiled, shyly, and could think of nothing to say. He tucked a blanket around me, told me to rest and that later we would all consult together to determine what was to be done.

I was content to take him at his word, because I felt so appallingly weak. When we arrived at the house, I saw that Mrs Carson had been crying. I said awkwardly, 'Sorry I am, madam, to have brought such trouble upon you.'

'Chloe, thank Heaven you are safe. My husband was distraught! I must go to him; I must tell him you have not been harmed.'

She returned within minutes. 'The surgeon is with him now, he says the colonel will do very well. The bullet touched no vital spot, so we have much to be thankful for.'

She took charge of me, telling me that I needed to wash, drink and sleep and she was right. I allowed myself to be cosseted and it was not until the next day that I learnt how Sir Marcus had come so opportunely to my rescue.

My grandmother had begun to feel uneasy. Time was passing, she thought Bellamy must have learnt my elopement was a hoax, and she was troubled about what he would do. At the same time, Sir Marcus had the uncomfortable notion that Bellamy might, on returning from Scotland, choose to pass through Derbyshire.

'Perhaps he guessed you were here,' he said. 'When I considered the matter, I became certain he would. I cannot tell you how appalled I was! I had brought you to the first place he would think of looking. Oh, Chloe! I almost got you killed!'

He buried his face in his hands as though to blot out an awful vision and I, despite the presence of Mrs Carson, went to him and touched his cheek with my fingertips. 'Marcus, I beg you will not take on so! You came in time, you saved my life!'

'I shudder when I think of you, trapped in the mill with him and no one to help you . . . I think you saved your own life, no thanks to me.'

I shook my head. 'No, I was done, I could

fight no longer.' Sir Marcus took my hand and his own tightened around it convulsively. I said, 'Come now, I wish to hear the rest!'

'We decided to move you again,' he said. 'So I came.'

He had happened upon the wounded colonel, who heard the second shot and saw Bellamy. 'He realized you were in mortal danger and he contrived to mount the mare, meaning to bring his remaining strength to your assistance. I told him to have care for himself and leave Bellamy to me.' He stopped, looking grim. 'Not that I wished to kill the scoundrel. I would prefer to see him clapped in irons, and suffering the penalty of the law. He met his end too easily, upon my soul, he did!'

'He will be judged in a higher court, do not doubt it,' said Mrs Carson. 'I am astonished he made an open attack for, as a rule, he worked by stealth. What prompted him to act so?'

'I cannot say for certain, but I believe Chloe had been a thorn in his side for too long. Always, she stood against his ambition of possessing Oakwood Pascall and she has eluded him these many years. Had he been rational, he would know such an act could not avail him, but I think he was not.'

'I dare say you are right. Well, it does not signify, now.'

The rest of that day was fully occupied in telling my story, over and over. I was obliged to describe the circumstances of Bellamy's death to a local magistrate, I visited the colonel in his bedchamber and gave him an account of my adventure. Neighbours came to call: all were curious to learn the truth and, of course, I wrote to tell my grandmother everything that had occurred.

At dinner, Sir Marcus told me I should instruct my maid to pack because tomorrow we would set off for London, to join my grandmother and take part in the victory celebrations.

'How fortunate you are, Chloe,' said Mrs Carson. 'There will be grand dinners and grand balls and I have heard there will be a lavish display of fireworks. And so many foreign notables! Who knows, you may even be introduced to the Czar!'

'Indeed, it would be a shame to miss such an opportunity.' I smiled, but I was thinking of an interminable journey, cooped up in a chaise, with Jane sitting primly between us and all but the most trifling conversation between Sir Marcus and myself made impossible.

Before that happened, there were matters to be settled.

I said, 'Could we not delay our journey for one day? Because tomorrow I would like to visit Oakwood Pascall.'

Sir Marcus agreed to take me. Since it was a fine day, we went in the Carsons' gig, just the two of us. When we arrived, the housekeeper lined up the servants to be inspected and later showed me around the house.

A great curving staircase swept upwards from a spacious hall and the lofty, well-proportioned rooms were neat and clean. Twenty years earlier, the furniture would have been in the first style of elegance but now it was outmoded. Although there were no ragged carpets or patched curtains, the bright brocades had faded, the paint on the panelled walls had cracked and the gilded picture frames had tarnished. Everywhere had a cold feeling of neglect.

I was told that very little had been done since my parents' time, Bellamy being parsimonious. Repairs were needed and there were items which should be replaced and more servants required to bring the house into order.

'Mr Bellamy spent very little time here, miss,' she told me. 'He preferred to be in town, at his gaming clubs,' she added with a hint of disapprobation.

'He milked the estate for his own profit,' added Marcus grimly. 'I fear there is much to be set right, Chloe.'

The gardens were extensive and here, too, there was evidence of neglect. I knew very well how they could be brought back to their beauty, but I was overwhelmed by the amount to be done. I would need an army of gardeners.

As soon as I was alone with him, I asked Marcus about my fortune. 'Is there enough to do all that is necessary?'

He smiled, though there was a hint of bleakness in his eyes. 'You are a very rich young woman, Chloe.'

'Then later, you must advise me how to begin setting the place in order. But first . . .'

We had strolled down to the river and stood on the bridge, looking over the parapet, watching a family of ducks squabbling in the water, below. I turned to him, my heart thudding uncomfortably and when I saw the dark, brooding look in his eyes, my courage almost failed me.

A flash of orange and turquoise, a kingfisher diving for its prey. For all I had spent my life in the country, it was the first time I had seen one and it seemed like an omen.

A reckless feeling overwhelmed me and I smiled at him and said, 'Now, sir, do you not think it is time you paid your addresses in a proper manner?'

'Chloe!' He gasped and stuttered and looked stunned. I smiled my encouragement, but when he could find his voice, he said bleakly, 'I have betrayed myself, have I not?'

'Certainly, you have. Do not think to escape me now.'

'Escape you? I shall never— Oh, Chloe, do not torment me so! I am a pauper, compared with you! And you are young, only just come into your own, you have the world at your feet! How can I importune you with my proposals?'

'Where is the sense in having the world at my feet? All I wish for, all I have ever wished for, is my own fireside and someone I can love.'

He had scruples because I was young, because I had a fortune which outstripped his own and because I had not yet had opportunity to meet other gentlemen on my own terms.

'Believe me, there are scores of gentlemen who will love you, you can take your choice. Am I to deny you that? What a knave I would be!'

'Upon my soul! Do I wish for scores of gentlemen to love me? There is difficulty enough in managing just one of them!'

A laugh escaped him, but he said, 'Chloe, I am serious.'

'No, you are nonsensical. We are well suited to each other, you know we are. Scores of gentlemen! Well, I have met scores of gentlemen, and only one will do for me.'

'Oh, Chloe, how can you be certain? Nothing would make me happier, but you are young and I scruple to—'

'You may scruple to be happy, if you wish,' I told him. 'But what about me? Why should I be miserable, just because you have a few starched notions?'

'I—oh, hang it all! You are a determined

minx, are you not?'

'Yes, but I would like please.'

He stood before me, mine. His hands took n. my heartbeat quicken. It wa. the accepted manner but, to n. more pleasing.

He said, 'Shall we be happy togethe. and I?'

I nodded and blushed and a tear trickled down my cheek: his mouth claimed mine, gently at first, then he gathered me into his arms, touching his lips to my forehead, my eyelids, my cheeks before claiming my mouth again and tightening his embrace.

Tremors ran through me and I stroked his cheek, his neck, and I clung to him, laid my face against his and felt the warmth of his skin against mine.

My longing quickened into compulsion, my breath shortened and he, sensing the danger of overwhelming need, released me, and stepped back.

Our eyes met. We spoke no words. Each of us felt the beating of our blood, the sharp rush of urgency and we stood, stricken by the knowledge that, for the present, we must contain ourselves, we must subdue our hearts.

'I believe,' he said at last, with a shaky laugh, 'that a wedding has been arranged.'

I swallowed. 'Will it take long? We have to

London and there will be all
iresome victory celebrations, and
nother . . . I suppose she is my guardian
She will not withhold consent, but she
wish for all the trappings of a society
dding. I confess, I—'
'Your grandmother will wish you to have
what you wish for.' I sobbed.
'I wish only for you.'
He took my hand, kissed it, then tucked my
arm through his and we strolled through the
grounds of Oakwood Pascall, talking, making
plans, and setting our hearts and minds on our
future together.